IN THE EYE OF THE BEHOLDER

The year is 1857 and a young man, Peter Kersey, recently arrived in the village of Upton Market is found stabbed to death in the churchyard. When suspicion falls on the vicar, a man deeply disturbed by the death of his wife and two boys, his wealthy young sister, Maria Marston, seeks assistance from Augustus Westcott, a former Metropolitan Police detective.

Westcott packs his bags, puts his pet, Tom Cat, in the care of his landlady and goes to the village under the assumed identity of Charles West, a retired draper from Limehouse and the cousin of the Marstons' housekeeper, Constance Brown.

Unable to find suspects for the murder of a man who knew no-one in the village before his arrival, Westcott asked himself two questions. Was there anything in Kersey's behavior after his arrival, which roused antagonism? Why had Kersey come to the village?

In answer to the first of these, the detective found that Kersey had freely expressed radical views on religion and the rights of man, which, with fears fresh in their minds of the French Revolution and of Chartist unrest, might have driven some men of rank and privilege to see him as an enemy intent on spreading discontent and revolt amongst the villagers.

Knowing that character, like beauty, is in the eye of the beholder, Westcott was careful to look, too, at those who might have admired Kersey and those who might have been jealous of such feelings.

But it was not until Westcott discovered what had brought Kersey to Upton Market that he found the final clues pointing to the murderer amongst his suspects.

ISBN 978-0-9555497-2-4

Printed and bound in Great Britain by Harlequin Media Limited, 4 Victoria Works, 6 Fairway, Petts Wood, Kent BR5 1EG T: 01689 897777

Published by InHouse Publications
Rose Farm, Top Road, Wingfield, Diss, Norfolk. IP21 5QT

www.swubble.co.uk

IN THE EYE OF THE BEHOLDER

LILIAN SPENCER

HOUSE
PUBLICATIONS

Other books by the same author

THE ADVENTURES OF NATHANIEL SWUBBLE

THE OTHER SIDE OF THE COIN

www.swubble.co.uk

CHAPTER 1

This journey to Upton Market was one Maria Marston would always remember as the one on which she first saw the man who was to be murdered in the village churchyard within six months. But, as the coach turned out of the inn yard and set off along the road, her only thought was that riding in a coach gave her the feeling that she was a puppet, her limbs completely under the control of another being. A rut in the road jerked the top half of her body and forced her to throw her arms out to keep on her seat. Another jerk tossed her sideways, making her brace her foot against the floor to keep from falling into the laps of the other passengers.

Like most people now-a-days, Maria would never have contemplated making the journey from London by coach, but her brother James, who was her guardian, had insisted and there had been no point in arguing. Where once it had been working men who had raged against new inventions, it was now a section of the well educated gentry who condemned the railroad as an invention of the Devil.

Maria's fellow passengers seemed happy enough to be jolted and bumped along the road by a form of transport which she, at the age of eighteen and in the year eighteen hundred and fifty seven, felt belonged to an earlier era. Even though they all came from Upton Market, she had not, having been at school in London, met any of them before. Still, she felt she knew them well from the long letters her sister-in-law, Frances, had written to her each week.

When Maria had arrived at the last moment in the inn yard, the other passengers had been donning their coats and cloaks to board the coach. John Howard, a friend of her brother entrusted with the task of escorting her home, had been pacing up and down in obvious annoyance. Formally, he introduced the others, Mrs Amelia Carter, Mr Edward Skinner and his nephew Captain Ernest Skinner Montague and, lastly in order of proximity and of social rank, Mr Philip Bradley. Then he had handed her into the coach, hurried the others into joining her and they had set off.

Now Maria had a chance to examine them more closely and compare her impressions with her sister-in-law's comments. John Howard, at thirty, looked younger than the picture she had formed, but his clothes did make him appear older at first glance. The notch in the lapels, the trouser strap under the foot and the long, pointed waistcoat had not been the height of fashion for some years. His small beard and his moustache were, like his speech and manner, neat and precise. Together with his arrogant expression, they suggested he was certain he knew how to behave and was disgusted that, nowadays, no one else had the slightest idea what was acceptable and what was not. Maria had already realised that, by her lateness, she had not disappointed him in this view of human nature. How right Frances had been in saying that John Howard was quick to see the mote in another's eyes, while ignoring the beam in his own. She had considered it unfortunate that, in the small, enclosed society of the village and with his coming from an old, influential family which had held the same estate for generations, they would have to meet him so frequently at social events.

Of the two older men, Edward Skinner's clothes resembled those of John Howard. They were of the highest quality, but in the fashion of the forties rather than of 1857. Knowing him to be a self-made man, Maria could not be certain whether he was not interested in fashion or whether, having bought good clothes when he first made his money, he was now determined to continue to exercise economy and make them last. Frances, when she had written to say that Edward Skinner had rented their house, had not been able to make up her mind on this point, either.

As for Philip Bradley, as Maria had expected, he was still wearing boots and breeches in the style of John Bull. This, Frances had reported, was the role he liked to play. He saw himself as a plain-speaking farmer, the salt of the earth and the backbone of England.

There remained, for her closer inspection, Captain Ernest Skinner Montague, formerly of the Hussars, but, as he always managed to catch her eye and smile whenever she as much as glanced in his direction, she could only peep now and again. However, his dress had already impressed itself on her vision the second she had arrived at the inn. Her first thought had been that she would have preferred to see him in his uniform rather that his present clothes, which she found somewhat ridiculous. Her second thought, slightly more generous, was that a man brave enough to charge with the Light Brigade at Balaclava could be forgiven for being daring enough to wear fawn trousers in the peg top style – wide at the top and narrowing to the ankles – and a high buttoned coat which dropped open at the front, the better to reveal a bright tartan waistcoat.

2

The woman passenger sharing the coach was Mrs Amelia Carter, the widow of a prosperous draper, who, as Frances had reported, never missed an opportunity of telling how her husband had left her well provided for from the income of several shops now run by her sons. Possibly it was the draper's shop connection which, it appeared, made her feel it was her duty to use the maximum of material, ribbons, buttons, lace and embroidery on her clothes. Although some fifty years older, she wore, like Maria, a tight fitting, well boned jacket of satin. Fortunately for the other passengers, as Philip Bradley had mentioned in a loud aside, her ample skirt was supported by petticoats and not by a crinoline.

Again like Maria, Mrs Carter's bonnet was worn, fashionably, well back on her head and she wore gauntlet gloves and ankle-high boots. Around her pagoda sleeves, and every other seam and edge, were examples of the draper's wares and she far outdid Maria in these decorations. The light blue of her gown contrasted sharply with Maria's black mourning clothes. Mrs Carter, like the Captain, made it her business to catch Maria's eye, but gave a kindly, pitying smile instead of a friendly grin.

As Maria glanced around at the other passengers, her face bore a pained smile to convey her discomfort at the roughness of the ride, but they all, apart from the Captain, wore expressions of deep contentment. When they began to express their views on the old and new methods of travel, she soon learned why. All clung to the belief that coach travel was more civilized and much to be preferred to journeying by the, to them, new-fangled railroad, invented when most were passing their prime. The younger man, Howard, it seemed, went further and deplored all change from the Golden Days of the Past.

Mr Howard, given precedence as coming from a long established family, had soon made his view clear on these matters. "I cannot understand," he asserted, "why everything these days must be done at great speed. We were once content to laying claim to possessing the swiftest or boldest horse. Now every gentleman must boast of having travelled on the fastest steam engine or of having crossed the ocean by steam boat in the shortest possible time."

"I must say," Mrs Carter put in, to add her voice to the protests against steam, "when I ventured onto the railroad, my daughters were forced to push me into the carriage and hold me down until it started. Suddenly," she added, dramatically throwing out her arms, "I felt myself hurled forward.

I screamed, begging them to hold me fast and not let go until we reached our destination. Now, I hear, engines are propelled along at an even faster pace. I shall not venture onto one ever again."

Appearing to want to please everyone, Mr Skinner declared, "There's something to be said on both sides. There's no doubt steam has brought some benefits, but we must be careful not to destroy old traditions, which have stood the test of time. All things considered, I agree with Mr Stephenson – the engineer," he added for the benefit of the ladies, "that forty miles an hour is ample for the needs of any man. To go higher is to threaten the safety not only of the passengers, but of bystanders along the way. Not long ago," he continued, "we marvelled that a train could outpace a coach with its nine or ten miles an hour. Soon people will no longer be satisfied with twenty or thirty, but will demand fifty or sixty miles an hour."

"It can only lead to disaster," Mrs Carter warned, with a despairing shake of the head.

"Though," Skinner admitted, "I did myself no harm by buying and selling railway company shares at the right time."

"You make your money where you can," Bradley stated firmly, putting the matter, to his satisfaction, beyond contradiction. "I'll be the first to admit that steam has been a blessing to me on my farm. Does the job fast and well and doesn't keep asking for higher wages nor steal from behind my back. But I had my fingers badly burned dabbling in railroad shares. Rogues everywhere you turn today."

As the others carried on in this vein, wanting progress and prosperity without any drawbacks, Captain Skinner Montague leaned forward to speak to Maria. As he did so, she thought how right it was for him to wear just side whiskers, which did not mask his spontaneously charming smile.

"Like me," he confided, "I assume you had your mode of travel selected for you."

"My brother chose it," Maria answered, finding herself smiling warmly in return. "It was a case of 'he who pays the piper plays the tune'. As you will know, he is a clergyman and sees all steam engines as works of the Devil."

"They do huff and puff in a threatening manner," the Captain remarked. He continued to smile, but did not laugh in case this offended Maria. It was all very well for a sister to criticise a brother, but not for a stranger to join in.

Maria was still too annoyed by her brother's refusal to allow her to travel by the railroad to notice if anyone else laughed. She told the Captain, "It is probably not the huffing and puffing which upsets my brother, but the coals and furnace, which remind him of Hell fire."

Taking advantage of the attention Maria was paying his nephew, Mr Skinner managed to draw her attention to the fact that the Captain had taken part in the Charge at Balaclava.

Modestly, his nephew protested, "These neighbours are not interested in my doings in the Crimea, Uncle. That is over and done with."

"And all the better for that," Maria asserted without hesitation. As an outspoken, modern young lady she gave of her opinions freely. "It was all a great mistake and a tragedy for all concerned in it. For my part, I agreed with Mr Bright when he said in his speech that...."

Mrs Carter made it clear she did not hold with young ladies expressing opinions so freely by butting in with, "I have been meaning to ask, Captain Skinner Montague, did you ever meet Miss Nightingale?"

The young man hesitated, smiling. For a moment Maria thought, and hoped, that he was going to make up the kind of story Mrs Carter wanted to hear to repeat to her friends, but to her regret, he resisted the temptation.

"I could say that I did not have that pleasure, Mrs Carter, but, as most meetings took place in hospital, it might not have been so pleasant."

"How foolish of me," Mrs Carter laughed. "In that case, we must all say that we are sincerely glad that the meeting never did take place."

From there, the conversation flowed to and fro with all heavily dropping names of relations, friends, connections and, if important enough, mere acquaintances. It was all, Maria thought, like playing at cards, with clubs, diamonds, spades and hearts being replaced by occupation, rank, birth and education. Family and birth were always trumps, but wealth, if great enough, acted as a joker. But, in the game of social precedence, scoring was more difficult than it was at cards, where numbers were clearly marked. She had known some girls at school who knew exactly how to score a cousin twice removed in the aristocracy against a cousin who had made his fortune in India, but such matters had never been of interest to her.

As though reading her thoughts and sensing her contempt, Ernest Skinner Montague remarked in a low voice, "We must soon play this game ourselves, Miss Marston. I must find myself a bride who is wealthy as well as beautiful, while you must say, 'No!' to anyone with less than twenty thousand a year."

"Do not talk such nonsense, Ernest!" his uncle protested. Speaking to the rest of the carriage, he explained, "If my nephew continues to make a success of his life, as he has done so up to now, he will inherit almost every penny I have. His sister will have a decent dowry, but she cannot carry on the family name. I can assure you all that he is joking. He is no fortune hunter."

"Same with my eldest," Bradley was quick to say. "He will get everything. My grandfather built up the farm and my father followed his example. I've followed the same road and now we have just about the biggest farm in the county. We haven't built it up to see it fall apart when I die. And he's a good boy." Regretfully, the farmer added, "He takes after his mother more than I might like. But that can't be helped."

"Such matters," Mrs Carter admonished the young people, "are to be taken seriously." Then, deciding this was going to be her best opportunity to ask a question which had been on her mind, she was ill-mannered enough to inquire, "Miss Marston, have I not heard that you are the only niece and your brother the only nephew of a bachelor uncle who has made his fortune in the West Indies?"

"I have no way of knowing what you may have heard, Mrs Carter," Maria replied in her politest tone.

CHAPTER 2

The other passengers smiled to themselves to hear Mrs Carter put in her place, even if it were by a young lady a third of her age, but the smiles disappeared as she patted Maria's hand and said in almost a whisper, "I must express my sympathy at your family's losses. I can quite understand your brother's being so distraught and scarcely able to fulfil his duties. First his wife dies and then the baby to which she was giving birth. As though that were not enough for any man to bear, his two young boys follow their mother within two weeks. Measles, wasn't it? And the little girl catches it and survives. If only it had been one of the boys! That would have given your brother something to cling to. No wonder he remains so cast down."

Mrs Carter paused for breath, but she had not yet said her piece. Patting Maria's hand again, she advised, "You, my dear, must take the burden from his shoulders. You must take on the task of running the household. You are young and inexperienced, but it is a duty all ladies must take on in the end."

"Is it?" Maria demanded. The ferocity of her tone startled everyone. She was about to say more, when she saw the Captain put a finger to his lips and shake his head. He was right, she decided, she must not discuss family matters in this way. Instead, she gazed out of the window and fumed in silence.

Duty was duty, Maria tried to tell herself and, were she a kinder person, she would accept her fate with a better grace. But, once again, the image of herself as a puppet helpless to control her own life came into her mind. She had hoped for a few years of freedom before marriage. What harm would there have been in a few years in which to read, take long walks with the dogs and enjoy the beautiful countryside in which she lived? And what harm would there have been in a little dancing, meeting with friends and flirting just a little with men like the Captain?

As for managing a household, what had she learned at boarding school to prepare her for that? She had always supposed that Frances would have taken her in hand and taught her all there was to know about balancing a budget, preparing menus and dealing with servants. Now she would have to cope with servants who would see her as a slip of a girl and who would do just as they pleased behind her back. How she hated the thought of her future and how she would miss Frances.

To hide her tears, she kept her face turned to the window and stared unseeingly at a tall young man, well wrapped in heavy winter clothes, who was walking in the same direction and whom they were just passing. For a second, he stared back and then, seeing her tears, he smiled and touched his hat. His future, she thought, must be more appealing than hers. She did not acknowledge his greeting. The quality and style of his clothes were not those of a gentleman and, even if he had been a gentleman, he was not known to her. Nonetheless, Maria warmed to him, as she had done to Captain Skinner Montague and as she did to anyone who showed concern for her. Frances had been the only person to care for her and protect her against the world. Who was there to take her place?

As Maria had withdrawn into her own thoughts, she had been vaguely aware that the Captain had led the conversation back, perhaps tongue in cheek but certainly to save her from more personal comments, to the decline of morals and manners. Now she came back from her own thoughts, that subject having been exhausted. Mrs Carter was deploring the besmirching of the English countryside and English washing by smuts and smoke from every passing engine.

"However energetically the servants pound with the dolly, they cannot remove the grime," she finished.

With little or no experience of what went on where his servants toiled below stairs, John Howard moved on to one of his hobby horses, the new county police force.

"It is a threat to our liberty and privacy," he began, "and they would have had no case to make in support of it and to demand the taxes to pay for it, were it not for the railroad bringing thieves, vagabonds and malcontents into the countryside. Now-a-days any rabble-rouser can descend upon us and appeal to the ignorant and uneducated."

"Farm labourers," Bradley put in, "dream of saving a few pounds to cross the ocean to America or Canada. What it will do to wages if more go I not think."

"Better they go," Skinner reminded them, "than stay as a burden on the poor rates."

Considering it her turn to speak again, Mrs Carter lamented, "Tramps are threatening enough when they come on foot and alone ...." Suddenly recalling the man they had just passed, she explained, "Like that one.

Did you see his shifty eyes and furtive glance? Every inch a villain. He will catch us up at this rate."

The reference was to the fact that they were travelling slowly over the wet, icy ground along a bad stretch of road. Suddenly, a wheel caught in a deep hole opened by winter rain and frost and now hidden by the last snowfall. The driver urged the horses on, but the coach had shuddered to a halt and become a dead weight. The passengers were thrown first this way and then that, the women clutching the men and the gentlemen trying to support them. The driver's cursing and the creaking and clattering of the coach were replaced by a moment's silence in which they tried to gather their wits.

"Whatever has happened? Am I on my head or my heels?" Mrs Carter gasped.

"Is anyone hurt?" the Captain asked.

The gentlemen, having gallantly established that the ladies were not hurt, scrambled to the ground. Each had his opinion on what was to be done.

Ignoring them, Maria turned to the trembling Mrs Carter. "Do you still prefer road to railroad, Mrs Carter?"

"But think," the widow replied, not willing to give an inch, "How much worse it would have been had there been several carriages, one behind the other and full of passengers."

Captain Skinner Montague appeared at the door. "Come, ladies," he urged, "Let me help you down. While you are both, I am certain, as light as feathers, the carriage will be lighter still without you."

Laughing, he whirled Maria down as though she were, indeed, a feather and managed to convince Mrs Carter that she was no weight at all. But her pleasure at being treated with such consideration and charm did not prevent Mrs Carter from complaining about the cold. To hurry matters along, Skinner Montague called over the stranger whom they had just passed, but who had caught up with them again.

The man came hurrying forward and smiled at them all. This time, Maria smiled her gratitude and was promptly rebuked by Mrs Carter.

"Do not acknowledge his presence, my dear. Such beggars are so forward he will be at your kitchen door tomorrow morning convincing your cook that you told him to call for his reward."

With the addition of a young outside passenger there was soon a half a

9

dozen men ready and willing to help. Mr Skinner urged his nephew to take charge, but Mr Howard, seeing himself as the born leader, took it upon himself to give the orders.

"You, my man," he barked at the coachman, "go to that wheel and you, fellow, go to the other. There will be mud flung up when we move and your clothes are better suited to the task than ours."

The coachman stepped forward to show that he was ready to oblige any gentleman and avoid a complaint against him, but then he hesitantly pointed out that he must lead the horses. The newcomer did not move.

"I have only what I stand up in," he pointed out, all the more firmly for knowing the others would think him insolent. "Perhaps a gentleman with a dozen pairs of trousers could take the wheel."

"It's settled," Mr Howard insisted, "You are clearly born to manual work, even if you avoid it when you can." He glared angrily at the newcomer and continued, "Insolence is all one receives from your kind, these days. Have you no thought for the ladies standing shivering by the roadside?"

Laughing, Skinner Montague stepped forward and prepared to put his shoulder to the wheel. "It needs another man with the horses. You, my man," he ordered, addressing the newcomer, "look like a cavalry man. You have the job." He waited, as though for confirmation of his remark, but, receiving none, went on, "This young passenger and I shall take the wheels and the rest of you go to the back."

Just before leaning onto the wheel, the Captain called, "You are in command, coachman. Give the order when you are ready."

As the horses pulled and the men pushed, the coach moved forward, hung in the balance and then, as the men's strength ebbed, fell back into the hole.

"We nearly managed it," the young passenger, an eternal optimist, announced. "Next time, we shall succeed, you mark my word."

No one was marking his word, some thinking him too young and insignificant to utter one and others being busy rubbing their sore hands.

"Take a fresh grip, gentlemen and a deep breath," the coachman called. Then, half a minute later, he shouted, "Heave!"

The coach moved forward, balanced at the top of the rut and, this time, rolled forward.

"I said we'd manage it the second time," the young passenger claimed with pride, glancing in the direction of Maria. To his obvious satisfaction, she stepped towards him and thanked him for his efforts on their behalf. Ignoring the mud on his clothes, he climbed up on the coach and immediately asked the coachman and the other outside passenger if they knew anything of the ladies and gentlemen. He felt he had been one with them for a few minutes and would have a right to name drop when relating the tale to his parents.

The stranger who had stopped to help stood recovering his breath after struggling with the horses. His broad brimmed hat had been pushed to the back of his head and, caught by a gust of wind, it blew off. Before replacing it, he smoothed down his thick, red hair.

"Irish blood there!" Howard remarked. Mrs Carter nodded knowingly and disapprovingly, but Skinner Montague approached the man in a friendly manner.

"Are you travelling far?" he inquired.

"To Upton St John."

"You have friends there?"

"None, nor many in these parts, it would seem."

"Your name, sir?" the Captain asked. "Were you ever in the army?"

"Peter Kersey. No. And your name, sir?"

The Captain, as ever, took the reply in good part. "Ernest Skinner Montague, at your service, sir." He called to the coachman, "Take Mr Kersey along with us. You have room there, I see."

Thanking him for his consideration, Kersey climbed on the coach, where the other outside passengers made room for him.

"You should not encourage his insolence, Skinner Montague," John Howard protested. "If he does not know his place, it is our duty to teach him."

Not for the first time, Maria decided that she did not like John Howard. Captain Skinner Montague was more to her liking and, as he helped her up into the coach, she smiled warmly at him. Watching, Mr Skinner smiled too.

Mrs Carter was also observing them closely and drawing her own conclusions, but Bradley and Howard were still watching the red-headed newcomer.

"He needs an eye keeping on him," Bradley warned, "and my two boys are the men to do it. And the dogs will see him off if he comes to my barns looking for a bed."

About to reply, Howard happened to glance back along the road. "The cavalry to the rescue again," he laughed, looking relaxed for the first time on the journey. Here was Henry Storr, son of Lord Frederick Storr, one of his own circle, riding towards them.

Having greeted Howard and discovered what had happened, Henry Storr made a point of leaning into the coach and asking Maria Marston whether she had come to any harm. Learning she had not, he told her how much, once her family's period of mourning had passed, he looked forward to becoming better acquainted. Maria thought he had improved since the days, as a young boy, he had teased her at every opportunity. She had much preferred his older brother at that time, but he had been killed at Balaclava and his baby son was now next in line for the barony.

Next, Storr acknowledged Skinner Montague, with whom he had served in the Crimea and he gave the briefest of greetings to Skinner. Mrs Carter and Mr Bradley were sure he had greeted them, but, if he did, it was sufficiently brief to escape anyone else's attention.

The coach, late by now, set off again with little chance, in the poor conditions, of making up time.

CHAPTER 3

As James Marston raised his eyes from the blank paper at which he had been staring unseeingly for some minutes, his attention was caught by the snow falling so thickly and rapidly that, with one flake instantly taking the place of the one below, the sudden storm seemed composed of strands of snow falling to earth in endless lengths.

His thoughts, as usual now, turned inward, it had already slipped the vicar's mind that he had sent the carriage to collect his sister at the coaching inn and he was unaware of how late she was. Memories crowded back into his head. They were so vivid it was as though he heard the voice of his dead son, Matthew, calling excitedly, "There's my snowflake, Father, and that one's Mark's." or sadly saying, "Oh, Papa, I've lost it." Mark's eager, childish voice came next. "I can still see mine, Papa. There it is in the middle pane."

Glancing towards the top panes of the window, James tried to pick out one flake for himself and follow its course down through the lower panes, but he soon lost it amongst the mass of seemingly identical ones. Even as the flakes became larger and fluffier, he lost each one he had selected as it disappeared from one pane to pass to the one below. While he longed to remain with his children in memory, he became irritable and frustrated with the effort of concentration. His mind these days, he feared, was less and less under his control, always coming back to the one question, which all his study of the Scriptures could not answer, "Why did God take my wife and children?"

Now-a-days, James reflected, he could no more take an interest in the progress of the souls in his parish than follow a snowflake down the window panes. He had never claimed any talent for consoling those in trouble with soft words and he had welcomed Frances's taking that burden from him. With her sweet smile and comforting words, she had brought strength and hope to others, but where was she now to comfort him? Angrily, he demanded, "Why did you leave me, Frances? I begged you to stay." Then, overcome with remorse, he turned his anger again on God. "Why did they have to die, O Lord? Why?"

Still forgetful of his sister's journey, the vicar tried, desperately, to concentrate on his sermon. In this age, more than ever before, the clergy, he believed, were called on to interpret God's words to sinful men. Now that so many of the common people could read, even if they turned to the Scriptures rather than to penny dreadfuls, they could not understand what they read. Wilfully, they twisted God's word to fit any passing theory or to excuse any sinful behaviour. They picked out the verses which suited them and ignored the others.

With his thoughts thus occupied and the snow deadening the sound of the carriage, James did not hear his sister's arrival. Suddenly, she was there before him, young and on the threshold of her adult life. Did she have ahead of her, he wondered, the sorrows he had known? As far as he was able, he must protect and guide her. He rose to embrace his sister and welcome her home.

Maria, her head buried in her brother's shoulder, wept, not from happiness or even unhappiness at returning home, but in sorrow at her brother's appearance. James' serious face had always worn the expression of a man dedicated to his work of bringing his fellow men to God and his dark whiskers and hair had enhanced the sternness in his dark eyes. But his bearing had always been that of a prophet secure and calm in his faith and confident in his God. Now, the dark restless eyes sunk in his thin face seemed to lack belief in the world around him or the world within. He seemed, Maria thought, torn between a yearning for some source of comfort and a search for some work of the Devil to root out and destroy. She did not realise these could sometimes be one and the same thing.

"Well," James announced, trying to behave as normally as possible and holding his sister at arm's length. "My little sister, Maria, is my little sister no more. I shall promote you to just being my sister and the mistress of my household." Nodding in the direction of the door, he added, "Mrs Brown will advise and support you, but you shall always have the final decision."

Turning at her brother's words, Maria faced the middle-aged house-keeper. On the woman's face was a pleasant smile, but Maria was sure she must resent having a young girl giving her orders. Maria's smile, in return, was a little distant, to establish the authority she was being forced to assume.

"And here is Alice," James announced.

The child had waited patiently at the door until noticed by the grown-ups and until she received permission to come in. She had wondered at her aunt's daring in walking straight into her father's study. Even when her aunt held out her arms, Alice looked anxiously at her father.

"Come in, child," he told her. It sounded like an order. "We shall make an exception this once." As she shyly took a step into the room, her father demanded, "Do you know what an exception is, Alice?"

"Yes, Papa." she answered quietly, pausing in her progress, "It will not happen again."

Having given his sister and daughter two minutes to complete their greetings, the Reverend Marston returned to his seat at his desk.

"Now you must leave me to God's work."

CHAPTER 4

The future, as it invariably does, unrolled to become the past and the questions Maria had asked herself about her new life was replaced with another – who had killed Peter Kersey, the man who had helped to free the carriage from the mud. The newly formed county police force not having produced an answer, a letter arrived from the Head Constable of that force at the home of Augustus Westcott, formerly a detective with the Metropolitan Police.

After subjecting the letter to a minute scrutiny, which stopped just short of opening it and reading it, his landlady placed it on the hall table. She prepared to lie in wait until his return and then question him closely on sender and contents. As Westcott had taken to a regular routine since his retirement, she knew, almost to the minute, when her lodger would be back.

The detective had found that, with a regular routine each day, he could convince himself that he not only always had somewhere to go, but even somewhere where he must be at a certain time. Every morning, having breakfasted, fed the cat and read the newspaper, he would set out along Salmon Lane to the Commercial Road and keep going into Narrow Street, passing those men who had found no work that day and receiving hearty greetings from them. Then, if feeling energetic, he would walk or ride to one of the docks, usually the London, the West Indian or Regent's canal, entering through one of the impressive gates built into the mighty walls. Other times he would just look out onto the Thames, always busy and packed with shipping. He would watch the ships, steam as well as sail, chugging and gliding through the narrow channel between those anchored on either side and have his eye caught by the cranes swinging their heavy loads high in the air as though made of feathers. And there were always lighters scudding to and fro, dodging the stately sailing ships and the steamers, which bore down upon them with scant regard for their safety.

Westcott did not have to lip-read the oaths the lightermen shouted as the steam ships bore down upon them at speeds they had never experienced in their youth. Nor, as he shut his eyes and listened to the sounds around him, did he hear their words. But he could pick out the creaking and clanking of cranes, of masts and of anchors, the clatter of coal being unloaded from the colliers, the hammering of coopers, the foreign tongues of sailors and

16

the orders delivered by foremen, anxious to complete their tasks. And, Westcott always thought, if he went blind and deaf, he would still be able to enjoy the closeness of the river and of the docks. To prove the truth of this, he would focus on the smells around him, so familiar that he hardly noticed them without making this effort. Some, like the stinking smoke from funnels, the stench of hides and horns and the sickly scent of rum, he found oppressive, but he breathed deeply of the smell of timber and fragrant spices.

Usually, wherever he stopped, there were old salts, pilots and tidewaiters ready to tell their tales. He would listen to the same stories over and over again, happy to provide an audience for lonely old men. At noon sharp, he would enter one of his favourite dining rooms or chop houses to be greeted warmly by the waiters and fellow diners. The waiters, knowing his likes and dislikes, always knew what to recommend so that he was never disappointed in his meal. Finally, he would make his way home to doze for an hour or two in a chair.

On his way through the hall, Westcott always looked on the table, in hope rather than expectation. Today was different. There was a letter. Like a guilty schoolboy stealing fruit, he grabbed it and scurried into his room. He felt a quiet triumph in out running his landlady, whose rheumatics must be playing her up.

Living alone and not wishing to share his confidences with his landlady or another lodger, Westcott had long addressed remarks and questions on his cases to his cat. He did not hesitate to do so again and read the letter out loud to share its contents with Tom Cat.

"My dear Westcott,

"Although we have not met or been in touch for some time, I hope you will recall how grateful I have been for your help in the past and how much I admired your clear-headedness, intelligence and, above all, your discretion. Such virtues are very much needed in a case before me now and, having heard that you occasionally emerge from retirement to conduct private investigations, I have put your name forward to Miss Maria Marston of the Vicarage, Upton Market, a young lady much in need of your assistance.

"In brief, a young man, Peter Kersey, newly arrived in the village, was found stabbed to death in the churchyard. He was a working man and our investigations led us to believe that he was killed as the result of a brawl with another of his own kind, but no sufficient evidence came to light against any particular man.

"What is causing Miss Marston great distress is that rumours have begun to circulate pointing the finger at her brother, the Reverend James Marston, as the killer while he was deranged by grief at the death of his wife and children. He is now in a private asylum, where he may remain for the rest of his life, but his sister feels it important to clear his name. I might mention that the Marstons are well connected and have powerful friends. The brother and sister have recently each inherited a half share in a very large fortune amassed by their uncle in the West Indies.

"If you take the case and come to Upton Market, you may read all the reports collected by us on the case. You may wish, too, to talk with the local constable, George Harris. He leaves much to be desired, but the new force is not popular with local people and few men of any worth have come forward to join our ranks."

The letter was signed, after a friendly personal message trusting in Westcott's good health, by John Croft, the Head Constable.

Suddenly, Westcott became infused with a new energy and with it came a new honesty. He could admit that he had been fooling himself into thinking that he was content with his lot in life. He knew that his mind was aching for activity over and beyond that of watching the rest of the world at work and listening to oft repeated tales. And he knew that, as much as he loved his river, it would still be there, even more appealing, after a break in the country.

Flattered by the letter, Westcott reread words such as 'intelligence' and 'discretion', but the cat did not even twitch an ear. Nor did he respond by a flick of his whiskers to his master's comment that, "Reading between the lines, that man has no wish to offend the gentry, and possibly the local aristocracy, by digging too deep into the vicar's actions. He is putting yours truly right in the firing line."

To provoke some response from his pet, the detective tried a promise of fresh fish from Billingsgate, to be paid for out of his fee. There was no reaction, the cat knowing that his master took little interest in fees and took on cases just for the challenge. Giving up, and eager to get started, even though he knew it would take a little while to settle plans, the detective took a basket from the cupboard and announced firmly," I know you hate steam engines, Tom, but, if you stay behind, you'll have to dodge dogs

18

chasing the horses and I know you hate that just as much." The cat stirred at last and, reading the signs, pointedly curled up in the cupboard in the place left vacant by the removal of the basket.

The packing had not been completed when another letter arrived, driving the landlady to a frenzy of curiosity. Westcott took it from her, thanked her politely, and calmly shut the door. This time, thinking it silly to read to the cat through the cupboard door, he read to himself. It was from Miss Marston.

"I understand from Mr Croft that he has written to you concerning certain allegations against my brother, the Reverend James Marston, vicar of Upton Market. My brother is a true Christian and a dedicated priest and, however deep his troubles, could never murder another man, whom God had created. Please, please help me. Mr Croft has spoken highly of you and I shall willingly pay anything you ask if you clear my brother's name."

Forgetting the cupboard door was closed, Westcott spoke aloud. "And what if I don't clear his name? What if I prove his guilt beyond doubt? Will this young lady be able to face the truth? In any case, I'll just take moderate expenses and a small fee. I don't like money to cloud my judgement. We'll consider it a holiday in the country, Tom. I know you think I'm silly, but there you are. That's my nature and a leopard can no more change his spots than a tabby can change his stripes."

Replying to Maria Marston's letter, Augustus asked for details of her friends, relations and household and, receiving a prompt reply, he wrote again asking for a cottage to be rented in his name by the housekeeper, Mrs Brown, whose cousin he would claim to be while in Upton Market. While he could not imagine meeting anyone he knew in the back of beyond, he also informed Miss Marston that he would be known as Charles West, a retired draper from Limehouse, who was considering settling in the area. This name, he had found before, had the advantage of being sufficiently like his own to allow him to correct the error of starting to give his real name. He could cough, repeat 'West', and apologise for the frog in his throat.

The occupation was one which could be mastered, at least to fool anyone who was not himself a draper, without a long apprenticeship or extensive study. Being retired and of independent means allowed him to be, in the eyes of all except the gentry, a gentleman and suitable company for the higher servants who knew what was what in the neighbourhood. He would have liked to pose as a true gentleman born and bred, but he knew he would not get away with that. He had too much of the cockney in his accent and too little money in his pocket. But, as Mrs Brown's cousin, he would have access to the vicarage and to Miss Marston without causing comment.

When the morning for his departure arrived, Westcott awoke early, threw back the bedclothes saying, "Right foot forward, West." The fact that he put his left down first did not worry him. He was not one to pay attention to omens and signs.

Making one last attempt to keep his master at home, the large tabby approached and rubbed his head on the foot on the floor. Westcott brought down his other foot and tickled the cat's ear with his big toe and then walked over to pick up the basket again. The cat walked off, tail in the air, and jumped onto the window sill, clearly ready to watch Westcott walk down the road.

"That's right," the detective said, "Stay if you like. You be your own man, just like me. We own nobody and nobody owns us. You ask nothing of me and I ask nothing of you, or of anyone."

That was not strictly true. Most evenings the cat would be found in the window or on the front door step gazing in the direction in which his owner had disappeared in the morning. If the cat was not there, and this happened only when he had been shut in somewhere, Westcott called and searched and did nothing else until the cat was found and taken safely in to supper.

About to leave, the detective gave the cat one farewell pat. "It's the tender care of the landlady for you, my man. Don't let her win your affections. I've fended her off for twenty years or more and you can do the same." Reluctant to leave his cat in the largest city in the world, he thought of another warning. "Just watch out for that old tom across the street. He didn't get that torn ear sitting on the doorstep and you know that he's jealous that you are Tom Cat with capitals and he is just an old tom cat like any others."

CHAPTER 5

As Westcott alighted from the train at the Uptons, the guard and another official looking man fussed deferentially around an old man, who already had four servants apparently attending to his every need. As the detective made his way past the group and unintentionally obstructed its progress, he was requested in hushed tones, as though it were an honour for him to do so, to stand aside while Lord Storr's party left the platform. Thinking 'when in Rome' he did so, imitating any local man who owed his job, his cottage and his living to the Big House. As he watched, he observed a younger man hurry forward and give his arm to lead the baron to his coach.

"Is that the next Lord Storr?" Westcott asked the guard.

"No, that's Henry. Just pipped at the post by the arrival of a baby son to his older brother's wife. The brother died in the Crimea, you know."

By the time Westcott left the halt, which he decided had obviously been built for the sole convenience of the local bigwigs, the coach was just disappearing out of view.

Westcott stood and took in the sights. The countryside was just as the poets described it. The sun shone in a blue sky across which tiny clouds scudded, chasing, but never catching, each other. Birds fluttered in and out of the hedges or collected on the ground, pecking at invisible delicacies. Butterflies and bees dipped from flower to flower and then back again, for fear of having missed a sip of nectar.

The detective took in a deep breath, then coughed. A sheep behind the hedge coughed, too, making Westcott jump at the harsh, rasping sound. "It's strong stuff, this country air," he agreed, setting off to walk the mile or so to the cottage rented in his name, or rather, in the name of Charles West. He reminded himself that he must take on the character to go with the name. He must be polite, ready to chat but even more ready to listen, perhaps a little ingratiating, but, above all, harmless. If he played this role, the detective was convinced, people would trust him and open their hearts to him.

As he walked, the detective reflected how, since his retirement from the police, he had discovered the advantages and disadvantages of working alone on a case. To his disadvantage, he was usually too late to examine the body, let alone the scene where the crime was committed, and he had no

21

authority to examine witnesses. Once people knew who he was and his purpose in coming, they could just ignore him or keep out of his way. To his advantage, he would not have half a dozen fresh faced, flat-footed young constables trying to gain promotion by pointing out facts which they considered important, while distracting him from those which really were. Best of all, he had no superiors demanding immediate results, directing him up blind alleys and taking credit for themselves when he followed his own, more productive route.

So, as he walked along the lane, he was quite content with his lot. He would keep an open mind, just look and listen without any preconceived ideas and trust that, as often happened, he would wake up one morning to find that the mass of facts he had collected had sorted and sifted themselves at the back of his mind, allowing the solution to surface at the front. He planned to spend a couple of days just wandering around, looking at the church, admiring people's gardens, eating at the inn and stopping to talk to everyone he met. The villagers would be full of the murder and all too ready to talk. For a day or two, he decided, he would not even visit the vicarage in case Miss Marston was too persuasive in convincing him of her brother's innocence.

It did not take Westcott long to realise that he knew little of the countryman's character. As he walked along, a gang weeding in a field all stood up, held their backs and stared at him, unsmiling and in utter silence. A labourer even walked past him with three feet between them without responding to his smile – unless a suspicious stare could be termed a response. The detective recalled that he had often heard it said that it took forty years to be accepted in the country. He suddenly feared that he might not live long enough to persuade anyone to smile at him, let alone talk to him.

As a cart came clattering towards him, Westcott waved cheerily and was glad to see it pull up beside him.

"Where you going, then?" the man demanded, looking the detective up and down. As Westcott recited his piece, the man's expression remained unimpressed. "Last stranger 'ere got 'isself murdered," the man commented, cracking his whip, urging the horses on and laughing at his own joke.

For another half mile, Westcott saw nobody except a shepherd inspecting a sheep's foot and a woodman chopping branches from a tree. Predictably, both stopped, stared and watched the detective until he had disappeared

22

from sight. Did they, Westcott wondered, go home and say, "Saw a man walking down the lane today," before snoozing all evening? If the wives asked what he was wearing and what he looked like, they would be able to give a detailed description down to the colour of his eyes.

Soon, Westcott found he was crossing a bridge over a canal and an inn beckoned on the other side. The Pig in a Poke. He saw this as a challenge, as well as a source of much needed refreshment and, possibly, of information. There were men seated outside and men coming to and fro from the boats. A woman smiled at him and was probably surprised at the warmth of Westcott's smile in return. A few of the men nodded a welcome in reply to his. He feared that they might be travellers from afar and not the native population.

With an amiable smile fixed to his lips, Westcott entered the inn, only to find that, at first, little was visible, the ceiling being low, the windows small and the smoke thick. As he tripped over an outstretched leg here and there, he tried to remember that he was Charles West and not Augustus Westcott. That is, he apologised rather than cursed. Eventually, he found an empty seat and dropped into it.

A man at the next table immediately called, "Come and sit yourself here," in a voice which suggested that he was used to everyone falling in with his wishes. "Leave your bags," he added.

Acting like West the draper, the detective moved to the other table. Acting like Westcott the policeman, he took care to take his things with him and keep them close to him.

"Not as stupid as he looks," another man at the table mocked. "Buy us all a drink and we'll leave you what you stand up in."

As Westcott looked around the table at the three men seated there, longing to challenge these bullies, but wanting, at all costs, to avoid a scene, he was amazed to see that the third man wore a swallow coat and had a top hat on the chair beside him. So this was Constable Harris, who clearly did not know about his visit.

Harris spoke next, using his authority as a police constable. "And when you've ordered the ale, I'll trouble you to tell me what your business is in these parts."

"I'm simply about my lawful business," Westcott answered.

"And what's your lawful business?" the constable asked, sitting up straight and trying to intimidate Westcott with his height. As the detective

23

himself was tall, this did not work, although the detective was impressed by the constable's girth.

Obligingly, Westcott recited his name, occupation, reason for coming to the village and his relationship to Mrs Brown, housekeeper to the Marstons. As he did so, he sensed, rather than saw, the leading man of the group signalling to the others to change their approach.

"Now, sir," Harris said, changing his tune, "I was only asking for your own good. The last stranger we 'ad visiting us was murdered. If you was connected to 'im we wouldn't want the same thing 'appening to you, would we, sir?"

Smiling gratefully, Westcott thanked him for his concern and then asked deferentially, "May I be so bold as to ask your names, sirs?"

"Joshua Mansfield," the leader replied at once. "I work for Mr Skinner, who you'll find has an estate nearby." Indicating the man next to him, he went on, "This is Samuel Rimmer. Works for Mr Howard – another gent lives here in Upton Market. The quiet one, over there, is John Blackburn. He's gamekeeper to Lord Storr. And this, as you'll guess from his daft top hat, is constable Harris. You might say as how he works for all the gentlemen."

They all laughed, but Westcott thought that, when Harris realised who he really was, he would have the last laugh on the constable.

"A 'ighly respected woman, Mrs Brown," the constable commented. "And the Marstons are one of the best families around."

"And the richest!" Rimmer reminded them.

Mansfield rose and the other two, as though attached by strings, did the same.

"We'll tell the landlord to take good care of you," Mansfield said. "Try the steak pie. You'll not regret it."

Expressing his warm thanks and hoping that he was not overdoing it, the detective asked in scared tones, "Have they caught the man who did it? The murder, I mean."

Mansfield's large hand dropped coins onto the table and then rested on Westcott's shoulder. "There, we were only joking, asking you to pay. Don't you worry. There's no danger here for a law abiding man like yourself."

"But who killed him?" the detective persisted.

"It was just some brawl – probably about a woman. You know what young fellows are like these days."

Turning to summon the landlord, Westcott came face to face with a boatman at the next table, who had obviously moved his chair close enough to eavesdrop on the conversation.

"Murder they say," Westcott said, still trying to appear concerned. "Were they pulling my leg?"

"No joke, Mr West," the man answered, revealing he had, indeed, been listening. "Killed in the churchyard 'e were, a few weeks back."

"Who did it?" Westcott asked, turning his chair right round to face the two men at the table.

One opened his mouth to answer, but the other nudged him and replied hastily, "Some boatman moving up and down the canal. A tramp. A local swain crossed in love. A good few names were put forward, but none of them stuck."

The detective would have liked to ask, "Whose names?" but, as he knew nobody locally, he realised this would arouse suspicion. As it happened, he did not get the chance. The men stood up to leave, but before they went, one stood with his back to the landlord and said in a low voice to Westcott, "One name was the Reverend Marston's, but the police turned deaf when 'e were mentioned."

"Watch out," his friend warned, "Jack Cant is coming over." They made off before the landlord arrived.

"So," the detective thought, smiling at the landlord, "one more publican who listens to his customers and sells the information to the highest bidder or to the one who can do him the most good."

"My apologies, Mr West," the landlord smiled. "Mr Mansfield told me to take good care of you, as belonging to the Marston 'ousehold, as it were. Now what will it be? First meal on the 'ouse, sir. 'Ope you'll be one of my loyal customers in the future."

Westcott accepted with many thanks and ordered the steak pie. He did insist that the landlord joined him in a drink. The detective hoped to tap the mass of information in the landlord's head, but he was disappointed. All Jack Cant would say was that Kersey had been a ruffian of the sort who got himself into trouble wherever he went. He had been in a brawl a short while before his death.

"Probably," Jack Cant told Westcott, "the fellow came up against another ruffian, who used a knife instead of his fists."

Perhaps a bullying ruffian like Mansfield or Rimmer, Westcott thought.

CHAPTER 6

His meal over and the steak pie sitting comfortably in his stomach, Westcott was more than ready to accept the landlord's offer of the loan of a boy to carry his bags and show him the way to the hired cottage. The detective did not have to tell the name of the cottage – everyone knew which one he had rented.

"I'm off," the boy said on reaching the door and not wanting to be given anything else to do by a man who might not be a generous tipper. As it was, he stood long enough to make it clear that he expected at least tuppence for carrying the bags and hoped for sixpence. He received a sixpence, Westcott thinking that if word went round that he was mean with his money, the villagers might be mean with their information.

Perhaps it was the change of air or the lack of foul air to which his lungs were accustomed, but Westcott found his energies sapped and he did little more that day than explore the cottage and walk in the garden. He found a meal set ready for him on the table, flowers in every room and everything provided that a man could want. His bed had been aired and made up with the finest linen and he dropped into it gratefully.

Westcott had hardly roused himself next morning when he caught sight of Harris marching up the path with a parcel under his arm. The constable had clearly been sent with the reports and now knew who he was. The detective intended to assert his authority from the beginning and keep the man waiting at the door, but the constable walked in as bold as brass, sniffed the air, found the smell of breakfast very appealing and clearly expected to be given some. Sensing that the constable saw himself as taking orders from those of rank in local society before those of superior rank in the police, the detective thought it time the man learned where his duty lay and ignored the constable's envying glances at his ham. Instead, he left the man standing, awaiting instructions.

This, in Westcott's experience, never failed to leave a constable holding his top hat under his arm and looking as awkward as a ghost carrying his own head. It was as if, he had always thought, constables carried their authority in their tall hats and looked indecisive and sheepish without them. Little did he understand the rural constables of the new county force. Without more ado, Harris put his hat down on the table amongst the food, helped himself to bread, butter and ham and sat down, fixing Westcott with a cheerful gaze.

If, the detective decided, he ordered the constable to return the food and stand to attention, the man would be sullen and unhelpful. A man with local knowledge could be useful to him. But he could not let the man get away scot-free.

"I require some explanation, Harris," Westcott said, in his sternest voice. "You treated me, a member of the public, with disrespect yesterday. What is your explanation?"

"Well, sir," the constable answered, not in the mood to acknowledge any guilt, "I 'ad to know whether or not you was a respectable member of society. I 'ad to know 'oo you was before I knew 'ow to treat you."

"When I was a constable, Harris, we were taught to be polite and respectful to all members of the public, whatever their rank or occupation."

"Well," Harris said, with a superior smile which suggested he knew more about his own patch than any city policeman, "that were in London. 'Ere in the Uptons we 'ave the aristocracy, the gentry, tradesmen and then the lower orders, some of the said lower orders given to poaching and thieving. You 'ave to take all that into account, sir." With an even more knowing smile, he added, "You don't treat the criminal classes like you would respectable people, would you, now?"

Knowing when he was beaten, Westcott accepted the documents Harris had brought him from the Head Constable and read them while Harris finished his meal. Report after report, written in a spidery hand which Westcott took, along with the spelling mistakes, to be Harris's, pointed to one or other labourer who might have had a grudge against Kersey. Much of the information seemed to have been provided by Mansfield and Rimmer, possibly to divert suspicion from themselves.

"Doesn't Mrs Harris mind you spending so much time at the Pig in a Poke?" the detective asked, pointedly.

"The Poke we call it, sir. Best if you get to know the local names, I think, sir, if you're to be accepted around 'ere." Receiving Westcott's thanks with a gracious nod of the head, he added, "No, Mrs Harris knows 'er place, as all good wives should, sir."

"I see that Kersey was badly beaten a short while before his murder. Did you find the culprit?" the detective asked. He had decided to leave the constable's training and education to the county force.

27

"Don't really count brawling as a crime, sir. 'Appens too often."

"Did Kersey make a complaint?"

"Not what you'd call making a complaint, sir. Just reported it to me like."

"And you took no action?"

"Didn't see the necessity, sir," Harris answered. "'E just mentioned it in passing, you might say."

"Is it not possible, Harris, that the same men beat him as later murdered him? Might you not have saved his life had you investigated?"

It took the constable a little while to sort out the complicated construction of these sentences with unusual negatives implanted in them. "Shouldn't think so, sir," he eventually answered, giving up the struggle and being noncommittal.

"These reports give the impression, Harris, that the man was always in trouble. What were these fights and squabbles about?"

"The usual," Harris replied. "A girl. Ale spilt on a jacket. Not showing respect to someone bigger than 'im. Usual things like that, sir."

"But any particular cause important enough to provoke murder?"

"'Oo knows?" Harris asked. "Any cause is enough to a man 'oo's drunk or jealous."

"And which particular drunk or jealous man was the culprit do you think, Harris?" Westcott asked. Stopping himself adding, "If you think at all."

"Could be 'alf a dozen always in trouble of one sort or another," Harris answered, stifling a yawn. Seeing that the detective was becoming impatient, he added hastily, "Tom Osborne's name kept coming up."

"Where is the report of your conversations with this fellow Osborne?"

"Should be there, sir," Harris mumbled, looking just mildly uncomfortable. "But it isn't."

"I remember," Harris said brightly, pleased at his own facility in thinking up lies on the spot. "'E 'ad nothing new to say and we couldn't find no definite evidence against 'im."

The detective tried a new tack. "One name I have heard, which isn't mentioned here, is the name of the vicar, James Marston."

"But," the constable protested indignantly, "it isn't up to me to put the name of a gentleman in a report for any Tom, Dick or 'Arry to read. 'E's not only a reverent 'isself, sir, 'e's related to the aristocracy. 'E's got friends in 'igh places on the bench and up in London."

Suddenly, Westcott longed for London. He had heard that many country people were protesting about paying rates for a new police force from which they gained little. The detective had every sympathy with them.

"So you did not investigate the allegations against the Reverend Marston?"

Harris's indignation was righteous. "It's me duty, as I sees it, sir, to 'arris the criminal classes, not to 'arris the gentry. The gentry, especially clergymen, sir, don't go around thieving and murdering, do they, sir? By nature, it's the criminal classes as commit crimes."

Westcott felt sure there was a fault in the man's logic, but he was also sure there was no point in trying to argue with him. He contented himself with stressing to the constable that he must not discuss these matters with anyone or give away the detective's identity. From Harris's expression, Westcott guessed his advice might have come too late.

CHAPTER 7

It seemed to Westcott at five o'clock next morning that a thousand birds, of mixed varieties and song, were greeting the new day with wild joy. After late nights on cases he had learned to sleep through street din and clatter, but these sounds were new, penetrating and impossible to ignore. He left his bed and stood at the window, breathed in the cool morning air and watched a hare zigzag across a field. Then, as the memory of Constable Harris intruded upon the scene, he sighed. The best thing, he decided, was to forget the policeman and start again with his own investigation. It was clear to him that, so far, only people willing to accuse tramps, vagabonds and village labourers had been questioned and their replies noted. Those accusing the Reverend Marston had been discouraged from speaking up, but, the detective reminded himself, there were awkward customers everywhere who would still have their say and he was bound to come across them sooner or later.

It turned out to be sooner rather than later. Constable Harris's report on the finding of the body and on the scene of the crime had, like the coroner's report, been perfunctory, to say the least. Kersey, the little evidence available suggested, had been killed in the churchyard near Mrs Marston's grave late in the afternoon while an exceptionally thick fog blanketed the whole village. The corpse had not been discovered until the next day when half the village, it seemed, had searched around the churchyard and trampled into the earth any evidence of the crime which might have remained. Kersey had been stabbed first in the back and then in the chest. No knife had been found. It puzzled Westcott why the search had been made in that particular area and his curiosity had been sufficiently aroused to take him next morning to the graveyard.

The detective had scarcely arrived at the lych-gate when a man, nmistakeably the grave-digger, in battered hat, mud stained clothes and sacking bound around his legs, beckoned him over. The man was leaning heavily on his spade, contemplating the hole he had dug and, seemingly, estimating the minimum depth he had yet to go before throwing his spade aside and sitting with his feet dangling over the edge.

"Come to see where it 'appened, 'ave yer? Draws people 'ere it does. Don't 'ave many strangers in the village, but them as does come ends up 'ere." Spitting on his hands and wiping them on his jacket to prepare a clean palm ready to receive any monetary consideration offered, he went on, "Jenkins' me name, gravedigger of this parish, you might say. I'm your man to show you round and tell you all the details without missing out none."

"Well," Westcott said hesitantly, playing his role as Charles West, retired draper, "I must say that I am not normally interested in morbid details." Then he went on, rattling coins in his pocket, "Just this once I'll indulge in a little gossip."

"Ain't nobody don't like gory details," Jenkins asserted. "And you won't learn nothing from that cousin of yours, nor from nobody else around 'ere. Told to keep quiet we was. But if that pair, Mansfield and Rimmer, thinks two drinks'll keep me mouth shut forever, they're very much mistaken. If I can make a few coins," he added, pointedly, "by telling the truth, what's the 'arm in it?"

"None, none, Mr Jenkins, but why should people want to keep you silent?"

"No mystery about that, is there?" the gravedigger replied. Westcott waited, but soon realised that was the only answer he would receive.

"'Ere, follow me," Jenkins ordered, leading Westcott to a monument close to the church itself.

The detective just had time to realise that the carved figure of a mother with a baby in her arms and two boys at her skirts was the grave for the Reverend Marston's loved ones, before Jenkins, with surprising agility for a lethargic looking man, threw himself backward across the grave and stared wide-eyed at the sky.

Scrambling up again and standing close to Westcott for maximum effect, the gravedigger whispered, as though the ghost of the murdered man was nearby, "They say you can see the murderer reflected in the dead man's eyes – the last face 'e saw fixed there for eternity."

Refraining from his first instinct to say that he would have been out of a job long ago if that were the case, Westcott asked in a nervous tone, "Who did you see?"

"Didn't need to see the murderer then, did I? Saw 'im in the flesh a minute later, didn't I?" Jenkins answered. "But I'm coming to that, sir. Got to tell you about the body first. Got to see," he added self-righteously, "that you gets your full money's worth."

The detective having apologised for interrupting the story, Jenkins continued, "Stabbed in the front he were, right 'ere." Swinging back his arm, he illustrated his words by punching his fist into his chest. "And they say 'e were stabbed in the back" he added, using Westcott's back to receive the imaginary knife. "Done a good job, the vicar did. Very thorough, like 'e always is. Deathly white, the corpse was. Never knew the meaning of that till I see 'im laying there. All 'is blood drained out onto the ground. Still be there, now, in that dirt. They say as 'ow a blood stain stays for ever."

"He was on his back when he was first found?" Westcott asked, trying to establish which blow was struck first.

"Was me as found 'im. Staring straight up at the 'eavens, 'e were. I never touched 'im, nor turned 'im over."

"What makes you so sure the vicar killed this man?" Westcott inquired in a hushed voice as though horrified by all he was told.

"See 'im, didn't I? Day it must 'ave 'appened. Fog were so thick you could 'ardly see your nose in front of your face let alone the 'and at the end of your arm. Never seen one like it in all me life and never want to see another. I swear as God is me witness, I couldn't even see the bottom of the 'ole I were digging. Usually, when I'm working, I don't 'ear nor see nothing – too busy on me job. But this day I were just resting me spade when the clock struck four. One! Two! Three! Four!" the gravedigger repeated slowly and solemnly. "Sounded more like the church bell tolling a death than the old church clock. Seemed muffled and distant. Unearthly, you might say, just as if it come from the other side of the grave. 'Alf thought I 'eard voices, but I told meself they was in me 'ead."

The gravedigger looked intently at the detective and, on cue, Westcott looked duly impressed. He must have made the right noises, for Jenkins continued, "I were scared, I don't mind confessing, sir. There were evil in the air that day. Weren't just the smell of the dank earth I'd raised from the 'ole, I'm used to that. The damp was as cold and chilling as 'ands running up me spine. And not a single ray of light got through the fog. The 'ole world were greyish white. Couldn't really say if it were day or night. There were cracking and snapping, creaking and groaning coming from 'ere, there and everywhere. It were all closing in on me from all sides."

While he decided that this whole tale had been rehearsed in the gravedigger's mind, Westcott was convinced that the man had been frightened at the time. He continued to listen intently as Jenkins went on, "I told meself not to be daft. I were a man, not a silly old woman. Didn't

32

make no difference. It were like four walls closing in on me and I 'ad to get out. I made for the Poke.

"As I moved forward, other thoughts come uninvited into me 'ead. Were I really in the churchyard? I could 'ave bin anywhere in the world for all I could see. What if someone come at me? I couldn't see to run away. I began to feel 'ands clutching at me arm, then at me legs. What if a bony 'and come up out of a grave and toppled me in? God, I were frightened."

Coming back to the present again, an embarrassed smile crossed Jenkins' face. "Sounds daft now, don't it sir, in this sunshine and clear air?"

"Any man would know what you mean," Westcott assured him. "It's a liar who says his imagination has never played tricks on him in a pea-souper."

"Then you can imagine 'ow much worse I felt when I suddenly come across 'is body laying there. I stumbled on along the path. And what 'appened then? I'd lost all sense of direction, 'adn't I? Should I go this way or that? I stood still. Then I 'eard this noise. Like someone moaning. Gawd, I were frightened, I can tell you. I were froze rigid and trembling from 'ead to toe."

Jenkins took a much needed breath and then continued, "I prayed, sir, me, Jenkins, I prayed. 'Please, Gawd,' I said, 'don't let me see it. Don't let me see no ghost. Let it pass by in the fog without me setting eyes on it.' I thought," Jenkins explained, "if I see a ghost I'd lose me reason and me 'air would turn white in a second."

"But you did see something – or somebody," Westcott prompted.

"I did, sir. I see I were near the wicket to the vicarage. This shape rose up. I breathed again. It were the Reverend. A second later, I wished it 'ad been a ghost what I seed. 'E were so close – closer than I'm standing next to you now. I could see 'is face as white as a sheet and 'is eyes burning in 'is 'ead like coals. There were dark patches on 'is coat and I knew they was blood. The knife were in 'is 'and. 'Olding it out like this, 'e were, like 'e wanted to throw it down, but couldn't let it go."

This time, the gravedigger stopped for breath and effect. "Then 'e said – and I could 'ear every word clear as if 'e were speaking in the pulpit – "'E's dead. Quite dead. It's the vengeance of the Lord.'

"With Gawd's 'elp' I took meself orf to the Poke. Don't ask me 'ow I done it. None of 'em believed me. Well, they said they didn't 'cos then they didn't 'ave to go and search in the fog, with it getting darker every minute. Next day, the fog 'ad lifted enough for 'em to believe me and come with me to the churchyard. Then we found the body, just as I've related to you, sir."

"And related many times," Westcott thought, but he looked duly impressed. He had noticed that, as the gravedigger had been talking, a woman was peering at them through a window of a cottage beyond a small pasture beside the church.

Following Westcott's gaze, the man said, "That's Mrs Jenkins – the wife. Don't like to be left out of anything, she don't."

"Was she here then? Did she hear anything?"

"Not orf me that day. I slept at the Poke – that's what we calls the inn around 'ere. Calls it me sty, Mrs Jenkins does."

"And often," Westcott thought, "tells you she got a pig in a poke when she married you." Aloud, he said, "I meant, did she hear the murder being committed?"

"Not 'er. She were sitting over a warm fire. Mind you, she 'as some cock and bull story as to why the feller come 'ere in the first place."

"Who was this man who got himself murdered?" Westcott inquired.

"Peter Kersey, that's what 'e called 'isself. Only got 'is word for it."

"Passing through, was he?"

"Passing through!" the gravedigger laughed. "Where would you be going to pass through Upton Market? It's at the end of the road to nowhere, Upton Market is."

"So you don't know why he was here? I was told," Westcott added quickly, "by someone I was talking to that he was a stranger, but most people have a reason for visiting a place – like I'm looking for a cottage with a view to settling here."

"You'll 'ave to ask Mrs Jenkins that one," the gravedigger answered.

Westcott had every intention of doing so. While he wanted to keep an open mind and not limit himself with questions and answers, that one question kept coming back to him. What, or who, had brought Peter Kersey to Upton Market?

"Do you mind if I walk over to your cottage and talk with your wife?" Westcott asked. "When my friends in London know I was at the scene of a murder, they will want to know all about it."

"I ain't got no objection, but per'aps you'd better give me 'er money along with me own. Can't trust a woman with money." Having long since given up all pretence of working, the gravedigger pushed his hat to the back of his head. "Anyway, I've got lots more to tell, if you've got the time and

34

the money to listen."

"I'll just give you your money and keep Mrs Jenkins' to give to her." The detective put a coin in the gravedigger's earthy hand, thanked him and hurried off. He thought he had heard the truth so far – truth not recorded in police reports – and he had no wish to stay and have Jenkins make up yarns just to earn more.

"You don't want to believe a word the woman sez to you," the gravedigger advised. "She went to school and learnt to read. Ain't done 'er no good. Just reads any rubbish she can get 'er 'ands on. All about dark, tall, 'andsome strangers, most of 'em. As though they'd look at 'er," he laughed. "Some days when I gets in, if I want to see me dinner on the table, I 'ave to knock the book out of her 'ands."

Poor woman would need some fantasy to take her mind off reality, Westcott thought.

CHAPTER 8

As Westgate approached the gravedigger's cottage, Mrs Jenkins came to the door and stood, arms folded, fixing her eyes on him with a cold, unyielding stare. He did not doubt that this was the attitude reserved for all her husband's friends and acquaintances, whom she had come to know as lazy, drunken, good for nothings.

"Mrs Jenkins?" Westcott began, smiling.

"What d'yer want?"

It would have to be, the detective decided, his helpless act. That usually softened the hardest woman's heart.

"I wonder, Mrs Jenkins, if I might trouble you for a cup of water. I'm not as young as I used to be. Retired, you know," he explained, breathing heavily, "through ill health." Westcott tapped his chest to indicate, without actually saying so, that his heart had little life left in it.

Mrs Jenkins was wise to all the tricks men could employ to win favours or get themselves out of trouble. She continued to stare, with eyes narrowed.

He would, the detective decided, have to go as far as uttering a lie. "My ticker," he muttered, smiling weakly, yet bravely, and wondering what to say if that failed.

"Wait there, then." Were, the detective wondered, the words and tone a little less sharp, a little less like Mrs Jenkins and closer to Florence Nightingale?

Gratefully, like a dying man in the desert, Westcott took the offered cup and gulped the water. It was all he could do not to spit it out again with a look of utter disgust. They said London water was bad for you, but at least it tasted better than this vile well water.

"Saved my life, Mrs Jenkins," he spluttered.

"Don't like our water then?" Mrs Jenkins laughed delightedly, showing that nothing escaped her keen eye.

"It is a little strong, madam," Westcott said, not wishing to admit she had made a fool of him, "but welcome, nonetheless."

"What did you really come for?" the woman asked. "I've work to do. We ain't all retired like you, nor bone idle like me 'usband. Did 'e tell you I knows why that dead feller come 'ere? 'E says it's just my fancy," Mrs Jenkins commented, nodding her head in the direction of the churchyard.

"You look an honest, down to earth woman to me, Mrs Jenkins."

"What's it to you, anyway?"

The phrasing was confrontational, but, Westcott thought, this seemed to be her usual attitude.

"I'm here to find a cottage....."

"I know all that."

"Well, I'm just walking about for a day or two, getting the feel of the place you might say, and I happened to hear about this young fellow. Idle curiosity, to be honest, Mrs Jenkins."

"An honest man," the woman laughed. "That's a new one! With a man I knew it would 'ave to be idle something or other."

Westcott laughed, too. "Well, to be honest again, madam, I have found, over a long lifetime, that women are more honest than men and better at getting at the truth."

"That's 'cos we know what truth is, Mr West," she asserted, confirming she knew his name and all about him. "But it's quite simple and straightforward. 'E comes from London like Maria Marston. 'E comes from there to 'ere on the same coach as that young lady. And, second day 'e's 'ere, 'e goes to the vicarage to see 'er brother."

Westcott tried to look as though he were following, but failed.

Sighing at his stupidity, Mrs Jenkins continued. "Look, you come from London, you should be the first to understand. It's full of every sort of rogue the Devil put on this earth."

"Have you ever been to London, Mrs Jenkins?"

From the look of horror on the woman's face, Westcott might have asked, "Have you ever been to Hell, Mrs Jenkins?"

Her reply came promptly. "I know fire burns, Mr West. I don't 'ave to put me 'and in it to find out. And," she continued, "I know London is where all them rich girls is sent to school. Fortune seekers can pick 'em out like sitting pheasants. A young feller like Kersey could easily turn a young girl's 'ead. 'E were 'andsome enough and tall with it."

"But not dark?" Westcott could not help saying.

"Tall, dark and 'andsome," Mrs Jenkins laughed. "Most of us ain't lucky enough to get one. One or two out of three is enough to turn a young girl's 'ead – and many an old one, too. Anyway," she reflected, "'is 'air weren't ginger like a carrot – more dark ginger, you might say."

37

"So," Westcott summed up, trying to get back to the point, "Kersey worms his way into this girl's affections and follows her here. To elope, you think?"

"No!" the gravedigger's wife exclaimed in exasperation. She was beginning to think this man was as slow as all the rest. "She 'adn't got 'er money then, 'ad she? And I told you, Kersey went to see the vicar. Wanted to be bought off, didn't 'e?"

"Oh," Westcott muttered. It made sense. He asked, "But Kersey stayed. Was he waiting to be paid or had he been refused and was thinking what to do next?"

"Vicar sent 'im away with a flea in 'is ear, didn't 'e? Didn't get nothing, if you ask me."

Already, Westcott had taken in the layout of the church, vicarage and Jenkins' cottage and realised Mrs Jenkins, from her cottage, could see the front door of the vicarage, but not the back. It was unlikely that Kersey had gone to the front door and, therefore, unlikely that she had seen him emerge. If he asked the woman whether she had seen him enter or emerge, she was likely to say she minded her own business and could not say. But did she know, for sure, about the flea in Kersey's ear?

"You'd have seen him go by," the detective asked, tactfully.

"Right past the church and bold as brass up to the front door. Not the back door, mind you – the front."

"And was he let in?"

"Yes, it were a new girl didn't know no better. But 'e weren't in there more than ten minutes. Come by the church with a face like thunder and the Reverend shouting after 'im."

"Perhaps he was an honourable young man and asked to be allowed to see Miss Marston?"

It was a hoot, rather than a laugh, which escaped Mrs Jenkins' lips. "Lay a pound to a penny you ain't got no daughters. 'Oo'd let a penniless working man court their sister except another penniless man? She were about to in'erit a fortune. 'E wouldn't be allowed within a hundred miles of 'er."

"Dear me," Westcott ventured, not wishing to persist with direct questions, "so he tried to meet her in secret, spread stories about her and force the vicar to pay him to stop."

"Well, no," Mrs Jenkins murmured, not having thought that far. Thinking about it now, she argued, "If it were in secret, we wouldn't know,

38

would we? That's what secret means?"

"No secrets in a village," Westcott commented, thinking he knew all about villages, even if Mrs Jenkins knew nothing of London.

"Secrets everywhere," the woman replied, just to keep her end up. "Anyway," she remarked, tiring of the conversation and wanting to ask this draper about new materials and prices in London, "finish of it were she inherited a fortune. Vicar was frightened they'd elope so, out of 'is mind like 'e were, 'e stabbed the young feller to death."

Deciding there was nothing else to be learned here, Westcott raised his hat to take his departure, but this was delayed by a full half hour spent answering Mrs Jenkins' questions. As usual, in this predicament, the detective fell into the role of draper with some enthusiasm. He had always thought that he would be good at encouraging people to spend more money than they wanted, just as he was at persuading them to tell him more than they intended. He even promised the gravedigger's wife that he would have samples sent to her from London.

CHAPTER 9

Eventually tearing himself away, Westcott walked back to the church. Jenkins had departed, no doubt to the Pig in a Poke, but another villager was there to waylay him. A man stood by the church door, eager to talk. In need of food and refreshment as he was, Westcott recognised a lonely man when he saw one and greeted him warmly. The detective had often found that it was the lonely person, who claimed to keep himself to himself, who often knew more than people in the thick of things.

The small, unassuming man stopped wringing his hands and beckoned Westcott across. The detective walked over and the man turned and led him into the church. There, as though he were more at home in the dimly lit church than in the outside world in the daylight, he seemed to relax.

"You'll have been hearing all about our sad tale," the man remarked. "My name is Marcus Goodier and I'm verger of this parish."

"A very sad tale indeed," Westcott commented in reply. He waited, sure the verger had something to tell him.

"You'll have heard Jenkins' version and, no doubt, his wife's. He is quite accurate, as a rule, unless tempted to embroider a tale in hope of financial gain." He paused, eyebrows raised.

"Sixpence," Westcott confessed.

"Then you probably had just the simple truth. With many it's been a shilling for the more gory account. He has, of course, spent it all immediately in the Pig in a Poke."

"A strange name for an inn," Westcott remarked, trying, by chatting, not to arouse the verger's interest in his true purpose for being in the village.

"No stranger than most," Goodier replied shortly, not interested in that subject.

"True, very true," Westcott agreed, smiling. "Perhaps I shouldn't suggest it," he added, lowering his voice, "but the vicar's behaviour sounds so strange of late, had he sought comfort in ....?"

"Oh dear me, no!" The verger was horrified. "A good Christian in every respect. I almost went on to say that he believed in moderation in all things, but he was not – is not – a moderate man. Always demanding the most exacting standards of me, of parishioners and of himself, most of all."

Nodding to show that he knew the type of man being described,

Westcott remarked, "Not someone you could confide in. Not someone you could go to for a chat."

Glad to have someone who understood, Goodier seemed to expand in size and confidence. "How right you are, my good sir. A chat about sin and guilt Mr Marston would join in any time – no, that's not correct – he would never chat. Admonish, correct, lecture and preach, those are the words to use."

"A stern, strict man of God," Westcott suggested.

"Not if you believe in a merciful God," Goodier replied. "Now, as for Mrs Marston, she was a saint, an angel and she brought out at least a degree of gentleness in him. He worshipped her, but I really think that he felt guilt that he might put her before his Maker." Suddenly turning to Westcott, the verger said, "I sense that you are a bachelor, sir. Never found the right woman. If there were another like Frances Marston, I would marry her tomorrow."

The detective was sympathetic. "I am, indeed, a bachelor, Mr Goodier. I know the loneliness. No one in the house to welcome you home. No one with whom to sit in a comfortable silence after a busy and tiring day."

"Yes," Goodier admitted, "I am feeling it especially now."

Correctly, Westcott assumed the verger meant that he felt the loss of his beloved Mrs Marston. "I sometimes think," he commented, "that there are not enough good women to go round."

For a minute, Goodier was lost in memories of his adored angel. "Well, of course, to be honest the dear woman would never have looked at me in that light. She was so far above me in every respect."

For once, Westcott did not know how to proceed. He wanted to learn all he could from the verger, but he was unwilling to wring it out of the man by sympathetic comments and smiles. For a while, at a loss for words, he gazed around the church.

To Goodier, it must have seemed like a tactful, encouraging silence, for, as though suddenly making up his mind, he turned to the detective. "Come this way, Mr West. Now that I know you have no morbid interest in this murder, but, like any intelligent person, will puzzle over how it all came about, I think that this may add something to your understanding of the crime. I know many of the villagers have their own ideas of why the Reverend Marston should kill a stranger, but I think the real answer lies here, within this building."

41

After leading the detective along one of the aisles, Goodier stopped in front of a large painting. As he pointed towards it, Westcott stepped closer to examine it. It was not a good painting, by any stretch of the imagination, but rather like one that might have been painted by the local painter of inn signs. Its style harked back to medieval times and Westcott's taste had not yet caught up with that fashionable Gothic revival of former days.

The subject was unmistakable. Along the top of the mural, people with blissful expressions and clothed in white were bathed in a blinding light, designed, no doubt, to hide God, whom the artist either held in such awe that he would not dare to represent or had not the imagination and skill to portray. These were the ones who had walked the straight and narrow path on Earth to reach Heaven.

Below were a mass of bodies writhing in agony and guilt. Thumbs, hands, limbs, heads and bodies were twisted in the most unlikely directions, prodded and pierced by an army of small devils under the command of the Devil himself. There could be no doubt that these were the ones who had strayed onto the wide and easy path to Hell.

"Cast your eyes there, sir," the verger ordered. "Observe Satan in Hell."

While the artist had been too overawed or too incompetent to paint God, he had made up for this in his enthusiasm in painting the Devil. The figure was naked and the artist, no doubt wishing to protect the modesty of the congregation rather than of Satan himself, had painted him emerging from a mass of bodies. The half of the Devil which was visible was bright red with webbed hands and a long, thick tail curling along his back. His ears, to Westcott, looked rather like the ears of the elephant in the Zoological Gardens in Regent's Park and the weapon in his hand resembled an over-sized pickle fork.

"My! My! " Westcott exclaimed, no other words coming into his head. He wondered what all this could have to do with Peter Kersey's death.

"Mr Marston," the verger explained, "believed that, now the common people can read, they are misinterpreting the Bible, twisting the words to fit their own beliefs. This painting, he hoped, would turn their thoughts back to the Church's age-old teaching and warn of what lay in store for eternity if they went against God's commands."

Taking hold of Westcott's arm, the verger pulled him to one side. "You were blocking the sunlight from the window. There, now look at the figure of Satan again."

42

With the flow of sunlight and the change of angle, the figure of the Devil had disintegrated into a kaleidoscope of formless colours. He had disappeared from the picture. Westcott still had no idea what this had to do with Kersey's death and listened patiently.

"I spend a good deal of time here, Mr West being, as I have said, a bachelor. I observed that Mr Marston often dashed into the church. Sometimes he rushed straight up to the picture. At others he appeared to be attempting to keep away, but always ended up standing before it as we are doing now. Even during the services, I noticed his eyes were drawn to it. He appeared to be attracted to it like iron to a magnet. He could not ignore it."

Westcott, at a loss what to say, nodded. He apparently made the right encouraging noises, for the verger resumed his story.

"Often, after he had left, I would stand where he had stood. I thought that, perhaps, a figure reminded him of someone. Perhaps he thought that he saw his dear wife and children among the angels in Heaven. I could see no likeness."

As Goodier paused in his tale, Westcott leaned forward to examine the faces closely, then, realising that he did not know the people concerned, stood back. His head slightly to one side like a bird listening attentively to sounds in the soil, he conveyed the impression of an attentive listener completely engrossed in the narrative. The verger was encouraged to continue.

"Mr Marston solved the problem for me. One day, when he was, as usual, quite unaware of my presence, he began to talk to himself. They say," the verger commented, "that is the first sign of madness."

"Indeed they do," Westcott agreed. At least he talked to his cat. But was that, he wondered, better or worse than talking to himself?

"As the days passed, I am afraid Mr Marston talked more and more and spoke more and more loudly, until I could not help hearing all he said. I thought it best," the verger explained, "not to move or speak and embarrass the man by revealing my presence. As it happened," he continued, "I heard him say, 'I have no control of myself. The Devil has taken command of my limbs, my eyes and my mind.' Then I nearly banged my head on the pew where I was kneeling when, in a mighty voice, he shouted, 'Get thee behind me, Satan.' He walked a few steps and must have come into the position where the form of Satan is replaced by sparkling colours dancing in the

43

light. 'He has escaped,' he cried. 'He is free to roam the land tempting others as he is tempting me.'"

"The Devil was tempting the vicar?" Westcott demanded, imagining the man had thought himself urged by Satan to kill Kersey. Realising that he was showing too obvious an interest, the detective laughed and added, "No doubt even clergyman are tempted to sin from time to time like ordinary men."

Although he was eager to continue with his tale, the verger answered the question. "Mr Marston, as I have said, was guilty that he might have loved his family more than his God. It must have played on his mind until he thought the Devil, aware of his fault, tempted him to give his soul in exchange for the return of his wife and sons to life." Obviously thinking that Westcott might not appreciate the finer points of religion, the verger explained, "To sacrifice his God-given soul in this way to Satan, would mean that he did, indeed, put his family before his God."

Having paused to regain the thread of the story, Goodier went on, "In the blinding sunlight shining upon the mural, it must have appeared to the vicar that the Devil had disappeared. Who knows where he imagined God's great enemy had gone? But I think it was to pursue Satan that Mr Marston ran to the church door and out into the graveyard." Goodier paused at this dramatic moment in his story. "Who should be standing there among the gravestones but Peter Kersey? "

"Ah!" Westcott murmured, "and Kersey had red hair!"

"You are ahead of me, sir," the verger said, seemingly disappointed, but continuing nonetheless. "Satan, if not represented as black, is painted red. To you or me, such a connection would not have been obvious, but to Mr Marston, in his condition, it was all too clear."

Nodding, Westcott encouraged the verger to continue his story.

"Kersey walked towards the vicar. 'Are you well, sir?' he asked. Mr Marston looked demented. He was as pale as death and his eyes bulged in his head. He did not answer at once. No doubt he thought it was a trap. Was the Devil asking if he were sick and ready to give up his soul? Kersey came nearer and repeated his question. I must say that he appeared to show great concern. When he realised that the vicar was becoming more agitated at his presence, he held up a hand, saying, 'There, sir, don't worry. I'm just leaving.' He turned on his heels and walked away."

"And the vicar, did he follow?"

"Oh, no. He rushed back into the church only to find that, from the place where he now stood, the Devil was in the painting once more."

"It does appear," Westcott commented sadly, "that Mr Marston's mind was demented and his soul greatly troubled."

"I fear so," the verger replied with great sorrow, "and, in his madness, he found reason to kill the poor young man. I can only speak as I found, Mr West, and I found Mr Kersey polite and considerate, if misguided in his theories. People tended to like him or loathe him."

Before Westcott could take up these comments on the dead man's character, Goodier commented, "Perhaps it is better – safer, at least, – to be neither loved nor hated. Indifference may be hurtful, but it is not fatal," he added, laughing at himself.

"It takes all sorts," Westcott said, patting the man on the shoulder. He realised that Goodier was belittling himself and did not wish to say anything which the verger could interpret as agreement with this opinion.

The verger, coughing, seemed to be working up courage to say something else. "I suppose," he ventured at last, "that you would not care to join me for a simple supper at my cottage?"

"Of course," Westcott replied, unable to refuse, whatever his own plans. "But," he added, "we shall talk of other matters. However, just one last question on this sad affair. Why did Peter Kersey come to Upton Market?"

'That I have often wondered. The only answer I can suggest is that he came to be killed. Somehow, in some way, it fitted in with God's plan, as all things must do."

"I doubt that," Westcott thought. "Satan's plans, maybe."

CHAPTER 10

Lately, by early evening, Westcott was feeling his age and, by bed time, had decided that he had been right to retire. He had been exhausted. The conversations he had had with Jenkins and his wife and with Goodier had whirled around in his mind, but he had not been able to hold a fact in his head long enough to weigh one against another and come to any conclusion.

Overnight, his mind had cleared and, by morning, he had reached some tentative conclusions, while realising that, as ever, one new, small fact might collapse the whole edifice he was building. When the vicar had rushed out of the church looking wild and distraught, Kersey's behaviour, as reported by the verger, had not been that of a man who was trying to extort money. It suggested a considerate and puzzled man, who meant the vicar no harm. Mrs Jenkins had been wrong.

Of course, Westcott thought, playing the Devil's advocate to his own theory, Kersey, having failed in his plan by threats, might have been trying to ingratiate himself with the vicar. After all, a young man who had deliberately set out to catch himself an heiress would be capable of turning on the charm when required. Having considered this point of view, Westcott dismissed it. Kersey had been angry when leaving the vicarage after his visit there and yet had later been anxious to help the vicar in his distress. Possibly, the visit to the vicar had had nothing to do with Mr Marston or his family, but had just been made to ask advice about whatever had brought Kersey to the village. Perhaps, again, Kersey had gone on to ask advice of someone else. He must bide his time, keeping his eyes and ears open and not rush to conclusions.

A few yards from his door, Westcott found another person more than willing to talk. He bumped into Carrie Osborne, or rather, she bumped into him. She was twirling round and round in the lane until her apron and skirts flared out all around her and singing at the top of her voice. As she spotted Westcott out of the corner of her eye, she jumped in surprise and toppled into him.

"Gawd! I'm sorry, mister. Did I 'urt you?" Hardly waiting for a reply, she went on, "I've got meself a proper job at the vicarage. Not a rotten skivvy's job like I've got with Mrs Jakes. I'm just orf to get me things and tell 'er what I think of 'er. I know just what to say. I've been practising it under me breath

46

for months."

Westcott had not said a word. He did not have to. Smiling was enough.

"Thought they'd never choose me," the girl went on. "If you ask me, Mrs Brown had made up 'er mind to give it to that stuck up Jane Fisher, but Miss Marston said she'd decide 'oo got the position. They say," she explained confidentially, "there's a real battle going on there between the 'ousekeeper and Miss Marston to see 'oo runs the 'ouse'old.. Mrs Marston, God rest 'er soul, didn't believe in keeping a dog and barking 'erself. She left most things to the housekeeper, but I suppose, being young, Miss Marston don't know no better."

While Westcott continued smiling and nodding, Carrie continued to relate the events which had led to her appointment. "Anyway, we was all lined up, me, stuck-up Jane Fisher and that common Betsy Marsh. Betsy went first. She 'adn't even mended 'er dress. It were filthy and she 'ad a black line all round 'er neck and you could 'ave grown onions in 'er ears. Miss Marston asked 'er, 'What's your name, child?' For a minute, I swear, Betsy were going to say, 'Child yerself.' Then, when the lady asked 'er why she wanted to work there, do you know what she said?" Carrie demanded.

Laughing along with Carrie, Westcott replied, truthfully, that he had no idea.

"She said," Carrie spluttered, "'I don't, Miss. Me Ma made me come. Said I 'ad to work somewhere what with me Pa's bad leg and 'er carrying another.'" Pulling herself together, Carrie chatted on, "'Er Pa's bad leg! Gets 'im down the Poke quick enough and back again."

"No wonder Betsy wasn't given the job," Westcott put in, wanting to make this a conversation he could direct later before the child ran off on her way.

"'Oo'd be daft enough to give any Marsh a job? Not one of 'em's ever done a day's work. Then Jane Fisher were next. Fishers 'ave always thought they was better than anyone else. Well, Jane were scrubbed and polished like a new pin, weren't she? Me 'eart sunk. She answered up nice and clear and were as polite and well be'aved as though butter wouldn't melt in 'er mouth."

There was a pause for breath, which Westcott thought long overdue, and Carrie was off again. "Do you know what done it for me, mister?" Without expecting or waiting for an answer, the girl went on, "Two things. For a start, Miss Marston asked 'er if she could read. Now, there were a poser for 'er. She can read, I know, but she were afraid if she said she could they might not want 'er, 'cos she might read things what don't concern 'er. 'Er Ma 'adn't drilled 'er in 'ow to answer that one. She stumbled and stuttered, 'No, Miss Marston, but I could soon learn, if it pleased you.' They could tell she were lying and you ain't supposed to lie to your mistress – though I knows them as does."

For a moment, Carrie seemed to have lost her place in her story, so West helped her out. "What was the second thing, which turned the situation in your favour?" Then he added, "What's your name child?" and laughed, "There, you can't say 'Child yourself', to me, can you?"

"There, I knew it were my lucky day. First I get a job and then a gentleman asks me name. Most people just say, "Ere you.' Me? I'm Carrie Osborne, the great and famous Carrie Osborne 'oo's going to be a fine 'ousekeeper like Mrs Brown."

A sudden thought struck the girl. "My Gawd, I forgot. It's Mrs Brown's cousin, ain't it? 'Er cousin what's come from London. I shouldn't be telling you all this. You might tell 'em what I've said and you ain't supposed to gossip about what goes on in the 'ouse where you works."

"You can tell me anything you like, Carrie. And, by the way, I'm Charles West."

"'Appy to make your acquaintance, sir," Carrie replied with a curtsy

"And what," the detective prompted again, "was the second thing?"

."Second thing," Carrie reflected for a moment. "Oh, yes. I were in the work'ouse. I'm an orphan. Me and me brother, Tom. Then I become a skivvy to Mrs Jakes. Now it just 'appens that Miss Marston 'ates Mrs Jakes on account of Mrs Jakes 'aving been so unkind to 'er when she looked after 'er when she were a child."

"So Miss Marston rescued you, Carrie, from this awful Mrs Jakes?"

"And nobody never were more in need of rescuing than me, Mr West, and that's the Gospel truth." Carrie sighed deeply. "I'll be saying me prayers tonight and thanking Gawd for 'is great mercy, no matter what Peter used to say."

"Peter's your brother?"

"No, I said me brother were Tom. Peter Kersey. 'E's dead. Vicar murdered 'im, they say."

"Don't you think he did it? The vicar, I mean."

"To be 'onest, mister," Carrie began and Westcott thought she probably

48

always was, even when it was to her disadvantage. She went on, "I do. It all points in that direction. But Miss Marston and Mrs Brown, they don't. That's about all they do agree on. And Tom don't, not for one minute."

"Did you know Mr Kersey?"

"A bit, but Mrs Jakes never give me no time orf, so I never got to know 'im really. Me brother knew 'im. 'E stayed with me brother while 'e were 'ere."

They stopped outside a house.

"'Ere's where the old witch, Jakes, lives. I come out without telling 'er. There'll be 'Ell to pay. She'll try to stop me going. She'll say she 'ad me as a 'prentice from the work'ouse and I 'ave to serve me time. Ain't true. I never put me mark on no agreement nor nothing. Tom told me I mustn't. But old Jakes wouldn't know the truth if she tripped over it."

"Tell me if there's any trouble," Westcott urged, forgetting he was no longer in the police force.

"Thanks, mister," Carrie replied, smiling up at him, "but I can manage. They sez you should meet fire with fire, so I meets cunning with cunning. She don't stand a chance."

Westcott was not as confident in the child's power to outwit this unknown Mrs Jakes, but he was sure Miss Marston would win the day on her behalf.

"Perhaps I'll bump into your brother," Westcott said, hoping the girl would say where he was to be found.

"Doubt it. 'E lost 'is job and goes wandering far and wide looking for work. 'Bye, Mr West, sir."

"Good to have met you," Westcott called after the child, who was already skipping up the garden path.

At the window, he saw the stern face of Carrie's tormentor, Mrs Jakes.

CHAPTER 11

It was time, Westcott decided, to meet his employer. Although he would have liked to, he could put it off no longer. If he had anticipated the nature of this first meeting at all, he had imagined it to be in the nature of a courtesy call, with Miss Marston repeating her instructions to him and he able to assure her that he would go about his task with a completely open mind. But all he had learned in the short time he had been in Upton Market appeared to confirm her brother's guilt and he was beginning to feel that, in all honesty, he could not let her cling to the belief that his investigations would end with the conclusion she so badly wanted.

The vicarage, as he walked up the drive, he found large and imposing, with pillars supporting the entrance porch and a large, semi-circular bay window on each side. It had probably been built around 1800, almost sixty years ago, to house a man of some importance – a clergyman of good family and education, probably with some family connection to the local aristocrat in whose patronage the appointment lay. James Marston, Westcott thought, must be such a man. A little oddity in his behaviour, an aloofness and rigid code of behaviour would be no drawback to such a preferment.

As his eyes ran over the façade, his attention was caught by a rapid movement in one of the downstairs windows. He was nearly certain that a young girl had been observing him as he surveyed the house. That would be Alice Marston, he decided, as he walked up to the door.

He reached for the knocker, only to have Carrie open the door and then quickly close it again. Word had been spread around that Mrs Brown's cousin was coming to the door and, eager on her first day to do everything right, Carrie had rushed to open the door, only to be told not to open it until the visitor knocked. Carrie's tutor proved to be Sally, who, on first day of not being the lowest and youngest dogsbody, was putting on airs and throwing her weight about. In order not to be left out, she took Westcott's hat and coat, advising Carrie all the time on the finer points of completing this apparently simple act. For her part, Carrie was unusually subdued, having been told a dozen times that a degree of decorum and respect was required of all those who worked in the vicarage.

To impress upon the staff the supposed purpose of the visit, Constance Brown, instead of waiting in her room, came down to meet Westcott. She even allowed him to give her a quick peck on the cheek, displaying a warmth in the meeting which young Sally and Carrie had assumed was not part of a housekeeper's nature.

"Let's go to my sitting room, Charles," Mrs Brown suggested. Sally and Carrie stood watching and recalling how often cousins married these days.

"Perhaps, Constance," Westcott suggested, "I might be shown round the house on the way. It has such a beautiful façade that I am sure the rooms must be just as impressive."

"Of course," Constance replied, smiling, "Miss Marston is in the library, but you may certainly see all the other downstairs rooms. Miss Marston mentioned that she looked forward to meeting you later on."

If West had asked himself why he was putting off going with Constance Brown to her sitting room, he would probably not have given the full, honest answer that he had made it a life long practice to avoid being alone with spinsters and widows. Like many bachelors and widowers, he over-estimated the eagerness of those breeds to inveigle him into proposing and whisking him down the aisle. The answer he might have given, half of the truth at least, was that he wanted to see the girl who had been watching him.

As they walked through the well-proportioned rooms, Westcott noticed that the furniture was not new. The Marstons had not rushed to buy everything on sale at the Great Exhibition six years before, let alone renewed it once or twice since. Perhaps, he thought, clergymen still believed you could not serve both God and Mammon. Or perhaps it was just that they did not like the heavy furniture coming into fashion and preferred what they had. On the tour, Westcott did not exactly see the child, glimpsing only her foot, poking out from under a large cloth covering a table. Even that glimpse would have been denied him had it not been for two small dogs, who, sniffing a stranger, came rushing out, barking around his ankles. Believing that small, yapping dogs were more deadly than larger, barking dogs, Westcott stood still.

Without referring to the foot encased in a dainty, shiny leather shoe, Mrs Brown ordered the dogs to be quiet and return to their basket. In amazement, Westcott saw them obey immediately.

"I must have you train my cat, Constance," the detective said. "He never does a thing I tell him."

"You have a cat?" the housekeeper asked, with an interest which suggested he had risen in her estimation. Then, recalling the parts they

51

were playing, she added, "Still the same one?"

"Still Tom Cat," Westcott answered, raising an eyebrow and inclining his head in the direction of the shoe. The housekeeper led him out of the room.

"That's Alice. It is a very difficult time for her. First her mother dies, then her sweet little brothers and now," she added, dropping her voice, "her father as good as dead."

"Is she fond of her Aunt Maria?"

"They barely knew each other until Miss Marston returned from school. I could so easily and willingly have taken on the task of caring for the child and running the household, but Mr Marston felt his sister to be the better person. Miss Marston has been robbed of her youth. Perhaps he wished to take her away from fortune hunters."

"Anyone special?" Westcott asked, with Mrs Jenkins' story in mind.

"Not as far as we knew. No. I am sure there was nobody," she concluded, positively.

"So, the child, Alice, keeps to herself?"

"Yes and no. She seems to feel that nobody wants her. Mr Marston, I'm afraid, had little time for a daughter. She adored her mother, as everyone did who knew Mrs Marston."

Westcott's thoughts turned to Marcus Goodier. "She appears to have been very well liked."

"There was much to like – to love – about Mrs Marston. But," Constance explained, "Alice is hiding to make Miss Marston look for her. She seeks proof, I think, that her aunt really wants her company on her walk with the dogs. Alice is upset that, sometimes, Miss Marston likes to be on her own."

"How strange little girls are!" Westcott commented.

"To a man, perhaps. Miss Marston understands such feelings all too well, but she enjoys her own company and cannot let the child demand attention all the time."

By now, they had reached Mrs Brown's apartment and, however reluctant he might feel to do so, Westcott was forced to enter with good grace.

"Miss Marston," the housekeeper told him when they were seated, "will come in a moment or two. I'm not sure how you wish to arrange matters to talk to her on her own."

"Perhaps," Westcott suggested, "Miss Marston would invite me to see the garden. Has she taken an interest in that? The flowers are beautiful at the moment."

"Fortunately, yes. Perhaps you might talk to her for a short while here. That would not arouse any suspicion. Then it would, indeed, be a good idea to continue in the garden. But be warned, the gardener and his son have large ears."

"Does anyone know of my purpose in coming here?"

"Only Miss Marston and myself. I had to be told, of course, to play your cousin."

There was the sound of young, light footsteps on the stairs. Mrs Brown opened the door to her employer.

The young woman greeted Westcott with warmth and relief. "It is so good to have someone to lean on at last. I have had no one to turn to over these dreadful weeks. All I know is that my brother is innocent and so long as we do not know who committed the crime, I can trust no one. You must clear my brother's name and bring the murderer to justice."

Looking at the young, pretty heiress, Westcott felt safe enough to show compassion. She would have plenty of suitors and no interest in an elderly man like him. He could act as a father to her in this terrible time. For the moment forgetting Mrs Brown, who was older and rather plain, he gave the young woman his full attention.

"You must, indeed, lean on me, Miss Marston. I can guarantee nothing, of course. I had a good record in the police force, but I make no claim to have solved every crime I worked on. I can simply pledge that I will do my very best to find out who killed Mr Kersey."

"You do not say 'to clear your brother.'"

"I must start with an open mind, Miss Marston, but I trust my words and yours will mean the same." Suddenly, the detective's growing conviction that James Marston had been the killer seemed based on nothing more than the gossip of the gravedigger and his wife and the verger's imagination. While he clung to the need to keep an open mind, he now hoped against hope that he could bring this young woman the peace of mind for which she yearned. Gently, he questioned her.

"Have you any evidence, apart from your own knowledge of you brother's character, Miss Marston, that Mr Marston did not commit this crime? Was anyone with him at the time? Did anyone see him elsewhere?"

"No, I am afraid, to both questions, Mr Westcott."

"West," the detective corrected her. "You must not forget that I am posing as Charles West, a draper from London."

"I beg your pardon, Mr West," Maria apologised. She was suddenly overcome by the strain of the past weeks and tears came into her eyes.

"There, there," Westcott said, soothingly. "All will work out for the best, my dear. Mrs Brown, fetch your mistress some water."

"I am so sorry," the young woman sobbed. "I don't know what came over me."

Westcott saw his new cousin raise her eyes to Heaven and, for a few seconds, thought that she was mocking his soft-heartedness to young and pretty women, but her next words revealed the true cause of her frustration.

"Tiredness and worry and helplessness came over you," Mrs Brown declared in a voice which brooked no opposition. "Why, oh why, Miss Marston, don't you at least trust me to manage the household?" Her patience snapped at last. "I know you wish to take Mrs Marston's place, but all in good time. If you will excuse my speaking my mind, you are trying to run before you can walk. You have enough to do without trying to do my job as well. Concentrate on clearing your brother and helping Alice and leave the rest to me."

Seeing the young woman's weariness and recalling Carrie's words about the struggle for power, Westcott agreed. "That seems to me very good advice, Miss Marston. I have not known my cousin for long, but I am sure she is a more than capable housekeeper."

"I have tried so hard to be like Frances, but I have failed," Maria wept. "I shall leave matters to Mrs Brown in future."

"It is what Mrs Marston would have wanted," Westcott advised. "For your brother's sake and for Alice's." As he spoke, the detective could have sworn that he heard someone at the door. Having heard the same noise, Mrs Brown opened the door. There was no one there.

"Let us go into the garden, Miss Marston," the detective suggested, "where we can see who comes within listening distance."

"You had better join me for tea, Mr West, if we are to appear cousins," the housekeeper said.

Warning signals sounded in Augustus Westcott's mind. Why were not women satisfied with having been married once?

CHAPTER 12

In the garden, Westcott and Maria walked slowly along the paths, well away from the gardener and his son. Frequently they stopped, ostensibly to admire the plants, but, in fact, to discuss Peter Kersey's murder and the circumstances surrounding it.

"You have heard Jenkins' version of events, Miss Marston?"

"I am afraid so, Mr West."

"Then let us take it that your brother reached the churchyard just after the murder was committed – when the victim's blood was still warm and flowing." Hearing his own thoughtless words, the detective looked at Maria. She was deathly pale and appeared on the point of fainting. He took her hand in a way which would look to others as though he were inspecting a thorn in her finger. So, he thought, despite Miss Nightingale, young ladies still swooned at the mention of blood.

"My brother must have done. The murderer might even have heard him coming. In the mist, James would have seen nothing."

"Perhaps," Westcott remarked, someone wanted him to arrive at that very point. Did your brother receive any messages that day which would have taken him to that spot at that precise time?"

Maria thought carefully before replying. "I am sure no one called that day and there were no messages delivered to the house."

"And your brother often left the house, telling no one where he was going?"

"When his wife was alive, he would, naturally, have told her, but recently, he has acted on impulse and secretly. I understand on this occasion he went out without telling anyone."

"And no one saw him leave?"

"James often went into the church to pray and talk to God, Mr West, but he would not have walked along the drive. There is a path leading directly from the vicarage through the wicket into the churchyard."

Before he could ask another question, Maria continued, "I must tell you that my brother often went to his wife's grave to speak with her. I tried to dissuade him, thinking it would deepen his unhappiness, but it seemed to provide a measure of comfort, however small and fleeting. You may think, Mr West, that a clergyman would find it easier than most to accept the will of God, but my brother would not accept that he would never see his wife and sons again on this earth."

The detective examined a flower while Maria recovered her composure and then he asked, "At that time of day, was it more likely that he was going into the church itself and was attracted by a noise at the grave or that he went directly to the grave?"

"I cannot say, Mr West, one possibility is as likely as the other. And," she added, anticipating his next question, "he had no set time for visiting either church or grave, apart from going to services."

"How frequently did he visit the grave?"

"Recently, there had been less and less time between his visits. As little as twenty minutes, on occasions."

"Then let us turn to your brother's return from the churchyard. Jenkins claims that he was carrying a knife and his clothes were bloodstained."

"No one saw him return. I heard Sally, our young maid, complaining that water had been dripped all over the stairs. It seems that James had washed himself and his clothes under the pump. Then he came in, dried himself and put on dry clothing. His wet clothes lay in a pile on the floor. Sally gathered them up at once and washed them."

"How did your brother explain his behaviour?"

"He did not try. He repeated over and over again, 'God's work has been done. Satan is vanquished.'"

"Your brother's exact words, Miss Marston. Did he say, 'I have done God's work'?" Westcott stressed 'I'."

"I am sure that James did not, Mr West."

"His words were, 'God's work has been done'?"

"Mrs Brown and I agree on his words."

"Did you agree from the beginning or did one of you persuade the other as to his exact words?"

"From the beginning, I am certain."

"And he was just as agitated as has become normal for him lately? Not even more excited?"

"My brother struck us as unusually calm. He said that Frances and the boys would rest in peace, now, and he would see them again when it pleased God to call him to his Heavenly rest." Here Maria paused, as though reluctant to express her thoughts. Westcott waited patiently. "It may sound foolish," the young woman said at last, "but it is those words which totally convince me of my brother's innocence. As a true Christian he would know full well that, had he committed murder, he would spend eternity in Hell."

"And," Westcott added, "the hope of meeting his family again on the other side would keep him from such an act, were he tempted."

"Exactly," Maria agreed enthusiastically. Westcott did not express his thought that, when his mind is disturbed, a mad man can act against all his beliefs and habits.

The detective went back to his earlier line of questions. "Where was the knife?"

"A knife has never been found. We have only Jenkins' word that there was ever a knife in my brother's hand."

"Was one missing?"

"Mr West, if cook is to be believed, one utensil or other is always missing from the kitchen. When I have looked into her complaints against the young kitchen maids, I have been convinced that, with so many tools, no one knows what is to be found from day to day."

"But did cook complain that day?"

"No, Mr West. I am not trying to protect my brother by covering the truth. I am trying to explain that, even had cook not complained, a knife might have been missing."

"My apologies, Miss Marston. I am afraid that I know little about the running of a large household." Westcott smiled at Maria. "Just another question or two and then we can return indoors and your inquisition will be over. Now, I must ask, did your brother take a strong dislike to Mr Kersey?"

Maria, who had been looking directly at the detective, turned away and made great play of trying to collect her thoughts on that subject. "Not exactly to Mr Kersey," she began, at last. "James appeared to harbour the notion that Mr Kersey was the Devil himself. Like all good Christians, James hates the Devil and all his works, but no, Mr West, he did not hate Mr Kersey."

Westcott did not point out the fault in this reasoning. "If it is possible, Miss Marston, I would like to talk with Mr Marston."

"We are not allowed to visit at present, but I am assured that he is gradually being restored to better health with the treatment he is receiving."

"How did your brother come to be at this ....?"

"Asylum, Mr West. It is a private asylum. His admission was arranged by Mr Skinner and his nephew. I am so grateful to both of them and to all the friends who have supported me."

Westcott made no comment, but stored the information for consideration at a later time. With the gardener having taken up position within earshot on the right and his son on the left, they walked back towards the house. "Just two last questions, Miss Marston," the detective began and felt the young woman become tense. That, too, he stored away. "Why did Mr Kersey visit your brother soon after he arrived in the village?"

"My brother did not tell me. I know that he was annoyed that a man who was unwilling to attend his services should expect him to give him help and advice."

"But you have no idea of the subject on which advice was being sought?"

"None, Mr West. And the second question?" Maria added. She laughed to make light of it, but the detective was sure there were some questions she did not want asked.

"Have you any idea why Mr Kersey should come to Upton Market?"

"I do not know the purpose of his visit," the young woman answered, choosing her words carefully.

Westcott felt that, if he knew the exact question to ask, he could learn more from Maria. He did not know, but he did spring an extra question upon her. "Miss Marston, did you know Mr Kersey before the day of his journey to Upton Market?"

Relaxing and smiling, Maria answered, "No, Mr West."

That, at least, was the whole truth, the detective decided.

CHAPTER 13

With Carrie leading the way, Westcott was taken up to Constance Brown's apartments, which were up the back stairs, but not as far up as the attic with the lesser servants' rooms.

"How are you settling in, Carrie?" Westcott asked. "Are you enjoying your work?"

Carrie, displaying a natural gift for walking up stairs while turning her head over her shoulder to talk, replied that her new job was like Heaven. "Sally moans," she went on, "but she's never worked for old Mrs Jakes. After working for that old witch anything would be an improvement. 'Ere we are, sir. Knock and wait for an answer."

"I think that you are meant to do that, Carrie. Then you step into the room and announce me."

"Announce you?" the girl queried.

"Say who I am and that I am here," Westcott explained.

"Oh, I can do that." Carrie rapped on the door with great vigour, then looked at her knuckles and stifled a grumble. Pressing her ear to the door, she whispered, "I can't never 'ear if they answers or not." She listened again. "Was that 'er or not? I'll just 'ave to risk it."

To ensure that she was not disturbing the housekeeper in a private moment, she opened the door and called, "Oo-ee, Mrs Brown. It's me, Carrie." As the girl added, "Your cousin's 'ere." Westcott heard the housekeeper murmur, "It couldn't be anyone else but you, Carrie."

Coming forward, Mrs Brown said, "Thank-you, Carrie," adding as Carrie stood there smiling benignly upon them, "That will be all, my child, but try to remember what we said about speaking carefully and clearly."

Westcott stood aside to let the servant pass. "Oo-ee, I'm 'ere," he joked, correcting it to, "Oo-ee, I'm here."

"Come in and sit down, Charles. I'll call you that to establish the habit. As for Carrie's 'Oo-ee,' it's that or a formal announcement good enough for royalty. There's no happy medium with the child at the moment, but she is determined to better herself and become a housekeeper. I shall give her every help and encouragement."

"She's a good girl."

"I think you're right. I would not have chosen her myself, but I think that there is not an ounce of malice in the girl and you cannot say that of many people."

"You don't think much of your fellow man?" Westcott asked. Spotting a large tabby cat curled up in a basket, he added, "You prefer cats?"

"No, certainly not. There are good cats and bad cats, just like people," she laughed.

"Very true," the detective agreed. "My cat says the same."

Not sure if she was being made fun of, Mrs Brown turned the conversation to the refreshments she had made. Westcott tucked in with a will. Not being at ease eating and talking, he was content just to eat and make a few comments on the excellent quality of all he consumed. Finally, having voiced his appreciation again, he brushed all the crumbs from his lap to the floor.

Rubbing his hands, the detective began, "Now, let's get down to business."

"You are a bachelor," Mrs Brown guessed, making it a comment, rather than a question.

"How did you know, Mrs .....Constance?"

"There is something of the detective in all of us," Constance commented, dryly.

Deciding he did not like the way the conversation was going and that he must leave as soon as possible, Westcott put to the housekeeper the same questions that he had put to her mistress, only to receive the same answers.

"Let me ask a little more about how Mr Marston came to be in the asylum. Had there been any talk of it before the murder?"

"I do not know the ins and outs of it, Charles, but I do not think so. We all considered Mr Marston to be under great strain and, to be quite honest, he was never an easy man, but we all assumed he would recover with time. Time is a great healer."

There was a pause while Constance watched more crumbs swept to the floor. Then she suggested, "Perhaps you are a widower rather than a bachelor."

"Oh, no!" Westcott asserted with conviction. "I have no interest in marriage. The single state suits me and will suit me till I die. But you are a widow, I believe?"

"Yes," the housekeeper replied shortly. "To return to your question. When Jenkins met with Mr Marston and claimed to have seen a knife in his hand, some put it down to Jenkins' having lost his bearings and letting his imagination run away with him in the fog. With the fog so dense the body was not found until the following day."

"At that point," Mrs Brown continued, "all of Miss Marston's suitors rallied round. George Skinner Montague and his uncle did a great deal. I include his uncle as Edward Skinner is always pressing his nephew's case. Henry Storr was also a great support. And Mr Howard helped, but not as a suitor."

"Mmm!" Westcott murmured. "And it was these people who arranged for Mr Marston's speedy departure to the asylum?"

"So I understand, but I was, of course, not involved in the discussions." Mrs Brown explained, "The Marstons and the Storrs have a family connection through the female line. That is how Mr Marston came to be given the living of Upton Market. The Storrs have it within their gift." After a brief pause, she added, "Having thought the matter over, I think that neither the Skinners, with their hopes for the future, nor the Storrs wanted a convicted murderer in the family."

"They were willing to have an unconvicted one, or a madman, in the family."

"While there is no conviction, there must remain doubt," Constance commented, "and, as for madness, Miss Marston is Mr Marston's half-sister. Though I should not say it to anyone else, it was his mother who was considered somewhat eccentric."

There was silence for a moment and then Westcott said that he must be on his way.

"Just before I go, Constance, as you are my cousin, I should know a little more about you so that I am not caught out if someone asks me about you. What was your maiden name, for instance?"

"Constance Green." For some reason, she did not look directly at the detective as she spoke.

"And you married a Brown?" Westcott asked, before realising it was a silly comment to make.

Constance now looked very ill at ease. She seemed about to say something, but was silent. Westcott, who had expected a simple answer in the affirmative, waited expectantly.

"Well," Constance began and then stopped.

Kindly trying to save his cousin any embarrassment, Westcott hurried to her rescue. "You are not a widow? Your husband is not dead, but he lives elsewhere?"

"Yes, I am not a widow and yes, my husband is not dead."

Before a puzzled Westcott could bring the obviously embarrassing conversation to an end, Constance explained, blushing in her confession. "He is not dead, as he was never born. I am not married. I am that despised creature, a spinster."

"Not despised, I am sure," Westcott murmured gallantly.

"You know that is not true," the housekeeper said with feeling. Westcott saw that it was an angry Constance Green, not the efficient, self-controlled Constance Brown speaking. She resumed, "We are 'on the shelf', because it is thought that no one has ever cared to take us down. We are maiden aunts, prim and proper, to be forgotten if we are poor and visited on Sunday afternoons if there is a chance we have a little put by to leave to our relations. We are considered lower than any married woman however young, stupid or unhappily married, abused or beaten she may be. Any husband," she continued with increasing anger, "a spendthrift, drunkard, even a pursuer of other women, is considered better than none."

About to utter some words of denial, Westcott was given no time to speak even one syllable.

"Bachelors are seen as happy and carefree. Chased and adored by spinsters, widows and, even, wives. After all, they are single because they have never bothered to ask anyone to marry them. They are masters of their own fates. Spinsters are single because they have never been asked. They must sit on the shelf and let life pass them by." Constance paused at last.

"I have never stopped to think about it," Westcott murmured.

"I believe you. You, like everyone else have simply accepted the generally held opinion without thought or question."

Westcott considered the matter. "I am afraid that is true. But," he continued, trying to free himself of any blame, "I have met many spinsters whom I have greatly admired."

"Why? For bearing their lot in life bravely? For smiling as they crochet shawls for their nieces and nephews?"

Feeling he could not win, Westcott asked, "Is that why you call yourself Mrs Brown?"

"You must deal with the world as you find it. I would much prefer to be called 'Miss' and judged on my own character rather than one imposed upon me in the popular imagination, but that is not possible. Part of the reason for claiming to have been married is that it stops the young girls giggling and imagining I keep an eye on them, not for their own good, but to spy on them kissing their sweethearts and to make them do extra work out of envy. Mostly, it is because employers like their housekeepers to be unattached and able to devote all their time and energies to the family and yet – what shall I say? – remain normal."

"My goodness," Westcott said, feeling somewhat battered by the storm.

"There," Constance sighed, "now I am living proof that spinsters are nervous creatures, always giving vent to their emotions."

"Well, now," Westcott smiled, "there I am not guilty. I thought all women were like that."

They laughed, until Constance explained, "People don't believe me, so I don't usually mention it, but I have never wanted to marry and, certainly, never to have children. I could never, as I have seen so many women do, rich and poor, hand their minds and spirit over to the control of a man. I could never wait on one man hand and foot without gratitude or wages in return. And I cannot bear the thought of going through the agony of childbirth every two or three years, risking my life, only to have the babies die like the young Marston boys."

"But you admired Mrs Marston?"

"Mrs Marston was a saint. She was so patient, turning her husband's strictness and holiness with a light word or a laugh. And, while she encouraged him to spend time with the children, she stood between them when he was angry, showing, by her example, how to train and guide them with love and encouragement, rather than with harsh words and punishments."

"There, there, Constance," the detective said softly, patting her arm and reflecting that no one realised how devoted servants could be and how they, like the family, needed to grieve and be comforted. "Then we must do what we can for her husband and for Miss Marston." He thought that perhaps he should put off questioning the housekeeper further, but she had her own questions.

"Charles," she inquired earnestly, "do you think that Mr Marston murdered Peter Kersey?"

"Do you?" Westcott asked.

From her prompt reply, the detective knew that Constance had been giving the matter much thought. "No," she said firmly. "He is a strict man, sometimes to the point of unkindness. He is a thoughtless man, often to the point of riding roughshod over others' feelings. But he lives by the Ten Commandments; there has never been any doubt about that." Having been so sure of her answer, she added lamely, "Yet all the evidence points to him."

"The police view is that there was a falling out between Kersey and his friends. A jealous rival, perhaps. Or there was some talk of a beating he received only a few weeks earlier."

For a few minutes Constance considered her words, then admitted frankly, "It seems to me that such stories have been exaggerated to protect Mr Marston. His friends, I am sure, feel that now he is confined and watched over carefully he can do no harm. Everyone is spared the disgrace of a trial and Mr Marston escapes death, even if he is confined to the end of his days."

"I think that you may be right. The view that the culprit was some stray attacker was put to me as soon as I arrived in the village, by two men named Mansfield and Rimmer. No doubt they were expressing the view of their masters, Skinner and Howard."

"No doubt. Rimmer has worked for Howard since he was a lad. Mansfield arrived with Skinner a few years ago. Both have done well for themselves by unquestioning loyalty. Wasn't Henry Storr's man, John Blackburn, there? He is another servant of unswerving loyalty." Before Westcott could answer, she asked, "What will be your next step, Charles?"

"Let us say that, knowing Mr Marston's character, he could not have committed this crime. I think I must next look at Peter Kersey's character to see who might want to kill him."

"I did not meet with the young man face-to-face," Constance said, "but I hear gossip among the servants. By all accounts, they thought he was something of a rabble-rouser. He made a speech in the churchyard, you know, which offended many." She explained, "Here in the country, working men may laugh at their masters and grumble behind their backs from dawn to dusk, but to their faces it's, 'Yes, sir,' and 'No, sir,' until the cows come home. They know that is how it must be if they are to find work and keep out of the workhouse."

Pausing for a second, the housekeeper continued, "I am not suggesting for a minute that the farm labourers, the boatmen and others who work in the Uptons follow their masters against their own convictions. They, themselves, are deeply traditional, seeing radical ideas as belonging to the large towns and having nothing to do with them. They would be against a rabble-rouser on two counts, because they disagreed with him and because he might cause trouble for them with the masters."

"And the masters," Westcott observed, "would also dislike him on two counts, because they disagreed with him and because he might ferment discontent among the work people. Well," the detective concluded, "we have enlarged the field so that I must suspect everyone in the village."

"Not of murder, surely," Constance protested. "Of a beating, possibly."

"We shall see." Westcott returned to the point which troubled him. "Have you heard any gossip as to why he came to the village?"

"None. Your man who might know that, Charles, is Tom Osborne, Carrie's brother."

"I had heard that he was a friend of the murdered man."

"What will you do next?"

"Ask if you can spare an old bachelor a couple of those dainty sandwiches of yours."

"I can do better than that for a newly discovered cousin," the housekeeper smiled, ringing the bell.

A clatter on the stairs made them both exclaim, "Carrie," and laugh as she knocked a mighty knock and then peeped hesitantly round the door.

"Carrie, please make Mr Westcott a substantial sandwich. He is going on a long walk."

While the detective puzzled about the long walk, Carrie pondered the request made of her. Eventually, she asked, "A sub what?"

"A doorstep," Westcott told her and her face brightened as enlightenment dawned.

"Then," the housekeeper said, causing Carrie to pause in mid-rush, "you may go and see your brother, on condition that you take Mr West with you and set him on the way to Twilight Woods. It's a little way past Tom's, isn't it?"

He had never, Westcott decided when Carrie returned with a huge hunk of bread and cheese only two minutes later, seen any food prepared so quickly and efficiently. Placing a peck on Constance Brown's cheek, he followed the grinning servant out of the house.

CHAPTER 14

Unusually, as Westcott made his way along the village street with Carrie, he was not looking and listening to spot any clue which might pop up before him. Instead, letting Carrie's chatter wash over him and quite oblivious of the blacksmith and other tradesmen and their apprentices staring at him as he passed, Westcott kept going over and over the last few minutes of his visit to Mrs Brown. The woman had as good as told him what he was to do next. It might well be, if he stopped to think, that this was a good way of being introduced to Tom Osborne without arousing suspicion. Left to himself, he would have gone walking in the direction of the young man's house, but he had not been consulted on the matter. The woman was worse than his superintendent in the police had been. He had always tried to organise other people instead of minding his own business.

Recognising the signs of annoyance emanating from her silent companion, and having long ago learned how to avoid making herself the target of any grown-up's bad temper, Carrie had fallen silent too. It was a while before the detective caught up with the present and asked, "What did you say, Carrie?"

"I said that were Captain Skinner Montague's groom 'aving the 'orse shod, Mr West."

"Where?" Westcott asked, looking around.

"We was passing the forge when I said it, sir," Carrie replied, careful to keep her own justifiable annoyance out of her voice.

"Sorry, child. I had something on my mind."

"Nothing's wrong with Mrs Brown, is there, sir?"

"No," the detective replied without conviction, thinking of all he could say. "We were talking about old times and my mind was still on that."

"I ain't got no aunts, nor uncles, nor cousins, nor nobody as I knows of. Tom says as 'ow 'e can seem to remember some, but it were a long time ago. Me Pa died before I were born and me Ma died soon after – soon after I were born, that is. Then it were the work'ouse for us both, me in the Girls' and Tom in the Boys'. But 'e managed to get to see me. Where there's a will there's a way, eh, sir?"

"My cousin remarked that she was pleased with the start you had made," Westcott said and smiled to see the look of pleasure which spread across the child's face.

"Some don't like 'er," Carrie confided, "though most as work for 'er do. Strict she is, but fair and you can't ask no more than that, can you?" After a pause to reflect on her own words, the servant asserted, "It's 'cos she's a widder. Widders is more understanding – more ordinary, like the rest of us. Spinster 'ousekeepers is a problem. Dried up and bitter Sally sez. She used to work for one before she come to the vicarage."

"Is that so," Westcott commented. To test out Constance's theories, he asked, "But Mrs Brown isn't like that."

"No. Like I said, she's a widder. You can 'ave a good laugh with 'er and go to 'er with your troubles. Sally and me and the others all sez that. And she's very kind to Miss Marston, even when Miss Marston tries to take over 'er job. She tells us to mind the mistress, even if she is just a slip of a girl."

"A slip of a girl?" Westcott queried

"Well," Carrie laughed, "them ain't Mrs Brown's own words, but you know what I mean."

"Strict, but fair," the detective thought. That was just what the junior policemen said about him.

"Our Tom lives just up this lane, Mr West." Carrie took a sharp right turn into a narrow pathway. "Don't know if 'e'll be in, mind you, though 'e ain't 'ad no work lately. Where you're going is straight on past and up the 'ill. You gets a lovely view from the top."

From his London days, the detective had learned that most young men were suspicious of older men. They did not need a reason. The very sight of an older man made them hunch their shoulders, thrust their hands into their pockets and stare and scowl. If addressed, they grunted and, although the exact words could not be made out, they were clearly aggressive.

It was a surprise then, when a tall, fair-haired young man came out of a ramshackle wooden hut, greeted his sister with a hug and politely asked to be introduced to the gentleman. How did it happen, Westcott asked himself, not for the first time, that some children who were knocked and kicked about by life and fate could grow up to be so open and friendly, while others turned violent and evil?

When Carrie explained who her companion was, Tom greeted him and added, "Sorry you see me idling about, Mr West, but I were dismissed from me work by me master and now no one is keen to take me on."

Coming at once to her brother's defence, Carrie explained, "It were when Peter Kersey stood up in the churchyard and made 'is speech running down masters and all. We know as 'ow it were mostly true, but you don't go around saying things like that. Trust our Tom to 'ave to go and cheer 'im on."

"I've got me dignity and pride," Tom claimed.

"And no job and no wages," his sister pointed out.

"At least they didn't kill me," Tom replied. "I swear it were Skinner and Bradley and that 'Oward as killed Peter. Expect their men did it. They just let Mr Marston take the blame."

"You knew Mr Kersey, I hear," Westcott said, once again taking on the role of inquisitive newcomer.

"'E were the best friend I ever 'ad."

"You ain't got none now, 'cept me," Carrie observed, displaying an annoying habit of pointing out the truth.

"Why ever would they want to kill him?" the detective asked.

"'Cos 'e were calling on their workmen to demand decent wages and 'cos 'e were learning us about our rights. And," he added, glaring at his sister, "a man 'as to stick up for 'is rights or 'e don't deserve to 'ave none."

There were questions the detective wished to ask but, afraid of arousing suspicions, he waited to see what he was told. Fortunately, he did not have to wait long. Once he had murmured, "Kersey sounds like a good man. I wish I had known him," Tom provided some answers.

"'E were from London where you're from, Mr West."

"London's a big place, Tom," Westcott smiled.

"I know that," Tom said hastily, fearing he had shown his ignorance, "but 'e'd been all over London. 'E might even 'ave come in your shop now and again."

"Perhaps he did," the detective agreed, remembering his role as a draper. "Was he born there?"

"Yes. Some saint's name, the place where 'e lived as a boy."

As his mind ran through all the saints' names in London, Westcott's heart sank.

"England and St George," Tom muttered, trying to stir his memory. His face lit up. "St George's out east of London."

"St George in the East," Westcott suggested hopefully.

"That's it, sir. 'Ave you ever 'eard of it?"

"That parish is just near mine," Westcott told him. "You can start walking

68

in Limehouse, turn a corner and soon end up in St George in the East."

"Fancy that!" Carrie exclaimed, quite unable to imagine villages, as she saw them, without a long stretch of fields between them

"Peter weren't used to the country," Tom laughed. "Never knew which way 'e were going, north, south, east or west." It reminded Westcott that the town is as different from the country as the country from the town. To the villagers Kersey would have been a town bumpkin. "'E used to tell me as 'ow the streets were all lit up with gas lights. Were it true?"

"Yes," Westcott confirmed and then asked, "Did he talk of his family or any friends?"

"'E 'ad no family, 'e said and 'e never mentioned no friends, I'm sure of that."

Having waited a minute in case anything occurred to the young man, Westcott turned the conversation to another path along which he wanted it to go. "What on earth was he doing here?"

"Come to spread 'is ideas," Tom claimed. "Ideas don't usually spread this far. Our masters see to that."

"But why here?" the detective persisted. "Did he come straight here on purpose, or just happen to end up here?"

"Don't know the answer to that one," the young man said. The question had not occurred to him before. To him, Kersey had appeared like a breath of fresh air out of the blue.

"Do you think he knew he was in danger?" Westcott ventured to ask.

Tom gave the matter some thought. That question had never occurred to him either. "Looking back on it, I think 'e might 'ave. 'E often went off on 'is own. Wouldn't let me go with 'im. Now I see as 'ow 'e didn't want to place me in danger." Angrily, Tom wiped the tears from his cheeks. He was angry at what had happened to his friend and angry that he could do nothing about it except shed a tear.

"Now, Carrie," Westcott said suddenly, putting his hand in his pocket, "If you would run and get us some tea, a loaf and a large lump of cheese, perhaps Tom will invite me in to rest my weary old bones and tell me all these wonderful ideas his friend taught him about."

Carrie hesitated. She had brought some of the food from her own meals, which she had saved for her brother, and they had both had enough of charity to last them a life-time, but she was a realist and knew that Tom had no money of his own.

"It's not charity," Westcott assured her. "I'm hungry and I'm simply asking Tom to join me."

Receiving a nod from her brother, Carrie took the money and hurried off. Westcott followed Tom into the cottage.

CHAPTER 15

The interior of the shack was so dark Westcott could scarcely see the chair he was offered, but he did see enough to realise that its maker had never set eyes on the pattern books of the great furniture makers. Only two factors had dominated the design and they were the nature of the second hand pieces of wood which the maker had to hand and his practical experience of the purpose of a chair in the scheme of things. It had a seat, four legs roughly equal in length and a back made of sticks topped by a solid, oblong piece of wood. Some effort had been made to shape the back by shaving the edges of the sticks and of the solid block and to round them off, but Westcott very soon found that it was not to match his shape that the trouble had been taken.

"I was at the Chartist gatherings in London in 1848," the detective began, once Tom was seated on a wobbly three legged stool, the only other seating available in the room.

"So was Peter," Tom replied enthusiastically. "Though 'e were only young."

Westcott knew that he had made the right opening. He had the lad's confidence already. He continued, "Suppose it was Chartist ideas your friend was eager to spread."

So confident was he that he knew everything Kersey would have believed in that he looked all around the room while awaiting Tom's reply. The wooden interior had been lined with a mixture of mud, lime and horse hair, which served to keep out both the heat of summer and the chill of winter. He was taken by surprise when the young man finally spoke.

"I suppose they come into it, but that weren't all and 'e never made speeches, 'cepting one, Peter didn't."

"Oh," the detective replied, "I'm sorry. I misunderstood. I heard some-one describe him as a 'rabble-rouser' and I assumed he stood up and made speeches."

"No," Tom laughed. "'E'd 'ave blushed and stuttered if 'e'd 'ad to do that. But 'e said as 'ow it were 'is duty to pass on what 'e'd learnt from all 'is reading and 'e'd answer any questions or explain anything to anyone. And 'e'd argue it out with any master, if 'e 'ad to and put up with any amount of name calling."

Giving up his study of the room and his reflections on rural poverty, which was clearly little different from urban poverty when all was said and done, Westcott began to listen more intently.

"Peter said it were all in the Bible," Tom continued. "If you read it properly, that is. When I were at school in the work'ouse, they just taught us the bits what they said told us 'ow to respect our masters. It were all in the Ten Commandments, they said. But Peter said as 'ow that were the Old Law. The New Law were all in the Two Commandments. You was to love God and treat your neighbour like you wanted to be treated yourself."

Westcott passed no comment as he digested this and paid attention to what Tom still had to say.

"Peter said as 'ow 'e expected there'd always be men and masters, but if the masters see their men as neighbours they'd pay 'em a decent wage and do all they could to keep 'em on in good times and bad and in sickness as well. And," he went on, having paused for breath, "if the workmen sees their masters as their neighbours, they'd give a fair day's work and wouldn't steal nothing be'ind their backs."

It was no surprise, the detective decided, that there had been scorn poured on these ideas by some men as well as by masters. Tom said exactly what he was thinking. "There ain't many workmen as don't steal the odd turnip or bit of wood when they 'as 'alf a chance, you know, Mr West."

"I had observed that in life," Westcott remarked, leaving Tom to conclude that drapers' shopmen were as dishonest as farm labourers.

"And there ain't many masters," Tom pointed out, "as don't send you packing when the weather's bad and expect you to be back smiling and eager when things pick up again."

"It's a far from perfect world," the detective agreed. "So you'd say that Peter was more interested in religion than in politics?"

Tom looked puzzled. "You mean in church instead of Parliament?"

"That's about it."

"'E never went to church. 'E said as soon as people set up a church they become self-satisfied and set in their ways. They began looking inward instead of out and big ideas got lost in worrying about little, unimportant rules."

Those, the detective realised, were roughly his own views. Seeing that Tom was considering how best to express his friend's thoughts, he smiled and waited. It was quite a long wait. Clearly the young man, as perhaps Peter himself had done, found it difficult to sum up all that was included in

72

the command to love your God and your neighbour.

"Peter said as 'ow, if we loved God, it were our duty to make the world a better place. 'E weren't really interested in politics. 'E said each one of us 'ad to work to make 'Eaven 'ere on earth. But 'e said we 'ad a long way to go, so we 'ad to deal with life as we found it to start with. We needed laws to protect the weak – like not making little children work – and we need to change bad laws – like them as make people 'oo need 'elp in times of trouble go into the work'ouse, where they're separated, wives from 'usbands and parents from children. They punish 'em, you know, for being ill or out of work."

"So, Kersey was a Chartist, then," the detective suggested, still trying to pigeon hole the dead man. "Supported their six aims, did he?"

"Well, yes. Votes for everyone. Letting men with no property be M.P.s and paying 'em, so poor men can get a seat. And secret ballots, of course, so them as 'as money can't bribe them as 'asn't with ale." Tom counted on his fingers. "That's four." He asked himself, "What were the others? Oh, yes. making the constit... the places all the same size so rich men can't own them places as 'as only a few 'undred voters. But not electing new men to Parliament every year. 'E said the Members wouldn't 'ave time to get nothing done."

Westcott was about to speak, but Tom added, "And 'e wouldn't 'ave nothing to do with talk of revolution nor violence. Said it were always the innocent caught in the middle."

Having waited this time to make sure that the young man had finished, Westcott remarked, "Seems your friend was a good and thoughtful man."

Not willing to be seen crying again, Tom hurried outside to meet his sister, returning with the food. Both Westcott and Carrie suddenly decided that they were not hungry after all. Tom was free to eat his first good meal for weeks and still have something left over.

"Now," Carrie said to the detective, "I just 'ave time to show you the way before I 'urry back to work."

Having forgotten that this was the excuse Constance had given for his wanting to go by Tom's house, Westcott was slow to reply. "My old bones are too weary today, Carrie. I'll go up there another day."

"Just call in when you go past and I'll come and show you the way," Tom suggested.

"I'll enjoy your company, young man," Westcott answered, shaking

Tom's hand and taking his leave.

As he walked away, Westcott's mind went back to the Chartist demonstrations of 1848. Had he not lived through those days and witnessed the movement at the moment of its strongest flow and highest tide, he would have dismissed Tom's accusations against Skinner, Bradley and Howard as the words of a man in deep distress at his friend's death. But he had lived through those times, had taken a part, if only a minor one, in planning how to contain the thousands who would gather in the capital. He had listened to discussions on how to prevent matters getting out of hand when, in the tinder of many working men's aspirations and frustrations, a spark might fire a riot, which would flare into revolution.

The detective recalled those days when each report of revolution on the Continent was greeted with celebrations and cries of 'Long live the Republic', when reports came from all parts of the country of men arming themselves ready, if their petition was rejected, to fight for their rights. And he recalled the very day in April when a great demonstration had been planned to present the Chartist petition to Parliament. It had been forbidden, but the newspapers greeted the dawn with forecasts of great disturbances and everyone asked, "Will today see revolution in England?"

With the Queen safely tucked away on the Isle of Wight and Wellington at the head of a mighty force of troops and armed police to control the bridges, those who did attempt to gather were herded into small groups and shepherded out of the centre of London. Looking back, it had all been a bit of a damp squib, but there were many who were convinced that it was only the great show of force and the solidarity of the middle and upper classes which had saved the day.

In particular, the detective recalled the dozens among the wealthy and aristocracy who had answered the call to enrol as special constables and hold back the tide of revolution. They had returned to their mansions at the end of the day, congratulating themselves on having defended the Queen and the constitution and saved their country and all they held dear from the mob. And there had been many amongst them who said matters should never have been allowed to go so far. Why, some had asked, give the leaders time to arouse the rabble and the mob? Why not pick out the ring leaders as soon as they began to preach their seditious nonsense and hang them as an example to any other trouble makers? Were Skinner, Bradley, Howard and Storr of the same mind? Would they have considered it their duty to remove any threat to all they believed in and held dear by killing Kersey before he contaminated local working men?

CHAPTER 16

"Enjoying the sunshine, Charles?" a woman's voice asked. "The flowers look rather sad and in need of deadheading."

Had he not been expecting Constance Brown, Westcott thought, or recognised her voice, he would have known it was her by her instant attention to detail to bring everything up to her own high standards. At any moment, he feared, she would start on the job herself, but he was wrong. She sat quietly on the chair he had placed for her, anxious to hear all he had discovered. In the absence of Tom Cat, he found himself relating everything he had learned from Tom Osborne.

As he finished, she asked, "You really think that it is possible that Mr Skinner, Mr Bradley, Mr Howard or even the Storrs played a part in the murder?"

"On the one hand," the detective answered, "I find it hard to believe. A beating? That is possible. Murder? Now that's a different kettle of fish. Though I have to admit I have met people – and respectable ones at that – who believe English society was ordained by God on the eighth day. It is to be defended at all costs. Such a man would see himself not as a murderer, but as a Saviour of his Nation and Champion of Queen and Country."

Constance considered the names mentioned. "Bradley's sons are hot heads. They would set about anyone just because he came from Upton Market rather than Upton St John. Skinner? He so wants to be thought a gentleman that I cannot see his taking any risks ..."

"Unless he wanted to please those who are gentlemen."

"True, but I was thinking of any reason he might himself have for disliking Kersey. He employs only a few servants. He would not risk all he has worked so hard for just because Kersey was spreading discontent amongst them."

"Who would you favour as the murderer from the names I have listed?"

As usual, Constance did not reply without some thought. At last, she said, "Mr Howard. I favour Mr Howard as a man who bemoans any change and sees the country going to ruin since the Reform Act."

"That ...," Westcott began, but Constance had not finished.

"This raises problems for you, I can see. Even policemen do not have the freedom to question those with wealth and influence. Such people ask the Chief Constable to dine – no more often than they need, but frequently enough to learn all that is going on and make him aware of their standing and connections."

"You took the words right out of my mouth," Westcott commented, while Constance read his next thought.

"Of course," she remarked, "such men would not have committed the crime themselves. Their henchmen, Mansfield, Rimmer and Blackburn, would have done the deed or even paid some passing criminal to do it for them."

"My very thoughts," Westcott said dryly. "But how do we get round the problem of my not coming out of the top social drawer?"

"The very question I was asking myself," the housekeeper laughed. The complete lack of malice in her amusement allowed the detective to smile, too.

Equally without malice, he suggested, "I am sure you have an answer, Constance."

"The best answer I can think of is that you talk with the new curate, Mr Robert Hopgood. Now he is from the top drawer. He is a cousin of the Marstons and related to everyone who is anyone. I shall arrange a meeting."

Almost before Westcott could thank her, Constance continued, with obvious concern for his opinion, "Charles, I hope you will agree with something which I plan to arrange." She paused for Westcott's comment, but, not knowing what she had planned, he gave no other response than a quiet smile.

"If one of these men, or more than one if they are all in the plot, carried out this crime, then they have tried to put the blame on Mr Marston and have gone to the extreme of having him locked away to prevent further investigation. Miss Marston requires some male protection."

On the alert immediately against matrimonial advances, Westcott smiled guardedly. She was going to suggest that he moved into the vicarage.

"I am sure that you would perform the task perfectly, but it would be unseemly for you, as the housekeeper's cousin, to take on the part. I think it best if I persuade Miss Marston to invite the curate, who, as I've said, is a relation, to live in the house while he is taking over all of Mr Marston's duties."

Constance looked to the detective for his reactions. He remained guarded. To his surprise, now that she had not chosen him for the task, he felt disappointed.

"A very good idea," Westcott said, at last, summoning up all the enthusiasm he could muster. He might have guessed that a woman such as Constance, whose satisfaction in her work had come from serving the late Mrs Marston, would now transfer her protective concern to the young and vulnerable Maria.

"I have arranged something else which concerns you, Charles."

He had been right first time, Westcott thought smugly. She was going to ask him to move into the house, no doubt to protect her.

"I have spoken with Miss Marston," the housekeeper continued, "and she has agreed to lend Carrie to you to do your cooking and cleaning and her brother Tom as gardener and handyman."

"But...," Westcott began in surprise. This was not what he had expected.

Misunderstanding his reaction, Constance explained, "Miss Marston will give you the funds for their wages, but you must be the one to pay them and she will reimburse you in addition to your fee."

"Why ...?" the detective attempted to intervene.

"Why? To give you more time. No, let me be honest with you, Charles. It is a chance to allow Carrie and Tom to live under the same roof as a family. Apart from a few years before they were taken into the workhouse, they have been totally separated by the barbaric system."

"Of, course," Westcott agreed meekly. "That is very thoughtful of you Constance." He felt a little guilty for having been so preoccupied with his own concerns, but comforted himself by deciding that he would have thought of it himself had he been in the position to arrange such matters.

The housekeeper had planned all the details. "I'll send you Carrie and let her think that it is at your request. She will readily accept," Constance went on without allowing a trace of a smile to appear on her face, "that all men are helpless and cannot manage a house for themselves. Then you can ask her to suggest someone for the lad's job."

"What if she chooses someone else?" Westcott asked, realising as he did so that he would find no other hole to pick on in the plan.

"She will not."

Should he object, Westcott wondered, to being organised by a woman, even when it would add to his comfort.

Constance had something else planned for him. She explained that, if he wished to talk with Bradley, he might do worse than try to meet the farmer as he returned from market.

"I'll think about it," the detective answered grudgingly.

CHAPTER 17

"This is far enough," Westcott said to himself, slowly lowering himself on to the wide grass verge. His feet, in fact his whole body, had been urging him to make this decision for the last half mile, but he had resisted. He had struggled on until he was far enough from Upton Market to give himself time for a reasonably long conversation with Farmer Bradley on the way back. As the sign posts were indicating, he had come as far as Upton St John, the village dominated by the family seat of the Storrs, Upton House.

Sitting there and catching his breath, he meditated on the wide meaning encompassed by the word 'house'. How could a two up two down, dingy, decaying and damp building in Whitechapel be classed under the same heading as the vast edifice he saw standing imposingly at the top of the high ground before him? The warren in Whitechapel probably housed as many people in one room as Upton House contained in all its grand rooms. At this point Westcott stifled the thought that the Storrs no doubt had another mansion in the West End. He was in danger of allowing Kersey's view of things to infect his own. Life had jogged along happily enough for him until now with his just showing kindness where he could, keeping his feet on the ground, applying practical common sense to life as it was lived and leaving plans of Utopia to those with their heads in the clouds.

The detective had arrived here to waylay Philip Bradley simply because he could not think of a better way of contriving a chance meeting than the one Constance had suggested. She had pointed out that, as Thursday was market day in the nearby town, it could be predicted almost to the minute on any church clock when each traveller would return. First would come those hurrying home to put the money from their sales under the mattress, then those who were willing to spend just a little of their takings on bargains and essentials and next those who had stayed to dine well and would bring the wife a bonnet or trinket. All would finally be followed by either those who had no one to come home to or those who had a wife who was hiding and hoping her husband would be too drunk to beat her.

A few buyers and sellers returning from the market passed him and he replied in kind to cold stares or warm smiles. To those who offered him a ride he answered that he was just resting, but, when they were out of sight, he prepared himself to be scowling and inspecting his foot the minute

Bradley came into view. When that happened, the detective put on a pained expression, pummelled his foot and moaned quietly.

"Should have tough enough feet, you coming from London," the farmer called, all smiles and contentment. He pulled up the horse level with the detective. "I've been to London in my time, you know. Oh yes, we tramped round the Exhibition for days and didn't miss a single thing. Mrs Bradley saw to that. She's never been satisfied with anything in the house since. But I can walk many a mile here, day in and day out without a twinge. A few hours in London and I was sitting with my feet in bowl after bowl of hot water. Luckily the serving girl who brought it was a pretty young thing."

Before Westcott could reply, Bradley continued, in reflective mood, "Perhaps it's with walking slowly. Keeps your weight bearing down on your legs more, do you think? Or, perhaps, walking slowly you take more steps and that does it. In the country we stride around our land with pride. Not like all them slow city gents we see at the Exhibition."

"Perhaps," Westcott suggested, "they were looking at the exhibits. I think, usually, we walk every bit as fast as you country men." Realising that, to defend the city dweller, he was being dragged into a silly argument, the detective suggested, "Pavements are very hard. There are more pavements in London than I have come across in Upton Market."

"Yet you're having trouble here," Bradley pointed out, "but never mind, climb up and I'll see you get home without your feet having to touch the ground again. We'll soon have you home, Mr West."

"Not too soon," the detective said to himself. To Bradley he said, "I'll admit you country men are in touch with the essentials of life."

"You never said a truer word," Bradley put in, "No fancy ideas or airs and graces down here."

"Nothing like a stay in the country to blow the cob-webs off you," Westcott went on. "As you say, you've no place for fancy ideas here."

When the farmer replied, the detective almost felt guilty that he had caught his fish so quickly, without experimenting with several types of bait or struggling to bring him in.

"You'd think so, wouldn't you, Mr West?" Bradley asked, as he pointed out to Westcott the easiest way to climb into the carriage. "We tried to make that young feller as was killed see things our way – Nature's way, you might say – but he had no sense between his ears."

"Quite wild theories some say." Westcott surprised himself by not including himself in this group.

"Have you," Bradley inquired, smiling as he recalled the stories, "read those books by that naval feller Marryat?"

"Indeed. Very enjoyable yarns."

"And a good deal of common sense between them covers, sir. Can't recall if it were Peter Easy, or Mr Midshipman Simple, but one of them proved that this lad's father was an idiot for believing all this nonsense about everyone being equal and having a say in how the country is governed."

The detective, not wishing to prompt his witness, made a noncommittal noise. This sound served to make the horse prick up its ears, listening for instructions. Sensing the horse's hesitation, Bradley called, "Steady there. There's no need to rush for home." Turning to Westcott he confided, "To tell you the truth, Mr West, I take such pleasure in dining with my friends on market day that I'm never ready to go home to the wife."

The farmer sounded as men do who, having dined well and drunk deep, feel sorry for themselves and in need of a sympathetic ear. While more than willing to provide one, Westcott hoped the farmer would not forget the point they had arrived at in their conversation.

"Me, a grown man," Bradley complained, "a pillar of local society, well thought of by my neighbours, the best farmer for miles around, am kept on a very tight rein. I, Mr West, who have no wish to go wild, am kept on a tight lead, while those boys of hers ...."

"And yours," Westcott suggested, just to set the record straight.

Nodding, as though in disbelief, Bradley replied, "Well, I remember being there when they were conceived." Staring ahead, as though addressing the horse, he continued, "There were few enough times for me to have a chance to forget. Once she had her two boys she had no more interest in me. At least prize bulls are allowed to go on to pastures new. Not me. Those brothers of hers always seem to be around to keep an eye on me."

Suddenly, turning to Westcott, Bradley demanded, "Are you married, Mr West?" As the detective shook his head, the farmer commented predictably, "Wise man, sir, wise man."

Apart from the clip-clop of the horse's hooves and the crunching of the slowly turning wheels, there was silence for a while. Fearing that Bradley was falling asleep, Westcott prompted, "You were saying that Peter Kersey ....."

With a sharp jerk, the farmer forced himself awake and uttered, with obvious dismay, "I was talking about her boys. Don't tell me I let out that it was them as gave Kersey a hiding? What will their mother say?"

Thinking quickly, both to comfort the farmer and to elicit his views, Westcott declared, "To your mind, he deserved it, didn't he?"

"To everyone's mind. Oh, I'm not blaming them. All I said," Bradley explained, not having mentioned it before, "was that they can come home covered in blood and all Mrs Bradley does is fuss that they aren't hurt. Now if I come home in suspicious circumstances ....."

"When was the last time that happened?" the detective asked innocently.

"Man to man and to be honest, the last time was when that pretty little widow came to stay with her sister in Upton St John," Bradley confided.

Looking at the smirk on his face, Westcott felt sure that this was the only kind of suspicious circumstance the farmer was ever involved in, apart from battering poor Kersey.

"You were there, then, when this teaching a lesson to Kersey went on?"

Stirring himself again, Bradley looked hard at Westcott. "You seem particularly interested in that. Ninety nine men out of a hundred would rather ask about the widow."

"Murder, ghosts, that sort of thing have always interested me. Every place in the country has its own story to tell. Widows," the detective added with a nudge to Bradley's well covered ribs, "they're two a penny."

"Cost me a deal more than a happenny," Bradley quipped and, obligingly, Westcott laughed loud and long.

"I count you as one of us," Bradley confided. "Not like that policeman feller, Harris. They say he's in Howard's pocket, but I don't trust him. We used to be one big family. We sorted out our own troubles amongst ourselves, but the world's changing. Nosy parker policemen everywhere." Confidentially, he leaned over towards the detective and said softly, "Yes, I was there. Keep it under your hat."

"Can you trust the others not to tell?"

"They won't," Bradley replied, falling into the trap. "Mansfield and that other one – whose name's slipped my mind – they each held one of her boys' jackets. Wondered afterwards if that was why they'd been so generous in buying drinks all evening. Urged them on, you might say."

"You tried to restrain them, did you?"

"Me? They never listen to a word I say. Anyway, he deserved it. He'd been provoking us all evening with his views on this and that. Who was he to have a view, let alone come down here and force his daft ideas on us?"

"Did he make a fight of it?" Westcott asked.

"No and yes, in that order. That is, he tried to turn the other cheek, but the boys just hit that. He lost his temper in the end, but his strength was sapped by then and he was soon flat on his back. Mansfield turned him over with his boot to see that he was still alive and then we left him there." To put himself and his friends in a good light, the farmer explained, "We wouldn't have touched a hair of his head if he had agreed to leave us in peace and go back where he came from."

"Why did he come here?" Westcott inquired.

"Never heard anyone say and I never asked him."

Giving up hope of gaining any more useful information, Westcott faced the way ahead, ready to jump off the carriage if need be. It had become clear that the farmer was half asleep and it would be a matter of luck whether or not they were run down by something coming the other way.

But Bradley had one last piece of information. "Not that our boys are cowards." At last he felt able to claim a share in them in this connection at least. "They kept telling him to put his fists up and make a fight of it. As for murder, even if we hadn't all been at home together when the deed were done, I'd have known that it wasn't them. Nor yet Mr Marston."

The detective was listening intently, the oncoming carriages forgotten.

"Not in the back," Bradley went on. "That's a rogue's crime, or a fancy gentleman's."

"Any particular gentleman?" Westcott asked, as casually as possible, but Bradley had lost his train of thought.

"Talking of books," he mumbled, "now Tom and Jerry. Remember them? Always was my favourite book. Read it as a young man and many times since. Mrs Bradley, she can't see anything in it, but what woman understands men and their sport? Now was it Tom or was it Jerry as ....?"

The farmer's head fell to his chest and the horse, realising he was at last in complete control, set himself a faster pace to bring his master to his armchair and himself to his nosebag.

CHAPTER 18

It was two days later when Westcott called in at the vicarage and was shown into the library where the Reverend Hopgood awaited him.

"I gather," the young man said, smiling, "that I am here to show you books on the history of the Uptons." He swept a hand across the volumes laid out on the table. "Let me show you one, at least, so that, if anyone comes in, we can turn to discussing it with some conviction."

Already, Westcott had summed up the clergyman as a pleasant young man, who looked as though he had a little more experience of the world than many churchmen he had encountered. The detective was ready to believe that he had both intelligence and common sense.

"I am flattered Mr Westcott – or West, as you prefer – that I have been included in your secret. I am most willing to provide all the help I can."

"You realise," Westcott answered, "that I feel I have my hands tied now that suspicion has fallen upon Mr Skinner, Mr Howard and Henry Storr. They live in their world and I live in mine. I have seen them from time to time, but that is all. I'm depending upon you to be my ears and eyes."

"To be quite honest, sir," the young man confided, "when the subject was first raised by Miss Marston I felt it most unlikely that suspicion could fall on any of them. After all, one does not expect to find a murderer among one's acquaintances. But I have thought long and hard on the matter and have tried to study them in a new light. I now have an open mind."

"Let us take Edward Skinner first," the detective suggested. "Would he have killed Kersey, or had him killed, to stop him in his tracks?"

"Now on Skinner, Mr West, I feel less confident in giving an opinion than on the rest. I have not been brought up amongst men like him or mixed with them. Perhaps it is blind prejudice for me to say that, in my opinion, fortunes do not fall into people's laps or come from hard work alone. Somewhere a man who makes a large fortune has to turn a deaf ear and blind eye to the stirrings of his conscience. A man cannot worship God and Mammon. That is my firm conviction."

"Would you say he was sufficiently offended by Mr Kersey's opinions to kill him?"

"There I have my doubts. At one time, perhaps, when he was actively engaged in business. According to Mr Skinner, it is to the country's good that nothing should be allowed to stand in the way of the man with the enthusiasm and energy to make money. No doubt he equates the country's good with his own. But I understand that he has given up almost all of his business interests now, apart from a financial interest in the canal. He wishes to be seen as a fully-fledged gentleman. To be in trade would damage the marriage prospects of his nephew, whom he has groomed to marry into good society. A few of the workmen on the canal might have been disaffected by Kersey's opinions, but," the clergyman decided, shaking his head, "I cannot see Skinner as your murderer. While he might kill were it to his advantage, I cannot see his killing and risking all were it not."

"John Howard?" the detective asked, passing on to the next suspect.

"Now there, Mr West, is a different story all together. He sees himself as a pillar of society, a pillar of the church and a pillar of Great Britain, but he sees, everywhere, radicals and revolutionaries trying, Samson like, to pull down those pillars and bring church, state and himself crashing down. The man has not yet accepted Catholic emancipation – one never crosses his threshold. As for Jews! In his mind they have taken over the banks and, by holding the nation in their debt, control the country. One would never be invited into his house or to join his Club."

Westcott nodded. There were many with such opinions. He was seeing a clear picture of the man. "You have heard all these views expressed in his conversations?"

"Indeed, sir, in almost every one. Let us take the mutiny in India. Howard's view is that, had the first signs of discontent been dealt with firmly – by hanging the culprits no doubt – it would not have spread. The smallest concession is, in his eyes, weakness."

"To Mr Howard, I would guess," Westcott suggested, "there is no difference between an Indian native and a British workingman?"

"None at all," Hopgood agreed. "Mr Howard would be quite at home in the caste system. To him, the lower classes are a distinct species, almost sub-human. Breeding, that is birth, is everything to him in dogs, horses or men. I will say, in his favour, that he is not impressed by wealth alone or by success, as I fear most men are today. While others invite Skinner to dine in the hope of picking up tips and connections, that man is never to be seen seated at Howard's table."

Westcott nodded again. He saw the whole picture.

"Did you know," Hopgood asked, "that Howard was one of those who became a special constable during the Chartist troubles in London in '48?"

"From what you say, I am not surprised." Westcott thought back to those days, but could not place Howard in the ranks of special constables.

"I understand that it was not the first time that the Howard family had stood firm against riot and rebellion. He boasts that his grandfather trained his servants at the end of the last century to fight should revolution spread from France and his father revived the practice at the end of the wars in 1815, when there was so much popular unrest. I am told that Howard went to London as a special constable, claiming he was determined to stamp on the first spark of rebellion before it turned to a conflagration, which would have destroyed all he held dear.

"But I must not be a hypocrite in these matters. There is some truth in Howard's opinions. But, for myself," the curate continued, "I am for the steady, gradual extension of the franchise and, even then, education must come first. In native intelligence there are labourers here quite as quick as I, but they have not the education to distinguish good theories from bad."

"To return to Howard," Westcott asked, "he sees no good in any of the Chartist's demands?"

"I fear not. To Howard, breeding, together with wealth, must decide who votes in elections and leads the country."

"It was those very men of breeding and wealth who made such disastrous mistakes in the Crimea!" the detective commented with feeling.

Hopgood smiled sadly and nodded, but was intent on giving Howard's views. "As for secret ballots, Howard claims that any true Englishman would be ready to stand up and publicly declare his choice and take pride in casting his vote before the eyes of his fellows."

Anxious not to waste time going through Howard's thoughts on the whole Charter, Westcott said, "I can guess his ideas on the other points. They seem very predictable. Let's turn last to the third man on our list, Henry Storr. You know him well, I believe."

"Indeed, I was at school with him and his brother. To be quite honest," the curate said, and Westcott was sure that he always was, "I always felt a little sorry for him. He was — and I am sure still is — intelligent and hard working and anxious for everyone to approve of him, but his brother, without making any effort, outshone him in every way. And there was something more to Frederick, his brother, than mere brilliance. People loved him as much as they admired him. In their hearts, I fear, everyone is sorry that it was Henry and not Frederick, who survived the Charge at Balaclava."

"A man who might want to rid the world of Kersey?"

"Mmm! How can I express this without offence, West? I fear that we, from the upper ranks of society, tend to see all those below us as one great mass....."

"The great unwashed!" the detective laughed.

"Not quite that bad, although we must always remember Howard and those of that ilk. As I was saying, we do not see the minute differences someone lower down might observe between layers of the working classes. Perhaps those below, looking up, make the same mistake. But, in fact, in society's pyramid, with the Queen at the apex, The Storrs are close to the top and are acceptable at Court. Not royal blood, but the next best thing. They are one of the few families who have kept their titles and their estates, if not always their heads, since the Conquest. From his high pinnacle, Henry would scarcely be aware of Kersey. He would be a mere ant scurrying to and fro."

"And Storr would not be tempted to stamp on him?"

Chuckling, Hopgood replied, "I cannot think so, West. Those in the top ranks of society might pass legislation to kill all those with red hair, but they would not exert themselves to kill just one man. After all, what had Henry to fear from Kersey? The villagers depend on the Storrs for work and their cottages. They accept the facts of English rural society as readily as their masters. To them, as to the Storrs, matters have always been the same, created by God. I fear the Uptons provided stony ground for his preaching."

"Then why did he come here?" The detective demanded an answer from himself as much as from the young clergyman. "If only we knew why Kersey spoke to Mr Marston at the earliest possible opportunity."

"I'm afraid that I cannot help you answer that question, Mr West. I found no note of the meeting – no mention of it at all."

"So it seems," Westcott concluded, without conviction, "that I should turn my attention to John Howard."

"I cannot, in all honesty, see how Kersey would have presented a threat to Skinner or Henry Storr. Howard alone might have been tempted to rid the world of a man, who threatened everything great about his beloved country." He added, "But to be fair, again in all honesty, I cannot see Howard stabbing anyone in the back. That would go against all the moral virtues which he holds dear."

"But if he saw Kersey as less that human, would the same rules apply?" The curate did not answer. "Then tell me," the detective asked, "in all honesty, do you prefer Howard to James Marston as the murderer?"

Without realising it, the curate glanced towards the door, anxious Maria should not overhear his opinion. In a quiet voice he answered, "They would both abhor Kersey's opinions, but Mr Marston ......Mr Marston was not himself .... He ...." The clergyman gathered his thoughts and began from another direction. "What puzzles me, Mr West, is how the deed was done, if it were not Mr Marston. He could so easily have come across Kersey in the churchyard by accident."

"With the vicar carrying a knife?"

"Ah! You have me there. But how would anyone else have come across Kersey? He could not linger about the churchyard without attracting attention. And who would want to risk carrying out a murder in daylight?"

"Oh, I see what you mean," Westcott assured him. "I have gone over it a hundred times. No one had more than a few hours' notice of the fog gradually thickening enough to hide a crime and no one could be certain that it would not lift again as quickly as it had gathered. A chance meeting seems the obvious answer. Unless, of course, Skinner, Howard or Storr are particularly audacious men."

"They are not audacious in that way or foolhardy and rash, I would say," the curate commented. "But," he went on, using the voice with which he urged his flock towards Heaven, "You must follow up every path, for Mr Marston's sake."

CHAPTER 19

Reluctant as he was to see Howard as the murderer, Westcott was relieved when Constance sought him out and gave him a good reason for not following up Hopgood's suggestion.

"I am afraid, Charles, that I have recalled hearing that Howard was miles away at an agricultural show on the day Kersey was murdered. As a city man," she explained, as though to a child, "you might not know that such events have, in recent years, sprouted up everywhere and draw farmers, especially gentlemen farmers, from miles around. There they boast to each other about the size and weight of their bulls and pigs and cast envious stares at each other's sheep. You are," Constance commented, "as likely to see a painting of their prize bulls hanging on their walls as of their wives and children."

Westcott's expression suggested that nothing country folk did would surprise him. He was not sorry to have the case against Howard weakened so that he could turn his attention to other matters.

"I have always favoured Skinner over Howard," he said. "Men like Hopgood do not understand men like him. To men like Skinner the ends of making money justify the means, from petty dishonesty to murder. So far, I can find no reason for Kersey to have been a threat to him, but there will be one, you mark my words. I have dealt with such men for years."

"By the same token," Constance had the temerity to suggest, "you do not understand such men as Howard. In your heart of hearts you believe gentlemen do not commit murder."

Stung by what he saw as unjust criticism, Westcott claimed, "I can see the weaknesses in all men – and women. I look beyond the trappings of rank and claims of moral and religious righteousness to the man, or woman, beneath."

"Of course you do," the housekeeper said soothingly, "but, if I were you, I would not dismiss Howard simply because he was far away. Shouldn't a man be far away when he commits the perfect crime?"

To himself, Westcott thought, "Well, you aren't me." Out loud, he said, "We shall see."

Later, sitting in his armchair, Westcott felt, not for the first time, frustrated in his role as Charles West, retired draper from Limehouse.

Perhaps, he thought, it was time to reveal his true identity and purpose for being in Upton Market. At least he would be able to go about openly asking questions. It was doubtful whether all would give him answers, but some small remark might put him on the right track. The trail of Skinner and of Howard having cooled, he racked his brains for an idea of what to do next.

Once again, the detective came back to the question of why Kersey had come to Upton Market. If only, Westcott thought, James Marston could be questioned, but the doctors had forbidden it. Then, out of the blue, in his mind's eye, Westcott saw Alice's face peeping at him from the vicarage window and heard again all the creaks and footsteps outside of closed doors whenever he had visited the house. Suddenly, he was on his feet and heading for the vicarage. Fortunately, so that he had a chance to speak to her directly, Maria Marston was in the garden. She listened to his request.

"I'm sure you are right, Mr West. Alice does listen at doors and knows much more than is good for her. Whether she will admit doing so and tell me what she has heard is another matter."

"Please try, Miss Marston. We have very little to go on until we know why Mr Kersey came to the village," Westcott pleaded.

"Of course, I shall try," the young woman assured him. "At once, if you wish."

"In your own good time, my dear," Westcott said politely, hoping she would not take notice of this remark.

Maria knew just where to look for the child and found her immediately under the table. Tossing a cushion onto the floor, she sat down so that she was at eye-level with her niece. Then she reached out and touched the girl's hand. Alice did not respond This was not the first conversation she had had with her aunt like this. Although she would not admit it, even to herself, Alice had at first taken to this hide-away out of misery at her rejection by her father. Now she took up this position in the hope that her aunt would seek her out. She wanted her aunt's affection desperately, but she had loved her mother dearly and was not going to let her aunt take her place without first making her prove, over and over again, that she could give the same patient understanding and unquestioning affection.

Without hesitation, the dogs, who had thought nothing was going to happen for a while and had settled for a quick nap, jumped up, immediately wide awake, and put their paws on Maria's shoulders to lick her face with wild enthusiasm. Laughing, Maria pushed them off, looking for a responding

91

smile from Alice. None came. This was going to be even more difficult than usual. Perhaps, Maria thought, she had been too confident in thinking that the rejected child in herself could speak directly to the unhappy child in front of her.

As the dogs returned to her side, Alice, stiff and unsmiling ignored them. They, used to her moods, lay down and let their eyes close slowly into sleep. Maria looked at Alice's hand, restlessly touching the large, heavy claws carved into the bottom of the table leg. In her loneliness, the child had endowed it in her imagination with thick strands of smooth, golden hair. To her, it was all-powerful, all-loving and ever faithful. It never stirred away from her except in spirit, when she called on it to strike her enemies.

"Have you ever noticed," Maria asked, "that the lion's paw by your right hand is shinier than the rest? That's where I stroked it so often."

"It's a tiger," Alice announced defiantly.

Instinctively, knowing that it would not help to agree weakly with the child all the time, Maria examined the claw closely. "I think that it is a lion, but a lion, a tiger, whatever it is, I expect it has been many animals to many children throughout the years and will be to many children long after we are dead." Immediately, Maria knew what the girl's reply would be.

"I wish that I were dead and in Heaven with Mama and the boys."

"You know that God takes each one of us in His own good time, Alice. Your Papa has taught you that."

"When is Papa coming home?" Alice asked, tears, by this time, rolling down her face.

"We are hoping it will not be too long," Maria began, but the child interrupted her.

"I am not a baby, Aunt Maria. I am ten years old. I know that Papa must stay there forever or be hanged."

"Nonsense," Maria replied, all the more firmly as she feared that herself. "Your Papa has harmed no one. When we have proved that and he is better, then he will come home, just you wait and see." Realising that she must risk revealing her hand at some time, she went on, "And you can help, Alice."

"How? Grown-ups are not interested in children."

"That," Maria laughed, deciding to make a joke of it, "is why you can help. I know that when I was all alone and no one took any notice of me, I still took notice of them. I would pretend to be playing or looking out of the window or checking my shoe while, all the time, I was listening to what they were saying. I hoped that they would talk about me and say that I was to return home."

"What a silly thing to do!" Alice replied with contempt. "No wonder no one loved you."

Somehow, Maria resisted the temptation to shake the child. Thinking it was now all or nothing, she risked all. "Alice, I know that you heard your father talking to Mr Kersey the day he called to see him in his study."

Alice began to protest, but Maria ignored her. "I know, also, Alice Marston, that you were behind the sofa, where you often became trapped when you were looking through your Papa's papers and he came in unexpectedly."

"How can you say such things, Aunt Maria! Mother would never...," the child began in an outraged tone.

"Oh, yes she would, Alice. Your mother would have smacked you because she loved you and wanted you to grow up to be an honest, thoughtful young lady."

"Are you going to smack me?" Alice demanded. "You won't make me cry."

"No," Maria replied, "because, sometimes, we can turn wrong to a good purpose and, if we can, we must, to show our remorse."

Alice suddenly smiled. "Aunt Maria, may I have that lovely satin dress we saw yesterday – the green one."

"Yes, and if you tell me what you heard between your Papa and Mr Kersey, it will help us to do all we can for your dear Papa."

Testing her power further, the little girl asked, "If I promise to tell you, may I have a green satin ribbon?"

Maria hesitated, but Westcott put in impatiently, "Yes, my child. I shall give you one, myself." Would Alice demand that her aunt run six times round the pasture or swing from the chandelier?

Drawing the dogs closer to her, Alice began her confession.

"Papa was angry with Mr Kersey for coming to the front door. Mr Kersey said that Papa would be welcome at any of his doors at any time. Wasn't that a strange thing to say, Aunt Maria? No one had taught him his manners."

Maria smiled a gentle smile. "Then what did they say, Alice? Try to recall the words they used."

Alice, finding that she enjoyed the attention she was receiving, scrambled

93

from under the table, for a moment considered whether to stand like an actress on stage, but chose to lean back like a grown-up in an armchair. As the child patted and plumped the cushions, Maria found the encouraging smile she was giving her fading from her lips.

"Well, Aunt Maria," Alice began, with such relish that Maria prayed she was not making up the whole story. She took a deep breath, but something in her aunt's expression warned her she might go too far and should keep to the truth.

"Mr Kersey said that he had a story to tell and would welcome Papa's advice. Suddenly, Papa demanded, pointing his finger, 'Are you a member of my congregation? I have not seen you in church.'"

Now, the child did stand and act out a two character play, moving from position to position and adding actions and expressions to the performance.

"'No, Mr Marston,' Mr Kersey replied. His voice was quite – not quite quiet, but not too loud, not too soft."

Maria bit her lip until she thought it would bleed.

"'I have only just arrived here, sir,' Mr Kersey said, 'but I must honestly say that I am not a member of your church.'"

Alice moved to the position that she had allotted to her father. "'There is no other true church,' Papa said. He began to go quite red. I could not see," she added hastily, "but I know that he went red. He had started to go red very easily."

Maria found herself waiting for the adjective to be qualified as 'deep red', 'blood red,' or any kind of red that the girl could conjure up. Alice missed this opportunity to drag out her story and continued.

"'The Anglican faith stands as the only true Christian religion,' Papa said firmly. 'You do not wish to attend my church, yet you seek my advice as a minister of that faith.'

"Mr Kersey spoke firmly, too. 'No, Mr Marston, I seek your advice man to man. God need not enter into it.'

"Papa thundered, 'God enters into everything.'

"Mr Kersey spoke more quietly, 'I seek your advice, sir, on behalf of a man who was a good Christian and a member of your church.'"

Moving to her father's position and striking the attitude, without realising it, of a self-righteous priest, Alice continued, "Papa shouted, 'Then let him come himself.'"

Slowly, making the most of the moment, Alice moved to the spot from where she delivered Peter Kersey's words. "Very solemnly, Mr Kersey said, 'He is dead.'

"Papa was silent. He was surprised," Alice added, by way of commentary, "and was not sure what to say."

She moved her position. 'This is Mr Kersey speaking again. 'Please, sir, I need the advice of an educated, intelligent man.'

'Then, Aunt Maria," the child said with genuine sadness and abandoning her acting, "Papa had that wild look on his face. He stood up and said, 'Let me save your soul, here and now. Turn your back on the Devil and renounce his works. Follow Our Lord.'

"Mr Kersey looked sad. 'If you will not help me I'll leave you, now.'"

Suddenly having lost the taste for acting, Alice stood like a shy little girl being forced, against her will, to repeat her lessons. "Papa said, 'Not before you have renounced Satan and all his works. You have the air of the Devil about you.' Papa did not say 'air', but I do not know the word he used. It began with 'or'."

Familiar with her brother's language, Maria suggested, "Aura."

"Thank you, Aunt Maria," the child said, with excessive politeness, anticipating that, once she had told her story, she might have to pay the penalty for having listened to the conversation. "I think that was the word Papa used."

Alice looked to her aunt, who encouraged her to continue. "What did Mr Kersey do?"

"He asked Papa if he could get by and leave. Papa was standing right in front of him and was in his way. Mr Kersey was very polite. He asked Papa to move several times and he always said, 'Please.' In the end, Mr Kersey said, 'I have as much right to my own beliefs as you have, sir.' Papa said he had no right to hold beliefs which were put into his head by the Devil."

In tears, Alice ran to her aunt. "It did not sound like Papa speaking, Aunt Maria. He was so excited."

Maria wiped the child's tears and kissed her cheek. "You are a very brave little girl. What you have told us will help your Papa. Be a brave girl just a little longer and tell me how the meeting ended."

"Will I be punished, Aunt Maria?"

"No, my darling."

Sitting on the floor, with her arms about her aunt's neck, Alice finished her story.

"Papa told Mr Kersey that, without God, he would not exist. ...."

"Try to remember your Papa's words, my love."

Alice thought carefully. "I think that he said, 'Without God you would not exist. He created land, sea and air and all the creatures therein. Finally, he created Man to worship and serve him. Had Eve not tempted Adam.....'

"'My time is precious,' Mr Kersey said. He was beginning to sound very impatient. 'You are not a man whose advice I require. You are not intelligent and well educated if you believe that nonsense about God creating the world in a matter of days.'

"Papa was muttering. He was really angry, but Mr Kersey just went on, 'Everyone must know by now that different spee.....'"

"Species," Maria suggested.

"'species have evolved, died out and changed over thousands of years.'"

Alice clutched her aunt more closely, recalling her fear as the argument raged. "Now Papa was almost speechless with anger. I really thought that he would choke. He rushed to the bookcase and took out his book of dates. He found the date in which God created the world and pushed it into Mr Kersey's hands. 'Can you read?' Papa screamed. 'There it is in black and white.'

"Do you know, Aunt Maria?" Alice continued, in shocked disbelief. "Mr Kersey laughed at Papa."

"Did he leave straight away, Alice?"

"No, Papa would not move from the door. I think that annoyed Mr Kersey. He began to shout, too. "We know from bones, which have been found, that different species inhabited the earth and have died out to be replaced by new ones over the centuries.'

"Papa shouted at him, 'I must protect my parishioners from the Devil. They are my flock and I am their shepherd.' Then Papa laughed. 'God is all-powerful. Have you not thought that He may create new creatures as he thinks fit. He will defeat the Devil.'

"Mr Kersey just smiled. He said something about not believing there was a bearded old man in the sky who could make new animals just when he felt like it, but I can not remember it all, Aunt Maria."

"Try, my dear."

"They argued about books by a man with a funny name...."

"Erasmus Darwin," Maria suggested.

"It might have been. And Charles Darwin, I think. I am tired, Aunt."

"Did Mr Kersey go, then?"

Alice thought carefully. "Papa said that the books were the works of the Devil and that Mr Kersey had the mark of the Devil upon him. Mr Kersey walked past Papa and left."

"What did your Papa do then, Alice?"

Alice hung her head. Her aunt asked her again. Tears came into the child's eyes. "Papa sat down at his desk and picked up the photograph of Mama and the boys." Alice dropped her voice to a whisper. "Papa cried, Aunt Maria. He cried and cried. Don't be angry with me Aunt Maria. I did not make it up, but I can't recall the exact words. I might have put in some wrong words."

Then the child asked suddenly, "Is it true what Mr Kersey said that God did not create all the animals in the world on one day, Aunt Maria?"

No one in the room answered the Alice directly. They were all leaning to acceptance of Charles Darwin's new theories, but they were reluctant to destroy a child's belief in the church's teaching.

Later, as Maria and Westcott walked again in the garden, he asked, "Do you think the child was making it up?"

"Oh, no!" Maria claimed. "Do you?"

"No, it has the ring of truth about it and I feel that a story teller would have added bits, not left so much trailing in the air. But to recall so much!"

"Alice is a very clever, lonely, little girl. She would have repeated the conversation over and over to herself until she knows it by heart."

"Do you think, Miss Marston, that when Kersey said that the dead man belonged to your brother's church, he meant to this parish church or to the Church of England?"

"I cannot say," Maria answered. She went on, anticipating his next question, "And I have no idea who this dead person might be. I understood from Peter that he knew no one here before he arrived and why would he come all this way to ask James about someone in London?"

It had not slipped Westcott's notice that, intent on what she was saying, the young woman had referred to Kersey as 'Peter' and had been told by him that he knew no one in the village. Nor had it slipped past his keen observation that, when she realised what she had said, a flicker of anxiety passed through her eyes and she hurried him on to consider, "Do you think that you have learned anything new, Mr West?"

"We have learned," Westcott said, "that Kersey had concerns about the affairs of a person who is dead, or, perhaps, about the death itself. We know that the man was a member of the Church of England, but not whether he worshipped in this parish."

The detective did not add that the conversation raised more concerns about James Marston's own hatred of Peter Kersey. He did ask, "I am no theologian, Miss Marston, but I understand from those that are that men like your brother, and they form a majority, think that talk of evolution, of the development of new forms of species, threatens the whole basis of their faith. No creation, no Garden of Eden. No Garden of Eden, no Fall. No Fall, no Redemption through the death of Christ."

Maria shook her head sadly in agreement.

On the way back to his cottage, Westcott walked through the churchyard. He had little hope of finding any clue there to this mysterious man who was dead, but he looked at the graves on either side of the path. He found signs that a few bodies had recently been buried in the paupers' common grave, their only possession, their names, having been taken from them. And there were some new graves, a few with headstones with carvings and inscriptions to remind the relatives of their beloved dead and of their own mortality.

As he walked along the path, Westcott was greeted and then passed by a mason and his tool-carrying apprentice. He went over to where they had been working and saw a simple stone, lightly carved with a representation of Christ addressing the multitude and the name, "Peter Kersey. Servant of the Lord." Westcott added to himself, "Or Devil's disciple? It all depends on whose eyes you are looking through."

Hurrying after the men and knowing that they had probably been well paid not to betray a confidence, he said, as though all were known to him, "A fine job of work, gentlemen. Miss Marston will be well pleased."

"Oh, yes, sir," the mason replied, "She has watched us at every stage of its making and much admired our work."

He had been right, Westcott thought, pleased as usual with his own powers of perception. He closed his mind to the thought that, if Maria had known Peter Kersey, she might have had a reason to kill him. Questioning her could wait until he returned from London. Whatever had brought Kersey to Upton Market had happened there and it was time he found out who else knew the secret.

CHAPTER 20

As the train approached slowly and deliberately, the driver taking great trouble to stop exactly where any member of the Storr household would board, the breeze blew the steam and smoke towards Westcott. He did not move, but, delighting even in the sight of black specks settling on his hand, let it wrap its dampness around him. Breathing deeply, he almost closed his eyes to enjoy the hot, stinking, choking smoke in his lungs. The town had come to the country in the form of this shuddering, snorting engine and the coaches rattling behind it. How he had missed London!

Once seated in the carriage, for a while the detective surveyed the passing countryside and, as he turned to the task ahead, he continued to stare, with unseeing eyes, out of the carriage window. Knowing the habits of the policemen who patrolled the streets, he planned to wait for them at their customary haunts and ask his questions concerning Kersey. Eventually, with the steady rocking of the train and the melodic clickety-clack of the wheels on the rails, he dozed off. He was just dreaming that his old superintendent and Constance Brown were shaking him for not paying attention to their orders, when he awoke to find that the shaking, in reality very gentle, was being done by a young man leaning over him with concern. Thinking Westcott new to the Metropolis, the man asked him whether he needed any assistance. As soon as Westcott replied, he realised that he did not and apologised.

They walked along the platform side by side chatting about the weather, the pleasure of railroad travel and were on the subject of the mutiny in India before they realised that they were well out of the station.

"I do hope," the young man said, "that I have not absent-mindedly brought you out of your way. My name, by the way, is Philip Robertson. I am always rather absent minded when I return from my parents' home in the country. It is quite a shock to come back to the bustling streets of London."

Westcott assured him that he was going in the right direction and asked what business the young man had to undertake in this part of the Metropolis.

"I'm working in Christ Church, trying to spread the word of God and a little food and comfort to poor people there."

The detective was glad to hear him talk of 'poor people'. So many saw them as 'the Poor', as though they were no longer ordinary people. "A very difficult task. The first one, that is."

"You know, Mr Westcott, I have been surprised, though I should have expected working men to be like any other. Some are saints, who have no need of me. Some are evil criminals with whom, I fear, I shall never succeed. For the rest, in each there is good and bad and, with patience and the grace of God, I may help the good to rise above the bad in their hearts."

"Having been a detective," Westcott told him, "I take a different point of view. There are, admittedly, some saints, mainly women who bear the brunt of poverty, and certainly some rogues determined to get themselves hanged, transported or confined in penal servitude. But, in between, I find that those who are a mixture of good and bad are all too readily drawn into petty crime and dishonesty."

"Perhaps your point of view arises from the nature of your work," Robertson suggested. "Look at the streets through which we are walking now. Neat two rooms up, two rooms down houses, rented by people who fight to stay respectable and out of debt by letting a room to a young clerk or shopman."

"And," the detective said, "not two minutes away, you will find filthy courts with rubbish and slops left to rot in front of miserable houses not fit for animals, with no doors, with paper and rags stuffed in the broken windows and so many people to each room, that the children are forced out to roam the dirty streets day after day."

"I must confess," Robertson admitted, "that my heart sinks when I turn off the Commercial Road and into a maze of courts and alleys. Hell, Mr Westcott, cannot be worse than being condemned to walk such alleys for eternity."

"I am sure," Westcott comforted him, "that your work helps to save many from prison and from Hell fire. Are you a clergyman, may I ask?"

"I am just down from Cambridge. My parents wished me to go straight into the ministry, but I decided to work here and see life without the barrier of ordination."

The young man looked earnestly at Westcott. "Tell me, sir, you must have considered the question sometime, whose fault is this poverty and degradation? I sometimes think that charity is not the answer. It makes men less self-reliant, less inclined to take life by the scruff of the neck and," he laughed, "pull themselves up by their boot strings, if you understand me."

"We all know what Samuel Smiles says, Mr Robertson. Any man in England may rise by his own efforts and perseverance."

"But then, you see, I cannot agree with that. It is against the evidence of my own eyes. I have seen respectable mechanics save every spare penny, only to fall into poverty when illness or accident strikes. And yet," Robertson sighed, "I am always asking myself why some cannot clean their homes, use a little whitewash on their walls and send their children to school."

"It all comes down, in my book," Westcott claimed, "to the central question of how you help the deserving poor, without rewarding the undeserving. That question has been with us for centuries and will remain for many more. The man who solves it will deserve the Victoria Cross or to be made Prime Minister."

"Indeed, sir, indeed, that is the crux of the matter. I wonder," the young man ventured to say and Westcott knew what was coming, "if you have retired from work and live hereabouts, whether you would have any spare time to help us in our work. You might frighten off the worst of the criminal element, who are a great trial to us."

"I never have done before," Westcott laughed. "You are probably too young to remember, Mr Robertson, but there were few who wanted a police force in the beginning. The criminals certainly didn't and all other classes saw us as interfering, spying destroyers of English liberty. Peel won the argument by saying that the police were just there to deter criminals. You know how it ended. Crime goes on and our work is to track down the culprits."

"How interesting, Mr Westcott!" Robertson said, rather absentmindedly, not wishing to rush his new acquaintance, but having arrived at his lodgings. "I have arrived at my destination. I am sure we shall meet again and I look forward to that." The young man glanced up and down the street and sighed. "If my parents could see where I worked, they would demand my immediate return to the family home. There are matters I look forward to discussing with you, sir, as a man who has seen the evil here, but has not been contaminated by it."

"Not contaminated. I hope that is true. But, sometimes, I think that I have become too used to these surroundings. I accept them too readily."

"And should we, as Christians," Robertson asked, "teach these unfortunate people to accept their present unbearable circumstances in return for their reward in Heaven?"

They shook hands and Westcott turned to continue on his way. His mind coming back to the purpose of his visit, he turned back and said, "I wonder whether you have ever come across a young man who also worked for his fellow men in this area. His name was Peter Kersey."

"Peter! I am more than happy to claim him as a friend and ashamed to say that he was my first friend from the working classes." As he slowly took in the full meaning of Westcott's words, Robertson commented anxiously, "But you say 'was'. I trust no harm has befallen him."

Westcott came straight to the point. "Peter Kersey was murdered in the village of Upton Market, by a person or persons as yet unknown."

"Please, Mr Westcott, come in and tell me the whole story."

When he had finished his tale, the detective observed, "If there is anything you can tell me about your friend, which would give us a motive for the crime, I'd be most grateful to hear it."

"And I would be happy to help James Marston in any way I can, though I fear, from what you say, that he appears the most likely culprit."

While Robertson brought his mind back from his stay in the country-side to the streets and people of St George in the East, the two men sat in silence for a few minutes. Then the young man began to talk of his dead friend.

"Peter and I met soon after I arrived here. We often visited and worked together and being a very honest and outspoken man he shared his views with me. Most I agreed with and I found myself, to my father's horror, becoming a radical. But Peter hated labels. He preferred to judge people by the fruits of their labour, rather than by their philosophies. Of course, I saw his work as inspired by God, but Peter was still searching, still questioning. In my eyes, it was love of God and his neighbour which illuminated his life."

"What did he tell you of his life, his family and his friends?"

"It seems that he was born in Limehouse, when that place was full of neat little villas, before the area went downhill and the respectable people moved out to Essex. His father was a cabinetmaker, in a good line of trade with one or two journeymen working for him. He produced furniture that he was proud to sell and have recognised as his. Then, it seems, his father fell ill. It was just as we mentioned before. His savings were soon used up and they were too proud to ask for charity. The mother took in washing, but there are few people here who can afford any but the cheapest skivvies to work for them."

By now, the detective realised that there was no need to ask questions. Robertson, with an ordered mind, would relate the facts in chronological order and, with the odd pause to refresh his memory, would tell all he knew.

"By the time Peter's father had recovered – although, I understand, he remained in poor health – he had lost all his customers and could not afford to buy the quality of wood he once bought. He had no choice but to set himself up as a garret master, working for himself with the cheapest wood he could lay his hands on. Along came a slaughterman – you are familiar with the term, Mr Westcott?"

"Only too familiar," the detective confirmed. "A slaughterman sets a workman up in a tiny room with the poorest quality wood to make small tables and bits of furniture, which look shiny and attractive at first sight, but which turn out to be shoddy and of little worth. He demands speed rather than skill and, knowing the man cannot afford the time to hawk his own goods, buys them for next to nothing. Then he deducts from his payment the rent of the tiny room – where the family often have to live – and the price of the materials. Both prices are excessive."

Shaking his head sadly in agreement, Robertson said, "Such a man, Peter told me, was Ebenezer Skinner."

Westcott sat up with a jerk. "Ebenezer Skinner?" he interrupted.

"That, I am sure, was the slaughterman's name," Robertson said, hesitantly, checking his memory. "Have I made a mistake?"

"No, no," Westcott assured him. "Please go on."

"There is not a great deal more to tell, to be truthful. Deprived of his health, his pride in his work and his ability to feed and clothe his family, Peter's father died, broken hearted. Mr Skinner turned the family out onto the street. Mrs Kersey was not long in following her husband to the grave. Living on the streets, Peter had to earn pennies any way that he could – running errands, taking messages, minding horses or sweeping up in workshops.

"One of the men for whom he worked, Mr Thomson, a Quaker, took him in and gave a home to Peter and his younger brother, Mark. He gave them an education and put Peter to work as a clerk in his business. He encouraged Peter to read – some would say more widely than was wise – and so our peaceful revolutionary was moulded to the man he became,"

Robertson sighed. "I shall miss him, Mr Westcott, for his work with us, for which he received a pittance, and as my friend."

"There are some in Upton Market who miss him greatly," Westcott remarked, "but what of his brother?"

"Mark? I did not know him. He joined as a soldier. He died in the Crimea, I am afraid. Peter was heartbroken when the news was brought of his death. He had been so against his brother's going to war. After that, Peter seemed restless and to have some serious matter on his mind. One day, out of the blue, he told me that he had to go into the country, but would be back when his business was completed."

"Mr Kersey gave no hint of what this business could be?"

"None. I must confess that I was curious, but he offered no reason and I did not press the matter."

"Would anyone else know?"

"To my knowledge, no one knew. I'll make inquiries for you."

"This Ebenezer Skinner you mentioned – the slaughterman – is he still in the area?"

"No, although one hears rumours. He flourished some time before I came. My impression was that he moved somewhere else ten or more years ago. Perhaps that was for the best. Peter held a deep dislike for the man. It was his father's experiences which made Peter so dedicated to encouraging workmen to band together into unions. On that score, some manufacturers complained of his activities. Fortunately, none of the people he most offended gave to our work and we were able to ignore them."

"Would your friend Kersey," the detective asked, "have tried to trace Skinner to exact some sort of revenge?"

"Vengeance? I truly think Peter was above that."

"What were these rumours about Skinner, which you just mentioned?"

"Rumours? Ah, yes. There are persistent rumours that Skinner works through other men to wring pennies from the poor. He wants the profits, but it no longer suits him to have his name associated with the work."

"In that case, might Kersey not have been tempted to discover the men who slaved for him and persuade them to act together against him?"

"It is possible," Robertson agreed, though there was doubt in his voice. He added, "Peter would have known that for every man who refused to work for Skinner, three others in dire straits could have been found."

"What if," Westcott asked, feeling some excitement as he framed the idea, "he realised this man was living as a gentleman and keeping his history from his neighbours? When he heard of the death of his brother, might he not have been tempted to find Skinner and reveal all?"

"When a man is made distraught by the death of a loved one, who can say what he will do? I fear, Mr Westcott, it seems that you now have two such men – Peter Kersey and James Marston. One, certainly, was the victim, but was the other the culprit? Your questions suggest that you suspect this gentleman, Skinner, of being your murderer. As a Christian, Mr Westcott, I should not wish ill to any man, but I hope that you are right. From what you say, Skinner appears a more deserving case for the hangman's noose than poor James Marston."

CHAPTER 21

"So, Tom Cat, my old and trusted friend, that is the story so far."

The cat did not even glance up at Westcott. This was the way it always was. Having been deserted and abandoned, albeit in a warm home with more food than he could eat, Tom Cat was not even going to acknowledge Augustus Westcott's presence, let alone forgive him. Since, from his seat in the window staring at the spot where he had last seen his friend, the cat had spotted his reappearance, the animal had sat without moving a whisker. When Westcott patted his head or tickled the cat's chin, Tom Cat remained impassive. When Westcott picked him up, he hung like a limp dish-cloth until he was put down and could return to his pose of a statue of an Egyptian deity.

"Now," Westcott went on, "we have the first signs of a real suspect other than James Marston. Ebenezer Skinner now passing as Edward Skinner!"

There was still no response from the cat. Tom's claws did not work in and out on the blanket, nor did the usual contented purr come from his throat at the very sound of Westcott's voice.

"I give up," Westcott announced. "I don't expect this trouble from a Tom Cat. Should have taken that little sister of yours I was offered at first. I'm off to be a detective, see you later."

The detective walked in the direction of Shadwell to an address given him by Robertson. It was that of an old lady whom Kersey had made a habit of visiting once a week. He had been informed that she was possibly a relation, but certainly an old acquaintance. As it turned out, Mrs Maine was not a relation of Kersey's, but had known him from birth.

Reluctantly and kindly, as he always was in breaking terrible news, the detective explained as simply as possible, without going into details which would haunt the old woman, that her young friend was dead.

"Nicer people than the Kerseys you could never 'ope to meet," she told him, once she had dried her eyes and asked how she could help. "Give a 'elping 'and to anyone when they was in trouble. Mind you, they was respectable people and kept theirselves to theirselves. Not always in and out of other people's 'ouses borrowing this and that, if you know what I mean. I'd 'ave taken the lad when they was in trouble, but I never knew things was so desperate. Weren't exactly a moonlight flit, they never owed

106

no one nothing, but it were done on the quiet."

"But," the old lady continued, as the memories flooded back and tears returned to her eyes, "Peter remembered me. Started to come and visit me every week and never missed, even in the worst of weathers or the thickest of pea-soupers. Brought me a few bits and pieces to see me through. I'm seventy-five, Mr Westcott, and see no point in being proud. My only cause for pride is that I ain't in the work'ouse and I'll keep out unless I lose me wits like some do and they lock me away."

"You seem to have your wits about you, Mrs Maine," the detective assured her.

"None of that flannel! Peter used to try it on. I know, I don't look no more than fifty and me memory's better than yours. That's 'ow it used to go. 'E didn't just bring me a bit of food, you know. 'E give me 'is time and there ain't many as does that."

"Did he know Ebenezer Skinner, the slaughterman?"

"'Oo didn't? Everybody did. Most of 'em worked for 'im. Gained from their labour and from their rents, 'e did. Never done a good deed and never missed a chance to do a bad one."

"What happened to him?"

"Mm. Now you've got me, Mr Westcott. It's there in my 'ead, but finding it, that's the difficult part. When you're my age, your memory's like Old Mother Hubbard's cupboard. You go there and, as often as not, it's bare. And it's no good searching, it's not to be found. Then, if you're lucky, next day, next week, next month, there it is again."

"Well, when you remember again, Mrs Maine, you tell Mr Robertson and he'll write to me," the detective suggested, with little hope that anything would come of it.

"Let's 'ave a cup of tea and see if it comes back," Mrs Maine told her guest. "Me daughter brings me tea from where she cleans for a grocer's wife. They only use it once and it's as good as new."

Westcott, thinking the woman lonely and eager for company, agreed. In his time, he had drunk pints of tea of second or third brewing, but as he sipped the drink he was offered and struggled to hide his disgust at the taste, he realised he was already spoiled by the new life of plenty brought by contact with the Marstons.

"Skinner, Ebenezer Skinner," Mrs Maine muttered to herself every now and again, trying to jog her memory.

"What was he like – in looks I mean?" the detective asked, helping her to focus her mind on the slaughterman.

"Not quite as tall as you. Thin. Wasn't going to waste 'is profits on food, were 'e? Clean shaven. Mousey coloured 'air."

It did not help much, Westcott thought. Skinner now was of an age to put on weight, eating at other's tables if not his own, and his hair was white. It was true that Skinner was a little shorter than he was.

"Blue eyes," the old woman recalled suddenly. "Struck me as you always think of angels 'aving blue eyes. 'E weren't no angel."

Westcott had not noticed the colour of Skinner's eyes. He had happened to notice one day that Constance's were blue.

"Did he have a sister?" the detective asked, recalling what he had heard of Skinner Montague's parents.

"Now you jog me memory, 'e did, but bless me if I can recall 'er name. Know she married above 'er station, everyone said. Still, she were a good looker and beauty in a woman is as good as money in the bank. Mind you, she 'ad that, too, from 'er brother. They said at the time that the gent was 'eavily in debt and Skinner paid up as 'er dowry. Bet 'e never paid another penny after the marriage."

"Did they have a child?"

Mrs Maine smiled knowingly. "Now you come to mention it, she did. They said that was all 'e wanted, to raise the Skinner name in the world."

"Why didn't he marry and have children himself?"

"'Oo'd 'ave 'ad 'im? Never 'ad time for anything 'cept 'is business."

"When did the sister's marriage take place?"

"Now you're asking! Must 'ave been before the Queen come to the throne."

So far, Westcott was pleased to note, everything fitted in. What he needed was one conclusive fact that Edward Skinner was Ebenezer, the slaughterman.

"I'll tell you 'oo would know," Mrs Maine suggested. "That sergeant, Davidson's 'is name, 'oo keeps an eye on the constables around this way. 'E always wanted to catch Skinner up to no good, but Skinner always seemed to keep on the right side of the law. That's not so difficult when you're one of them with a vote to make the laws to suit yourself."

"I'll see you again, Mrs Maine," Westcott promised, "when this is all over and I return home." He pressed a shilling into her hand, smiling and saying, "Now don't spend it all at once. Save some for a rainy day."

"It rains 'ere every day, Mr Westcott. No," she corrected herself, "I mustn't say that. I must keep me spirits up not down, though it's 'ard when you've got nowhere to go but to the grave. You know, Mr Westcott, when you're young it's a good idea to live every day as though it were your last – so you get the most out of life without doing no one no 'arm what you'll 'ave to explain away when you meet St Peter at the gate. But when you're old, you 'ave to try to live each day as though you 'ave another ten years a'ead of you. Otherwise, if you dwell on the short time you've got left, it 'ardly seems worth getting out of bed in the morning. Might as well save yourself trouble and give up right away."

Patting the old lady's arm as he left, the detective had one more question. "Do you think Peter might have searched Skinner out to get some sort of revenge for the death of his brother?"

"'E did always blame Skinner for Mark being a bit wayward and joining the army, but it doesn't sound like Peter." As she watched Westcott walk down the road, she shrugged and added to herself, "But 'oo can tell what any man will do, if driven far enough?"

Waving to the old woman, who watched him disappearing down the road, Westcott made straight for the place where he knew Sergeant Davidson would be checking up on his constables.

"Well, well," the sergeant boomed, "fed up with retirement again, are we?" This referred to the times when Westcott, missing the company of his colleagues, had sought out his friend since his retirement.

"No," the detective said, nose in the air, "I'm on a case, a private one."

"Let's hope it pays better than the public ones, then. You'll soon be too good for us poor coppers."

"I'll never forget my old friends," Westcott promised, "especially when they might be able to help me."

"Try me," Davidson challenged. "No better encyclopaedia of crime and criminals in this part of London than I carry in my head."

"Skinner," Westcott pronounced slowly and clearly. "Ebenezer Skinner. Look him up in that encyclopaedia of yours."

"Now there's someone I don't need to look up. I hope you know something to his disadvantage. I've been keeping a weather eye on that villain for years. Did everyone down, probably including his own mother, but never broke the law. Tell me he has and I'll nab him before you can say Jack

109

Robinson."

"Where did he go from here?"

"In a manner of speaking, he never left. He still sweats pennies and shillings out of anyone he can get his claws into. Leases more houses than you and me have had hot dinners. Pulls in the rent by letting rooms – Jews, Irish, any foreigner or Englishman. He makes no distinction so long as they pay up. Packs 'em in. Wonder the top floors don't fall in with the sheer weight of bodies."

Westcott felt his shoulders slump with disappointment. "You mean Skinner still lives hereabouts? Back to the beginning."

"I did say 'in a manner of speaking' he never left. His henchman runs the circus nowadays. People think that fellow is the landlord, but I know different. Most of the land around here is leasehold and I know who leases most of it – Ebenezer Skinner."

"If he's still here in spirit, where's his body?"

"That I'm not absolutely sure of. I've heard, but I can't swear to it mind you, that he changed his name to Edward. Moved around a bit. Went into Essex to live with his sister, who married above her station. She died and her husband went abroad to escape being locked up for debt. Their lad was left for Skinner to bring up. Heard he sent him to school with the nobs and made a gentleman of him. Ernest, that was the little feller's name, if I'm not mistaken."

A broad smile spread across Westcott's face. Then he had a thought. "Why would Skinner still be scratching around for pennies and shillings when he's living in the style of a man worth a few thousands a year?"

"'Cos pennies and shillings, if you've got enough of them, add up to pounds. He has streets paying him rent, each house packed from cellars to attics. There's even enough money in it for middlemen to rent a room off him and then charge some poor souls tuppence a night for the pleasure of sleeping on the floors."

"Or perhaps," Westcott said, half to himself, "he's not as rich as he claims and everything hangs on his nephew's marrying well to get his money. That would make him desperate to stop anyone or anything spoiling it all. I may have good news for you, old friend," he added with obvious pleasure.

Davidson looked less cheerful than the detective expected. "It won't be simple, mark my words. He always has someone else take the risks.

110

Whatever it is you think Skinner might have done, he'll have had someone else do it for him."

"Could be a hanging job," Westcott said.

This did not raise the sergeant's spirits. "It won't be Skinner as swings on the end of the rope."

As he turned to go, Westcott asked, "Did you ever come across Mark Kersey?"

"Boxed his ears a couple of times. Nothing serious, but you always had the feeling he might be led into trouble. He took the Queen's shilling and off he went to the Crimea. Why is it when these young men swagger about in their uniforms, they never think it will be them as gets killed? Heard a feller soldier brought his brother the news and soon after that the brother took off. Have you come across him?"

Westcott told the story of Peter Kersey's murder as briefly as possible.

"Skinner could be your man," Davidson agreed, "but take care. The only corpse we want is Skinner's dangling on the end of a noose."

CHAPTER 22

Having been cold shouldered by Tom Cat and not wanting to discuss this new information with Constance Brown until he had thought it through and thought of his own suggestions to make, Westcott closed his eyes and mind to the countryside flashing past the train and concentrated on what he had learned and how it affected the theories he had considered before. He had accepted, having seen in 1848 the hatred in the eyes of some of the special constables from the upper ranks of society for those from the lower orders, that Howard might have believed he had a reason to kill Kersey, but he had never felt in his heart that that was a sufficient cause for murder. Apart from murders committed for cruelty's sake, he had always found that self-interest, rather than principle, lay behind most murders.

Recalling Bradley's words on how Kersey had, at first, not fought back, but had done so when pushed too far, he imagined much the same happening with regard to Skinner. For some years, although Kersey had fought to improve workers' conditions, it had not been a personal fight with Skinner. Only having heard of his brother's death might hatred have driven Kersey to seek the man he saw as responsible for robbing his brother of a good upbringing and respectable employment and forcing him into the army to meet his death in battle.

The detective imagined how Kersey, finding Skinner living the life of a wealthy gentleman and working for the full acceptance of his nephew into society, could have decided to tell all he knew of the slaughterman's past life. That would undermine all Skinner had worked for over the years and be more than enough to drive him to kill the young man.

How did all this, the detective asked himself, fit into what Alice had revealed about Kersey's meeting with the vicar on his arrival in the Uptons? Quite well, he decided. According to Alice, the young man had referred to someone who had died. That would be his brother, Mark. And he had wanted the advice, not of a churchman, but of an intelligent gentleman. In other words, Kersey had not wanted advice about the rights and wrongs of what he planned to do, but wished to impart his information to someone of standing, whose word would be believed by Skinner's neighbours. He needed such a man to spread the word that Edward Skinner, gentleman, was, in fact, Ebenezer Skinner, slaughterman and tormentor of the poor, who had grubbed together his wealth from the gutters of London's East End.

Then facts which Westcott had put to the back of his mind before going to London pushed their way to the front. Maria Marston had referred to 'Peter', rather than 'Mr Kersey'. Could Kersey have seen which way the land lay and decided he could punish Skinner by making a play for the lady he wished his nephew to marry? If that were the case and he had set himself up as a rival to the nephew, Skinner Montague, then he would have to consider the captain as a suspect, too. And, he forced himself to half consider, if Kersey had led Maria up the garden path, then that young lady, herself, might ....

With a shudder, the engine pulled into the halt at Upton St John. Slowly and absent-mindedly, Westcott gathered his belongings and stepped from the train. He found himself facing Mrs Carter. For once, it was not the knowledge that an interest was being taken in him by a widow that concerned him, but that an interest was being taken in him by a draper's widow with evil intent in her eyes.

Raising his hat, he attempted to pass her with just a polite greeting, but, short of unfastening the grasp of the hand placed firmly on his arm, he was given no choice but to let the widow usher him outside and into the carriage waiting there. When they arrived at her house, the detective, grown man and terror of East End criminals as he had been, had no choice but meekly to accept Mrs Carter's insistent invitation to follow her inside for tea and pastries.

At least, Westcott found, the draper's widow was not interested in a cat and mouse game. She came straight to the point.

"Just answer me one question, Mr West, if that's the name you want to be known by, where was this draper's shop of yours?"

"In the Commercial Road."

Mrs Carter gave what she imagined to be a lady-like snort of contempt. "That doesn't tell me much. Stretches through one parish after another."

"Limehouse," the detective asserted without great conviction, "down near the East India Dock."

"The only draper in those parts is Mr Jones."

She stared at him, defying him to make up more stories. For a second, Westcott thought of saying that Mr Jones had bought it from him, but she anticipated the lie.

"And he's had that same shop for over twenty years." Mrs Carter fixed him with a look which asked all too clearly, "Now, what have you to say for yourself?"

"I give in!" the detective conceded, throwing up his hands and giving a sheepish grin like a school boy caught red-handed in a petty crime. This usually softened any woman's heart, but, if he thought it would satisfy Mrs Carter's curiosity, he was wrong.

"So what were you? You haven't been a man of independent means all your life. My guess," the draper's widow said, with the confident tone of a woman who was never wrong in her guesses, "is that you are a detective come to investigate Mr Skinner."

Westcott cleared his throat, this being the only noncommittal response which occurred to him at that moment. She was right on the occupation, but he sensed she was not right on the exact nature of the mission. She was dying to gossip about Skinner, so why not let her?

"You've a keen eye, Mrs Carter, I must say." The detective shook his head in astonishment at her perceptiveness, until it seemed self-satisfaction and pride might make the widow burst out of her tightly strained corset laces. "But, please, do not tell anyone else."

"As if I would! I've no great love for Skinner. Cost me a great part of my capital following his advice on railroad stock. Mind you, it was that old skinflint who first put me onto you – not that I'd ever have taken you for a draper. My husband had that air that all good drapers should have – neat and well-dressed, but not out to rival his best customers, who considered themselves a cut above us. They like humility and my husband was excellent in that direction. Not 'umbleness, mind you, as Mr Dickens portrays Uriah Heep. That's going too far and embarrasses all except them as put on the greatest airs and graces."

"You don't consider me well-dressed?" the detective asked, feigning disbelief.

Looking him up and down, Mrs Carter chose to take this as a serious question. This permitted her to give an honest answer. "I'm afraid not, Mr West. You need a good woman to point out the error of your ways."

As Westcott tried to think how to bring Mrs Carter back to the subject he was interested in without further arousing her curiosity, she helped him out.

"That man is as interested in you as you are in him. It's about Miss Marston, isn't it?"

Trying the old trick of simply repeating the question, the detective looked puzzled and queried, "Miss Marston?"

"All innocent," Mrs Carter laughed, seeing this as confirmation that she had hit on the truth that the detective had come to investigate anyone who appeared interested in Miss Marston's fortune. "Oh, yes, that man has set his heart long ago on his nephew marrying into money. If you ask me, he got to know teachers at some of those boarding schools in London and picked out Maria Marston as the one long ago."

For some years, Westcott had believed in the theory that the art of being a detective lay simply in making the right noises. He put this theory into practice.

It worked and Mrs Carter continued. "Knew Ebenezer Skinner – that was his given name – for many years."

"Ebenezer!" Westcott exclaimed, as though the name came as a surprise to him. "Edward, surely."

"Ebenezer, you mark my word," the widow asserted, further encouraged by the belief that she knew more than the detective. "Used to be a slaughterman, if you know what that is."

Westcott nodded silently, not to interrupt the flow.

"Anyway, he knew he couldn't rise to high society with a background like that, however rich he was. But he decided young Skinner Montague could, with the right schooling and a good marriage."

"Really!" Westcott remarked, in a tone which implied, "Tell me more."

Mrs Carter obliged. "He rented the Marston house – they'd moved into the vicarage – with one thing in mind, to have his nephew meet Miss Marston. Never missing a chance, he paid the clerk in the booking office to tell him which coach Miss Marston would be on. Then he books two tickets for himself and young Ernest. Wasn't any accident, you know, that they travelled together."

"Would Captain Skinner Montague be a suitable match for Miss Marston?"

"No young lady in their senses would refuse him. Charm by the bucketful, that young man possesses. Not treacly – genuinely charming. Always speaks to me as he passes, checks that I'm alright and nothing is causing me concern. There's no advantage in it for him. To add to that, he's now a hero of the Charge of the Light Brigade!"

"A young man with no faults!" Westcott exclaimed, trying not to sound envious.

"The only disadvantage he has is being related to Ebenezer Skinner."

"The young lady could do worse, then?"

Lowering her voice, Mrs Carter confided, "There was gossip that she'd set her cap at that young Peter Kersey, who had himself murdered, but I didn't believe it. He didn't compare with the Captain. Well, in looks, maybe, but no breeding. In my youth, I'd have thought him material for a little flirtation, but not for marriage. Much too far below her, I can tell you. The Captain would have been my choice."

"Yet you seem to have your doubts," Westcott pointed out, not surprised that Mrs Carter, like most women, preferred looks to character.

"Not about Skinner Montague, but about his uncle. I'm quite sure that Ebenezer Skinner is not as rich as he would have people believe. If I'd followed his advice on investing my money, I'd be in Carey Street by now. All these tempting schemes nowadays, offering vast interest with no risk. No such thing in my book. He might have made money in railroad shares, but I'd wager my last penny that he got too greedy and lost it all again. My sons tell me the word is that he isn't worth much and, in the drapery and tailoring trades, they know whose credit is good and whose isn't."

"So you think that, having invested so much in his nephew, Skinner will be looking to recover it, and his losses, from Maria Marston's fortune?"

"My very thoughts."

As the widow paused in her talking for a second, the detective murmured, "Most interesting, Mrs Carter. I thank you for your confidences."

"I think the poor child should be warned. Let her marry Skinner Montague by all means, but let the lawyers tie up her money so tight that skinflint can't get his hands on it. Mind you, her marriage chances won't be so good now, with her brother a murderer."

Ignoring the last remark, Westcott thanked Mrs Carter again for her concern. He was about to walk away, when she expressed her concern for him.

"You could do worse, you know, than marry Constance Brown. She's a good woman, if sometimes overbearing, and would make your last years very comfortable."

Embarrassed, Westcott muttered that he was not looking for a wife and he was sure Mrs Brown was quite happy as she was.

"Foolish, the pair of you," the widow commented. "How I miss the companionship of my late husband! He was no saint, but looking after him gave me a reason to get up every day. I even miss that stinking pipe of his!"

For a moment, Westcott feared she might shed a tear or two, but she quickly recovered. "I shall expect an invitation to the vicarage for my advice, even if it's only to tea with Mrs Brown. And," she added, "don't you be surprised if you receive an invitation to Ebenezer Skinner's. He wants to get on the right side of you."

The embarrassment caused by such a reference to Constance Brown almost put out of Westcott's mind a question he had wanted to ask.

"Have you told anyone else who Skinner really is?" In asking this the detective knew that, if all was already known, Skinner would have had no reason to kill Kersey to stop him telling all he knew.

"I know when to keep my own counsel, Mr Westcott. Nothing on the matter has ever been spoken between us, but he knows I know." Mrs Carter smiled slyly. "He also knows I shall reveal nothing as long as he keeps me sweet with little gifts from time to time.

CHAPTER 23

Amelia Carter had been right. Within a matter of hours an invitation arrived for Mr West to call on Mr Skinner and only a day passed before the detective stood at the great oak door of the grand house, which the slaughterman rented, and tugged on the metal bell pull. As the loud clattering rang through the house, Westcott was struck by the thought that, somewhere inside, Skinner would be listening, as tense and alert as he, himself, was. The prey listening for the approach of the hunter. Neither could know what the outcome of the meeting would be.

There was little, if any, doubt in Westcott's mind that Skinner was guilty of the murder. The detective had come across too many of his kind before, hard and unscrupulous men whose sense of their own importance and destiny drove them to destroy anyone or anything standing between them and their ambition. Somehow, without revealing the weakness of his own hand, Westcott had to bluff Skinner into incriminating himself, either as the man who had murdered Kersey or sent someone to do it for him.

When the door was opened and the housekeeper, who introduced herself as Mrs Maxwell, came forward to greet him, the detective, having expected to be shown straight in to Mr Skinner, could barely conceal his impatience. As she praised his cousin, Mrs Brown, and expressed her sympathy at the difficult time through which the Marston household was passing, he tried to smile and give the appropriate replies. When she told him that Mr Skinner was sure he would be interested to be taken on a tour of the house, his smile vanished and the housekeeper was not quite certain what he muttered in reply. She took it to be agreement.

Following her from room to room, listening to the history of the house and having his attention directed to this feature and that, Westcott feared there was no detail, however small, the housekeeper would miss out. Furnishings, furniture and paintings had little interest for the detective and he was more interested in recent history than in the lineage of the Marston family, from whom Skinner leased the house. However, he did pause at the portrait of James Marston's mother. To his eyes, she appeared sensitive and sad, rather than mad. Perhaps, he decided, the madness had resulted from marriage to the man whose grim and forbidding features were portrayed in the painting hanging next to hers.

Soon bored and a little mischievous, Westcott asked, "Are there no portraits of the Skinner family?" How, he wondered, would the parents and ancestors of Ebenezer Skinner be represented? Did the man come from a long line of sailors, dockers, coal-whippers and washer women, or just plain criminals?

The housekeeper did not hesitate in her reply. "Mr Skinner is proud to claim that he is a self-made man. He has risen by his own intelligence and effort and we are all privileged to serve him."

"Very commendable," Westcott commented, although 'intelligence' and 'effort' were not the words he would have chosen to account for Skinner's success in greatly improving his station in life.

"Mind you," Mrs Maxwell confided, showing her regard for the established order, "Captain Skinner Montague has old blood in his veins. His father was a gentleman."

"May I presume to ask," the detective inquired in his humblest tone, "how Mr Skinner made his money?"

Although the woman gave Westcott a glance which conveyed her opinion that only a retired draper from Limehouse would show such impertinence, she answered, "Mr Skinner has business interests in London and I understand that he was one of the few who invested in the railroad at the right time."

"And one of the few who didn't get his fingers burned?"

"It would seem so, Mr West."

"I've heard it said the young man is his uncle's heir."

"I believe that to be so."

"Good blood, good prospects and handsome. The young man will have the pick of the ladies."

As he was Mrs Brown's cousin, Mrs Maxwell lowered her voice and confided, "You will have heard that the Captain has picked out one already, Miss Marston. A real love match, they say."

"Indeed," Westcott remarked, for want of something better to say. He had heard of no such arrangement.

As they entered a room, the walls of which were lined with books, the housekeeper announced, rather needlessly, "This is the library, Mr West."

"What a well-read man Mr Skinner must be!" Westcott exclaimed, in mock admiration, well aware that Skinner had come up behind them.

"I make no claim to being well-read," the master of the house remarked.

119

"Life has been my teacher and there is none better for a man with spirit, determined to better himself."

Westcott was trying to think of a reply, which would approve of the general ideal of self-help without praising Skinner's particular brand, when Skinner, having dismissed his housekeeper, came straight to the point.

"I've had you come here, Westcott, because I know who you are and I am sure you know who I am. Am I right?"

"I'm Charles West, retired draper," the detective claimed, without much conviction, but playing for time.

Skinner laughed. "Augustus Westcott, that's who you are. Drop the acting and innocence and come clean. You're a bobby, a peeler and other things too rude to mention in my own house. You started when Peel first invented the breed and fouled up the streets of London with them. About twenty-five years ago that would be, wouldn't it?"

"Thereabouts," his visitor agreed.

"Then, when they decided to have nosy parker detectives a dozen years later, you became one of those. You know everything that happens in East London and everyone that does it."

"Not all," Westcott admitted. "I knew your man in London by sight and reputation, but I'd no idea who was behind him."

"Because I pay him well to keep his mouth shut. And then you come along. You know who I am, don't you?"

"Yes, Ebenezer," the detective gloated. He felt confident, in charge of the situation.

"It's clear you found out all about me on your trip to London. Don't let's beat about the bush. How much do you want to keep your mouth shut about my past and how I made my money?"

Taken by surprise, several replies went through Westcott's mind. If he said, "Murder's an expensive business," or "You'll have to pay well to keep my mouth shut over Kersey's death," would he trick Skinner into admitting his guilt? It all seemed too easy.

Then the detective's heart sank with disappointment. He heard Skinner's words again. "It's clear you found out all about me on your trip to London." The tension of the chase left him. He knew he was back to the beginning again. Skinner, like Amelia Carter, saw no other point in his investigation than that he was here to check on the nephew's suitability as a husband for Miss Marston.

Trying desperately to salvage something of his belief that Skinner was a murderer, he stated firmly, "I'm here to find out who killed Peter Kersey and you're top of my list. No money will stop me getting at the truth."

Now it was Skinner's turn to look amazed. "Murder?" He stared at the detective and shook his head in disbelief. "Me? I've spent years cleansing my reputation and distancing myself from any whiff of scandal. Would I kill a nobody like Kersey, who was doing me no harm?"

Grasping at the idea that Skinner was a good actor, Westcott tried to hold on to his conviction of the man's guilt. "He knew who you are. He could have done you harm in the only ambition you care about. Did you offer him a bribe not to tell the Marstons and kill him when he refused?"

"Well," Skinner smiled happily, "I can save myself a few coppers having to bribe you. I could ask you to bribe me to keep quiet about your real purpose in being in the Uptons, Mr Detective. You won't be popular around here when people learn you've been peeping and prying into all their lives. The murderer, whoever he might be, won't like it one little bit."

Dropping into a deep leather armchair, Skinner stretched out his legs and stared at his hands, which he held fingertip to finger tip like a child building a steeple. "I'm in a generous mood, Westcott, my old son. We'll make a simple bargain. You keep quiet about me and I'll keep quiet about you. What's more, I'll tell you all I know about Kersey between his arrival and his death." He indicated to the detective, with a wave of the hand, that he was to sit down.

CHAPTER 24

Smiling still, Skinner asked, "There's no crime in thinking murder without committing it, is there? If there is, you will be taking me in. When I spotted Kersey from the carriage, all kinds of thoughts went through my head. I recognised his face – the image of his father. I told myself it couldn't be, but then he took off his hat. With the colour of that head of hair, I knew it had to be him."

"Can you guess how I felt? No," Skinner concluded, having looked contemptuously at the detective. "You've no ambition – no desire to succeed at all costs. You've no aching to rise above those who think they are superior and despise you, yet envy you your money, accepting any you care to toss their way. I could buy out half the village and still have change for a dish of eel and mash. Since I was an errand boy, I knew I was destined for great things, but feeling the hand of fate on your shoulder doesn't mean you can sit back and wait for everything to fall at your feet. I've known what it was to work every hour God sends, year in, year out. Scrimped and saved for the day I could hold up my head in a house like this. Denied myself everything – everything but the dream of the day I could display the fruits of my labour to the world.

"But wealth," the slaughterman continued, now unsmiling and deeply resentful, "isn't enough for them, is it? Ambition, hard work, intelligence, dedication are nothing to those born with a silver spoon in their mouths. None of these count against blood line – against being born and educated as a gentleman. I've never had time to marry. Women at our level of society, Westcott, spend more than they bring to a marriage. But, long ago, I planned how to raise the family name in the world."

As Skinner looked at the detective to see that he appreciated his meaning, Westcott nodded and Skinner went on, "Married my sister to a gentleman. Her looks and my money made him blind to our humble birth."

Reading Westcott's expression as distaste, Skinner sneered. "Don't say you're a detective with a soft heart! Are you imagining a sweet young thing living down by the docks and in love with a sailor, torn away and forced into marriage to an ugly old man by a wicked brother? Nothing of the kind. Fanny was born a Skinner. She agreed to everything. Montague was a handsome young man of excellent family, but, unfortunately, only the second son with few prospects and an inclination to gamble beyond his means. I grieved, Westcott, when Fanny died and still do."

Sitting up and looking straight at Westcott to show there were, even so, no tears of weakness in his eyes, he said, "To cut a long story short, I bought her baby from Montague – yes, bought for a thousand pounds. I placed all my hopes, and Fanny's, on that boy, Ernest Skinner Montague. I educated him as a gentleman. I leased this house to give him the chance to live like a gentleman and meet the right people. I bought him a good commission. He's never known the hard times I have. Believes all this stuff about honour and bravery. Sometimes, I'm afraid he's not hard enough – not in the sense you and I have had to be hard, Westcott. Doesn't want the Marston girl for her money. Talks about love." Skinner laughed and was silent at last.

"And when you recognised Kersey?" the detective asked, returning Skinner to the point the detective thought the man was trying to avoid.

"I could see he recognised me. I swear he was as surprised to see me as I was to see him. There was no smirk, no knowing smile, just a flicker in the eyes. I was a distraction he didn't want to have to bother with. In short, we both found it convenient not to recognise each other."

"You left it at that?"

Sneers seemed to come readily to Skinner's lips. "Of course I didn't. I had too much at stake. Put my man, Mansfield, on to following him."

"And what did your man find Kersey was up to?"

"Preaching silly theories was all he could come up with."

"Silly theories?"

"Even you must have discovered by now that he was always going on in the Poke and anywhere else where people would waste their time listening. I heard him, myself, going on about working men combining together to raise their wages. 'Strength in unity,' he called it. You know how these radicals rant and rave. Though mind you, to be fair, he was a bit different from the rest. Talked about men respecting their masters." Skinner laughed as he related this. "And even suggested masters should respect their men."

"Didn't all this bother you?" Westcott asked, still looking for any sign that Skinner might have resented Kersey. "If your garret masters in London stuck together, you couldn't force down their prices like you do. Didn't you object to his 'silly theories' enough to want to get rid of him?"

Again, Skinner found some humour in the situation and laughed before answering. "In London, who knows? Here? He could have preached unity

123

to rural labourers until he was blue in the face. They'd just have chewed their straws, spat them out and got back to leaning on their spades. Get them really roused and they'll burn a haystack or two. Kersey preferred argument to arson."

"That's all your man caught him at, preaching silly theories?"

"That's about it. A few listened to him. That young Osborne lad thinks he was an angel sent from Heaven, but he's lost without his leader."

"Do you know of any reason why Kersey came to Upton Market?" the detective asked, not very hopeful of an answer.

"I'll tell you one thing, Mr Detective. He didn't come to Upton Market. I heard him myself, on the day he arrived, saying that he was on his way to Upton St John. So, yet another dent in your theory that he was after me."

"Upton St John," Westcott echoed. "What's there? Who's there?"

"Storr country, in a nutshell. Everything you see belongs to the Storr family."

"And who are they?"

"Came over with the Conquest, or thereabouts. Didn't all keep their heads over the centuries, but seem to have kept a hold on their land. Probably supplied a mistress or two to this king or that. The old Lord's been on the point of dying for a year or two and everyone took it that his eldest son, Frederick, would succeed. Hard luck on him he was killed in the Crimea just before his father died. Title was expected to go next to Frederick's brother, Henry. Instead, it went to Frederick's newborn baby son, Lord Storr's grandson. Put Henry's nose out of joint, I can tell you."

Having thought about the answer, Westcott commented, "Can't see Kersey having any interest in them." Then he asked, almost in desperation, "Didn't any report reach you of Kersey having made inquiries about anyone in the village?"

Having made a great show of searching his memory to keep the detective waiting for his reply, Skinner confided, "Now you come to mention it, there was something odd. My man said he seemed very interested in Mrs Jakes, a nurse of sorts, it seems. More like Mrs Gamp, they say, than Florence Nightingale."

"But she lives in Upton Market," Westcott said, thinking of the day he had met Carrie and seen her disappear into the house where she had worked."

Beginning to tire of the conversation, Skinner took out his gold watch from his pocket and told the time out loud. Westcott hurried to fit in another question or two. "Would your man have acted off his own bat? Taken it upon himself to remove any possible threat to you?"

"He does only what I tell him, no more, no less." Skinner could not have been more definite. He rose to bring the meeting to an end.

"One final question, Mr Skinner, if I may." Westcott rose, too, but took his time. "Young Kersey. Was he involved with any woman? They say ....."

As the door opened, the detective paused and turned to see a tall young man enter the room, dressed, by Westcott's conservative tastes, rather strangely. While he recognised Captain Skinner Montague by his likeness to his uncle, he noticed his features were more refined and his bearing more confident and relaxed. The union with Montague blood appeared to have paid off. On being introduced, the newcomer greeted Westcott as though he were someone he had been eager to meet all his life. It was easy to picture him in demand in the best society and still popular with the roughest soldier under his command.

Quite sincerely, Westcott declared that he must, like all true Englishmen should, thank him for his bravery and dedication to duty at Balaclava. Without false modesty, the Captain accepted his compliments, expressed his regret that so many good men had died and then turned his attention to his uncle, who was impatiently waiting to speak.

"The detective here, Ernest, is not inquiring into our suitability to be connected with the Marstons. He is investigating the murder of Peter Kersey. Maria must have hired him, although I'm sure he wouldn't admit that."

For a moment, a flash of annoyance broke across Skinner Montague's face, but then he came straight to the point. "The archdeacon, Mr Howard, my uncle and I, not to mention the Storr family with whom he is connected, have no doubt that James Marston killed Kersey, while his mind was in a state of excitement and confusion. He seems to have thought Kersey was the Devil come to torment him and his parishioners and saw it as his duty, as a good parish priest, to banish him from the Earth by one means or another. We feel, I am sure that I do, some guilt in not having prevented this from happening and not having saved the man from himself. We all agreed, therefore, that the wisest course of action was to have James taken to an asylum, where he could do no harm and be spared the terror of a public trial. In this, of course, we were also thinking of Miss Marston. How will it serve James or his sister to prove in open court that he is guilty? I have Maria's best interests at heart."

"You would have him escape the law?"

"As I say, what purpose will it serve? James can do no harm, now. He will spend his life there and, should he ever realise what he has done, will be in torment. Is that not punishment enough? A trial would do only harm to his sister and his young daughter as well as to the memory of the good, Christian man he was before the sad events of his life brought about this terrible affliction and turned his reason."

"What would you have me do?" Westcott asked, from curiosity, rather than any undertaking to obey.

"Let sleeping dogs lie, sir. No good can come of raking over this matter again. Had I known of Miss Marston's intentions to hire you, I would have persuaded her not to pursue it."

"I have been told that you and Miss Marston have an understanding. Do you have her agreement to this plan of yours?"

"Please do not speak to others of an understanding. Miss Marston, for whom I have the greatest regard and affection, has made it clear that she would not refuse me, once this whole sad affair is over and done with. You seem to be suggesting that we do not confide in each other. Obviously, Maria knew I would not countenance this investigation, which must lead to her brother's trial." He smiled indulgently, "She has a mind of her own, I am pleased to say."

"No doubt you will advise Miss Marston to drop the case?"

"Tell me, Mr Westcott," the Captain replied by way of an answer, "have you found any evidence against James Marston?"

"Yes," the detective was forced to concede.

"Have you found any evidence against anyone else?"

"No," was Westcott's grudging answer.

Laughing, the Captain gave the detective a light tap on the shoulder. "Investigate away, my friend, as long as you do not distress Miss Marston or report your discoveries to the police. Perhaps your conclusion – and on the evidence it can be the only one – that her brother is, sadly, guilty, will make her give up this wild goose chase and look to a happier future with me."

Skinner, pacing restlessly in the hall, was making it clear that their guest should have left long ago, but the nephew had one more point to make.

"My uncle, Mr Westcott, was concerned that you were here to prove the match undesirable. I have no such worries. My uncle's rise in the world is a matter of pride to me. I have no intention of keeping my bride in ignorance of his and of my mother's origins. If you do not tell her all you have learned, I certainly shall. But please, Mr Westcott, do not tell anyone else. I owe everything to my uncle and will not have him looked down upon for his humble beginnings."

When the detective had agreed to this, as he thought, very reasonable request, the Captain opened the door and ushered Westcott through it.

"Come, sir, let me drive you home."

"I trust," Westcott said, thinking of the friends he could impress, "that you will regale me on the way with a first-hand account of the Charge."

The Captain shook his head. "We were commanded to charge and we did our duty and obeyed. That is all. I cannot speak of it without sorrow for my fallen comrades." Smiling his most charming smile, he insisted, "But you shall regale me with tales of a London detective."

Westcott, unrestrained by modesty, did just that and, within minutes it seemed to him, he was outside his own front door watching the Captain skilfully turning his carriage in the narrow lane and saluting him as he urged his horses homewards.

Was it back to suspecting Howard, the detective asked himself? No, he was not going to retrace those steps again. Skinner had given him a clue in the name of Mrs Jakes and he would follow that next. Who better to ask about Mrs Jakes than Maria Marston? He felt uneasy at the prospect. There were other, more awkward, questions which he had put off long enough asking that young lady.

CHAPTER 25

For his meeting with Miss Marston, the detective had chosen a place where they were unlikely to be seen and where, if they were, it would appear that they had accidentally bumped into each other while out walking. The spot in the woods looked out over patchwork fields. It was itself sheltered by the trees, but gave a view of anyone climbing the hill towards them.

Westcott had noticed the place in his explorations around the village, his curiosity having been aroused by the dozens of tiny paw marks around the rough wooden bench placed there at some time by somebody to afford an opportunity for rest. Instinct told him this was where Maria had often met the man she referred to simply as 'Peter' and with whom rumours in the village had linked her name.

As he walked to this spot, the detective faced the fact, which he would angrily have refuted had it been made by a colleague, that his weakness lay in the very task he had ahead of him. While he could interrogate the toughest of criminals without fear and talk easily, as one of them, to men and women, young and old, in the streets of London, he was embarrassed and diffident when faced with a pretty young gentlewoman like Maria Marston. He knew that, to spare them and to extricate himself from the situation as soon as possible, he would accept half truths and evasions and fail to press home points he should pursue. Feeling protective of this young lady he would, in short, protect her from himself.

In an attempt to put himself in the right frame of mind, he forced himself to consider that Maria might well have known Kersey in London. If he, being poor, had been unable to resist a tempting offer from her brother to go away with money in his pocket, might she have been in despair at her abandonment? On the other hand, she might never have set eyes on him before, but had fallen in love with him and become desperate when he, an honourable young fellow, turned instead to a girl in his own level of society. In either case, a kitchen knife was as handy for a woman as for a man. If she had come up behind Kersey and taken him by surprise......

Westcott felt guilty even thinking such things about the young woman. It was no wonder that, in passing the vicarage, he had been tempted to pop in and ask Constance to make gentle inquiries of Miss Marston on his behalf. He had wanted to ask Constance, too, about any links between

Kersey's brother and Mrs Jakes. After all, he had no Tom Cat to try his ideas out on and he was beginning to view Constance as the next best thing. Perhaps, the detective thought, turning to these matters himself, Kersey had been going on a longer journey and had aimed for Upton St John simply for an overnight stay and been distracted by Maria or another young lady. Or perhaps, Westcott had to admit to himself, the murder was, indeed, the irrational act of some madman or evil-doer and nothing to do with any event in Kersey's life.

As he turned a bend in the footpath, Westcott saw Maria sitting on the bench, looking pale and sad in the hard light, which shone between the branches of the over-hanging trees. The two spaniels ran excitedly to him, sniffed around his shoes and then retired, disappointed. It was not the man they had been in the habit of meeting. The detective knew that he could not shirk the task ahead.

Greetings and niceties over, the detective gave an account of his findings in London and of his conversation with Skinner and his nephew. Maria listened in silence, holding back tears, but, at the end, simply remarked, "So we have made no progress, Mr West?"

Seeing a lead to one of his questions, Westcott asked, "You are not surprised, then, that Peter Kersey was interested in Mrs Jakes?"

"No, indeed, he asked me to tell him all I knew of her."

Seeing this as a lead into another question, the detective suggested quietly, "Perhaps you could tell me also about your meetings with Mr Kersey."

Looking directly at Westcott, Maria said, "I knew that I would have to tell you everything at some time. You have realised, have you not, that Peter was my true friend?"

"Then, Miss Marston," the detective replied gently, "you must grieve for him greatly and, perhaps, be happy for a chance to talk to me about him. In the circumstances, you will not have been able to confide your feelings to anyone else."

His approach had been the right one. Maria turned to Westcott and agreed earnestly. "I have had no one in whom to confide. Recently, I have talked to Constance – Mrs Brown. I am so afraid, Mr West, that all my memories of Peter will fade from the world and it will be again, as it was before, a grey, sad place."

"No, my dear," the detective assured her, equally earnestly. "The memories of those we have loved stay with us. I would even say that they grow stronger as we grow older."

"But his death was so unexpected. I had no time to store away his words and glances, his smile…….."

Producing a large, white handkerchief, Westcott gave it to the young lady to stem her tears and was silent. Then, once again, he assumed the tone of a detached, but gentle, questioner.

"You have told me about your first meeting with Peter Kersey on the coach, Miss Marston. The second was when he called at the vicarage to see your brother, was it not?"

Sitting up to her full height, which still left her small and helpless in Westcott's eyes, Maria began, "I must tell you, first, Mr West, that Peter was the most honourable of men and one of the few real gentlemen I have known. We did nothing sinful."

"I accept that, Miss Marston, and have never, for a second, entertained any idea to the contrary. I am also convinced that, in asking me to clear your brother's name, you are also asking me to find the murderer of your friend. Help me then, all you can."

"I did not speak to him when he called to see my brother. Alice has told you all that happened that day. Even later, Peter would never tell me why he had wanted to consult my brother."

"Then the next time you spoke to him, when was that?"

Maria did not have to think.

"It was a week later. Peter came to the vicarage. He did not even come as far as the back door. He stood just inside the garden at the wicket gate, which leads into the churchyard. He had been waiting there patiently until I happened to come into the garden. It was I with whom he wished to speak in particular."

"Why not bump into you on one of your walks? Everyone in the village knows that you regularly walk the dogs."

"I said, Mr West, that Peter was a gentleman. He did not think it right to stop me while I was alone. As he could not, on account of my brother's attitude to him, come to the house, this was his compromise. If I did not wish to speak to him, I was free to call someone from the house to send him away or would not feel impeded if I wished to retire indoors."

"Unusually thoughtful for a young man, or," the detective added, thinking of his contemporaries, "any man."

"Peter was, Mr West."

As the young woman dabbed her eyes with the handkerchief he had given her, Westcott pulled another from his pocket and removed something from the corner of his own eye. Small insects could be a bother at this time of the year.

After a minute or two, Maria resumed, "Peter stepped forward to speak to me, but, just at that moment, James opened the window of his study and ordered Peter to leave. Before he left, he whispered, 'Please let me speak with you on your walk, today, Miss Marston. I mean you no harm. I must know something about Mrs Jakes and they say you are the best person to tell me.' Immediately, Peter left, carrying his hat in his hand. My brother seemed transfixed, staring at his hair."

"When did you first notice that Mr Kersey had ginger hair?"

"Auburn," Maria corrected him. "It was a very cold day when we travelled from London and Peter wore his hat pulled down over his ears. As he pushed the coach, his hat slipped off and blew across the road. When he had finished moving the coach and walked over to pick up his hat, I saw his hair then." Looking straight at the detective, she added, "That would have been when Mr Skinner recognised him." It was clear that the young woman realised that one person's story was being checked against another and that she was not above suspicion.

Returning to the main thread of the story, the detective asked, in a voice which he hoped was free from censure, "You met the young man that afternoon?"

Obviously all too well aware how wrong her action had been, Maria read criticism into the remark, even when it was not there.

"I was very wrong, Mr West."

The detective tried to make light of it. "But Mr Kersey was a handsome young man and you sensed that you would come to no harm."

"No, indeed not. I mean yes, that is perfectly true, but I did not go for those reasons." Before Westcott could ask why she had gone, Maria burst out, "I went because I hate Mrs Jakes."

Westcott sat down beside Maria, realising there was much she was eager to tell to a good listener like himself, but that it might not all be relevant to the case. He urged her, "Tell me, Miss Marston, what you told Peter Kersey and what he told you."

The young woman needed no further encouragement. "When I arrived

131

here, Peter was already waiting. He was suddenly very awkward. 'I came here, Miss Marston,' he said, 'to be away from the open view so that no one could see us. Not,' he added in obvious embarrassment, 'that I …well, I mean…..'" Maria laughed at the memory.

"We laughed together about that many times afterwards, but at the time I simply said, 'You wish, Mr Kersey to know what kind of a nurse Mrs Jakes is, what kind of a person she is?' He had been told that, when my father died just before I was born and my mother just after, I was put in the care of a wet nurse, Mrs Jakes."

"You were too young, then, to recall much about her?"

Maria laughed bitterly. "You would have thought so, would you not, Mr West? But my brother was appointed my guardian. He had just been given the living here and was only too happy to take Mrs Jakes' advice to leave me in her care. I remained there until I was eight years old."

"And Mr Kersey wanted to know how she treated you?"

"Peter was surprised when I said that she was kind, that she showed me warmth in her hugs and kisses, which I received from nobody else. She fed and clothed me, listened to my joys and woes."

After pausing for a moment, to let Westcott take this in, Maria explained, "As I told Peter, sometimes I think that, however many books we read and however many conversations we take part in, however many words we learn and however much grammar we master, it is far from simple to put facts, let alone feelings, into words. Meanings compete with each other. They surge and whirl this way and that. If you put into words what you think is the whole truth, you find that you have missed out a small fact here, a little feeling there."

"You see, Mr West," Maria tried to explain, even though she could never sum up those years in a few sentences, "Mrs Jakes was the only grown-up to whom I was close. I relied on her alone for love and for my whole well-being."

Trying to return to the bare facts, the detective said, "Tell me how she treated you."

"As I have said, Mrs Jakes cuddled me, rocked me to sleep, singing lullabies. She spoke kindly to me and gave me treats. And this was not only when we were with other people. She was sweet and kind to me when we were alone. She was also," Maria went on, her voice expressing her anger, "cold and unkind. Suddenly, for no reason, she would shout at me, make me sit alone in the corner or smack me until I was sore and bruised. She would send me to bed in the dark and cold, refusing me a candle, however hard I begged for one, knowing I was afraid of the dark and laughing at my fear."

"Did you tell no one?"

"Not for a long time. You see, Mr West, as I explained to Peter, I thought that I had done something to displease her for her love to turn to hate. I tried, oh so hard, to be good, to be loving, to win back her affection. She pushed me away, telling me that I was wicked and ungrateful."

Just as Kersey had done, the detective spoke the right words. "How hard it must have been for you, Miss Marston, a child with no one in the world to turn to."

Hearing the words again, Maria recalled, "Peter asked me if I thought that Mrs Jakes was simply spiteful and given to moods or whether she might do real harm to a child — to a baby."

"What was your reply, Miss Marston?"

"Suddenly, with his question, it all came back to me so vividly. I burst out that she was a hateful woman, who tormented me for her own pleasure. She enjoyed hearing me beg for affection and seeing me rejected and alone. But above all, I came to realise, her actions were prompted by greed and the desire for gain. Making me appear unhappy and clinging on my visits to my relations, supported her claims that I was a difficult child, who took up all her time and attention for which she must be paid. She put it more and more openly to me over the years that I could regain her affection and care if I gave my new clothes to her to sell and wore old ones no better than those her children wore."

"My brother did his duty and allowed me to visit the family home weekly, but he never took me out or visited me in her house to see the conditions in which I lived. I never spoke with him except in that woman's presence. He was, of course, generous with gifts and money, but these she took from me 'for safe keeping' or persuaded me to give to her children. Then she would report to my family that I had lost or broken their presents and torn my clothes. These they would replace. My brother is a great believer in original sin, Mr West." Maria added bitterly, "He was all too ready to see it in me."

Unable or unwilling to stem the torrent of hatred against her old nurse, Maria barely took breath before continuing, "When I was three, the dreadful woman began a dame school and my presence there encouraged mothers to send her their children. The woman can barely read or write. By the time I was five, I had overtaken her and some of her children, who had picked up some sort of an education at Sunday school."

As Maria paused at last, the detective asked, "How did you answer Mr Kersey's particular question on whether she would harm a baby?"

Without hesitation, the young lady replied, "I told him that if it were to her advantage, Mrs Jakes would take great pleasure in smothering any child. I have no doubt," Maria added, as an afterthought, "that the woman spent many an hour weighing my value alive against my value to the resurrection men were I to die. She is evil and I hate and detest her."

The detective had watched Maria closely. She was lost in the past, in her childhood, and in her meetings with Kersey. At last, she paused and studied his expression. She feared it said that, in talking of Mrs Jakes, she sounded like her brother speaking of the Devil.

"I am not mad, Mr West, though Ellen Jakes would have everyone think that I am. She has been one of the foremost accusers of my brother. She has spread the belief that the Marston family has a strain of madness running through it, which touches us all."

"What did Peter Kersey say to all you told him?"

"He was greatly concerned, but would not tell me why."

Taking a deep breath and trying to avoid making a young lady cry, Westcott asked, as casually as possible, "And how did you come to know Mr Kersey, Peter, as a friend?"

"I liked Peter the very first time I saw him from the coach. As I glanced from the window, I was feeling so unhappy. He saw this and smiled, such a tender, caring smile."

Patiently, Westcott waited for Maria to continue. She was trying to sort out her thoughts and sum up those meetings and the times of happiness she had known for all too short a while.

"Sometimes, Mr Westcott, now that Peter is no longer here with his warmth, his smile and his gentleness, I think that perhaps he was just sorry for me, that he was responding to me as to an injured bird or a kicked dog. I wonder how I could have earned or deserved his love and whether Mrs Jakes was right in saying no one would ever love a horrid child like me."

Westcott, never having met her, felt he hated Mrs Jakes, as he would have hated anyone who made a child believe she was unworthy of love. Such childhood impressions were not easily erased.

"But, my child," he said, taking her hand, "you know that, when he was with you, you had no doubts that he loved you as you loved him."

Recalling those days, Maria said, "I know he smiled more readily, more deeply, more delightedly at me than at anyone else. He was always remarking, as he told me of the events in his day, 'I thought of you when .....' or 'Something reminded me of you ...' and 'I wondered what you would have thought ...' Always, he made himself notice and recall things I would have pleasure or amusement in hearing."

"And Peter said he loved you, my dear," Westcott suggested, hoping he was not blushing like a woman.

"No, he was too honourable to mention love without marriage or marriage without being in a position to support me. When I inherited my wealth, I proposed to him. Our Queen, I am sure, did that very thing."

Before the detective could even raise an eyebrow to inquire as to Kersey's reply, Maria went on, "He refused, of course."

"It is what any man of honour would have done," Westcott commented, recollecting the chance of a good marriage he had once refused on the same grounds. He asked, "Try and recall, Miss Marston, did anyone who might have resented it know of your regard for Mr Kersey?"

"A jealous rival!" Maria laughed in disbelief. "You will not find it beyond belief to learn that, since I have come into a fortune, many men have suddenly found me fascinating, beautiful and the ideal wife." She gave more serious thought to the detective's question. "Captain Skinner Montague and I have been good friends since my return here. He, too, is a gentleman and has always been kind to me. I hear his uncle has picked me out for his bride, but Ernest has always behaved with propriety and as a good friend. He knows that I cannot consider marriage until I have finished mourning for Frances, whom I regarded as a true sister. And I am sure that he could have known nothing of my meetings with Peter. Had he found out, he would have gone to Peter and asked whether his intentions were honourable. Ernest, as you must know, fought heroically in battle and would not stoop to petty meanness and jealousy."

Without any joy in her voice, Maria stated, "For the sake of the family and to have children, I may agree to marry him in time, but I shall never love any man as I loved Peter."

Lost in their conversation, neither Westcott nor Maria had heard Alice approaching and, when they suddenly heard her voice, they were startled.

As she was seeking attention, this was an encouraging beginning for her.

"I heard you talking to Papa about Mr Kersey one day, Aunt Maria," she announced, with all the bravado of a child determined to make mischief. "I shall tell Mr West about it myself, as I know that you repeat to him everything I tell you about Papa and Mr Kersey."

Continuing to speak rapidly, to prevent Maria's recovering and intervening to stop her, the child went on, "Papa was very angry. He told Aunt Maria that his parishioners were hinting that she was meeting Mr Kersey in secret. He said that it was most improper to be with any man, who was not a relation, on her own, but to be with a common working man who would not know how to behave to a lady was scandalous. She would make herself and her family a laughing stock among the gentry and make ordinary people lose respect for their betters."

"That is enough, Alice," Maria warned in an icy tone, which would have silenced any adult. It merely indicated to Alice that she had the power of hurting her aunt and was well on the way to doing so.

"Do you know what Aunt Maria said, Mr West?" the girl asked, with a smirk.

"I am sure, Alice," the detective answered sternly, "that your aunt will tell me herself, if she wishes."

As the child, not having expecting such a reply, hesitated, Maria said, as calmly as she could, "I said that, if he proposed to me, I would marry Peter."

"That was not all," Alice announced accusingly, trying to hang on to power.

"No, it was not," her aunt agreed. "I said that, if ever I received my inheritance and the independence that would bring, I would, myself, propose to Mr Kersey."

"Aunt said," Alice gloated, wringing the last drop of pleasure from the situation, "she would beg him to marry her and, if her money stood between them, she would give it all away to the poor and follow Mr Kersey to the ends of the Earth. Papa was furious." With her aunt moving towards her, she screamed, "Papa said that he would stop Kersey one way or another." Then she ran weeping back towards the house.

Having apologised for the drama, which had unfolded before them, Maria called the dogs and followed her niece, now screaming in the distance that she had meant no harm.

The child could feel well satisfied, Westcott concluded. She had not only distressed her aunt, as she had intended, but had also obtained revenge for her father's neglect by pointing the finger directly at him as the murderer.

CHAPTER 26

Feeling at the dead end of a blind alley with only James Marston staring him in the face, Westcott made his way to the vicarage. It would be a good idea, he told himself, to call and tell Constance all he had learned. He needed, he had convinced himself, to hear himself relating the facts to stimulate his mind into making connections and coming up with the right questions.

Sally opened the door, put on her most serious face and prim manner and asked, "Is Mrs Brown expecting you, sir? The housekeeper does not receive guests to tea without invitation."

"Is that the time?" Westcott demanded, consulting his pocket watch in disbelief.

As the detective hesitated and was about to turn on his heels, a voice, Mrs Brown's, called. "Show my cousin in, Sally. Family are exempt from the rules."

Upstairs, seeing the spread laid out on the table, Westcott asked, "I'm sorry if you were expecting someone, Constance. I won't take up much of your time. You can't have read my thoughts. I didn't know, myself, that I was coming."

"Oh, I foretell the future," Constance smiled.

"And the past?" the detective asked. "That is what I need to see through the fog on the day Peter Kersey was stabbed to death."

"It does seem," Constance began enthusiastically, revealing that she had already been told everything by Maria, "that we have a reason for Kersey's visit to Upton St John."

"Oh, yes?" Westcott queried.

"Yes, the Crimea links Peter's brother and the men, including Mrs Jakes' son, who fought there with the group who went with the Storrs."

"I couldn't fit in Mrs Jakes," Westcott admitted, too interested to resent her making the connection before him.

"Why should you?" Constance admitted generously. "You would not know that her son died there. Nor would you know that there are half a dozen other men from the Uptons who fought there, too."

"So you are suggesting that Kersey came to find out more about his brother's death?"

"Quite simply that, Charles. I have noted that, quite often, when someone

138

close dies away from home, relatives cannot accept he is dead until they know how, where and, possibly, why he died and how he spent his last moments. Even hardhearted Mrs Jakes was eager to know all the details of her son's passing from the men who returned."

"So," Westcott concluded, "if that explains away Kersey's being here, his death was unconnected to his reason for coming here. We are back to Mr Marston's being the chief – the only – suspect." He turned to Constance and, throwing his hands out in despair, asked, "Am I on a wild goose chase, Constance? Should I pack my bags now and go home?"

"Oh, no, Charles. You are Miss Marston's only hope. As you guessed, she wishes to know who killed Peter Kersey and she does not think it was her brother. Perhaps, as she was so close to the young man, her feelings tell her more than her reason."

While Westcott, who was not much given to belief in messages from beyond the grave, thought of a reply, the housekeeper continued, "Miss Marston told me of Alice's outburst. She is a very angry child, but even she realises she went too far. The poor child needs to know that her father is innocent."

The detective made up his mind. "If I am to continue, I must insist that I see Mr Marston. How can I be expected to solve this crime, without talking with the man at whom everyone, even his daughter, is pointing the finger?"

"I shall arrange it with Miss Marston," Constance assured him. "Captain Skinner Montague will not like it, mind you. He thinks that Miss Marston should forget her brother and live her own life."

"With him," I gather.

"With him, indeed."

"Would you approve?"

Constance took a minute to consider the question. "Ernest Skinner Montague is young, handsome, charming, and reputedly wealthy, always at hand to help a lady in distress. And a hero to boot!" She smiled a grim smile. "Why do I not like him?"

Normally, to such a remark, the detective would have politely commented that women saw things men missed, but, on this occasion, he replied, "Just how I feel."

"Could it be," Constance suggested tentatively, not to appear to be trying to influence her listener, "that Skinner Montague did know of Miss Marston's friendship with Kersey and wished to eliminate a rival?"

"Ah!" the detective stressed, as though to an apprentice, "You must not make the mistake of confusing your dislike and guilt. You must keep your feelings out of an investigation."

Too tactful to point out that the detective had not followed his own rule in the case of Mr Skinner, the housekeeper said not a word.

Concentrating on devouring the fare spread out before him, Westcott felt disappointed that it had not been prepared especially for him. Then something occurred to him, but, to avoid being seen to talk with his mouth full, he swallowed hard. "It will not do. If the connection were merely between Jakes' son and his brother, why was Peter asking about her willingness to do anything for money?"

"How," Constance exclaimed, "does a detective hold all these clues, big and small, in his head at one and the same time!"

"Experience," Westcott answered, taking the remark at face value.

"Then," the housekeeper, needing to get on with her work, stated, "the plan must be to visit Mr Marston, ask Skinner Montague if he did the deed and find out what Mrs Jakes may, or may not, have been ready to do for money."

"Couldn't have put it better myself." Westcott held out his cup and saucer. "How about more tea and another of those delicious pastries?"

"Certainly, Your Lordship," Constance replied, reminded once again of why she had always avoided marriage.

CHAPTER 27

Westcott had no very high opinion of private lunatic asylums. He had never visited one, but he had heard enough to convince him that, apart from one or two shining examples, the only difference between the conditions and treatment in such places and in the lunatic wards of workhouses was a better class of patient and of furniture. A patient from the aristocracy or gentry tended to believe he was Wellington or Prince Albert or, even, the Tsar of Russia, while the poor and ignorant fellow in the workhouse, who had often never heard of such illustrious beings, was content to believe he was Jesus Christ.

For the rest, the detective was sure both confined their inmates in straight jackets and isolation and left them in the care of idle and spiteful attendants, who mocked and bullied them. As for the physicians, you were as likely to find an enlightened one in the workhouse as in a private asylum, although the latter might be more fluent and imaginative in describing the theories on which their harshness was based. In truth, he had never been able to distinguish between the regime prevailing in such places and that of a prison.

As the coach bowled along the bumpy lanes, Maria told Westcott, "Dr Chilvers has great experience in these matters and a high proportion of success. Although, of course, he cannot reveal their names, he has treated many members of European royalty and members of well-known and respected families."

The young woman must have guessed that Westcott was not impressed, as she continued, "Several people assured me that placing James in Peace Haven was the best, the only, way to keep him from the hangman."

"Who was the first to suggest this?" the detective inquired.

"You think that someone wished to have James confined so that the truth of another's guilt was not revealed?"

"Quite possibly. With your brother unable to defend himself, his guilt could be assumed and inquiries dropped. And whatever he does say can be dismissed as the ravings of a lu..."

"You need not mince words, Mr Westcott," Maria informed him. "Dr Chilvers has confirmed that my brother has quite lost his reason and suffers from the severest form of melancholia. With the best care he can provide,

James may never recover."

The young woman was silent for a while and then asserted, "No, I cannot think that anyone acted but for James' true good. Mr Howard, Mr Skinner, Captain Skinner Montague and The Honourable Henry Storr were all in favour of James' move to Peace Haven. And they had the approval of the local churchmen and of the Bishop, himself."

Once through the imposing iron gates, the drive leading to the asylum was better maintained than the public lanes over which they had travelled. The gardens were well laid out and had every appearance of being well tended. The immediate impression was of good order and, even, beauty in the surroundings. But, here and there, Westcott spotted men and women, some being dragged or prodded along, others walking with great speed and animation. Each was accompanied by an attendant, but these made no attempt to speak to the patients and were intent only on aiming for seats around the grounds where they could gather and gossip together, ignoring their charges. Dismounting, Westcott was unable to hide a shiver, which ran through him at the thought of being confined and totally at the mercy of such ignorant men.

In the magnificent hallway, they were greeted by a servant, who said that he had been instructed to show them to Dr Chilvers' study as soon as they arrived. It was nicely managed, the detective thought, to indicate to the visitors that they must go to the doctor, who was superior to them in his knowledge of the mysteries of medicine, while assuring them of their own importance by not keeping them waiting.

"Ah! Miss Marston and ..er...Mr Westcott," the physician began, and Westcott wondered why doctors always seemed to be saying 'Ah!' or ordering their patients to say it. The doctor was making an obvious effort not to stare at the detective, who had been introduced as a friend. The wealthy, to his mind, could be friendly with anyone they chose, however strange or eccentric this choice, but, it was clear, this friend was the strangest to whom he had been introduced in all his years as a fashionable physician. He, himself, was dressed in clothes suitable for mixing with the aristocracy and the gentry, even if the only portion of these ranks he had the opportunity to know well were unfortunate lunatics.

"I wished for a word with you, Miss Marston," he smiled, "before your brother is brought in. Melancholia continues severely to impair his actions, thoughts and spirits. We must think in terms of his remaining here."

With Maria unable to reply through her tears, Westcott said, "Miss Marston wishes to converse with him now."

Giving a gentle, but derogatory laugh, Dr Chilvers repeated, "Converse with him! I fear that he has no interest in conversing with anyone but himself."

"Is there anyone here with whom he can converse?" the detective asked.

Staring at the detective like a man licensed to separate the sane from the insane and being certain of the category in which he would place Westcott, the physician smiled coldly.

"Our attendants, of the highest moral character, are encouraged to talk with the patients – guests, as we term them – and keep their minds from morbid thoughts."

"My brother has, or had, many interests," Maria remarked.

"What are the interests of the attendant who accompanies Mr Marston?" Westcott inquired.

A cold smile was, by now, fixed upon the doctor's lips. "His one and only interest is the well-being of the patient."

"Guest," Westcott reminded the doctor. "Perhaps we could see Mr Marston now." The wording was that of a suggestion, but the tone made it an order.

The doctor looked to Maria, who, for all her youth, was the wealthier and more influential.

"Please, Dr Chilvers, I wish to see my brother without further delay." The young lady, Westcott decided, had a streak of metal. Did it come from her harsh upbringing or Kersey's dislike of pompous authority?

An attendant, with gentle words and a tight grip, brought James Marston into the room. The clergyman was like a skeleton reluctantly commanded back from the dead. Over enthusiastic purging had made him as thin as a rake. Even his skin appeared thin, stretched over his bones without an ounce of fat. His hair and beard, except where a comb had been dragged over the surface, were matted and unwashed. His eyes fixed upon the doctor, as though seeking permission for every thought and act. Even before he responded to his sister's kiss and to Westcott's hand shake, he looked anxiously at Dr Chilvers and then at the attendant.

"Thank you, sir," Westcott said firmly, "Miss Marston and I wish to talk to her brother alone."

"It is most irregular, Miss Marston," the doctor protested, appealing again to the weaker one of the pair. "Perhaps, when the patient has been here longer and can be trusted."

"Now, if you please, Dr Chilvers," the detective insisted.

"But he may become violent. You know why he is here…"

"I can handle that," Westcott insisted. "And Miss Marston can blow him over if needs be."

Grudgingly, when Maria had given her support to Westcott, Dr Chilvers gave way. "I cannot take responsibility for your actions, taken against my advice."

"Of course you cannot," Westcott agreed, seeing that Marston was becoming agitated by the disagreement. "I take full responsibility and am willing to sign to that effect."

"That will not be necessary," the doctor replied, signally to an attendant to remain behind. Westcott dismissed him, too, with little ceremony

Taking Marston's arm, the detective led the bemused man to a chair and pulled up others, one for himself and one for Maria, to face him.

"I do not think," Maria whispered, trying desperately to stem her tears, "that my brother is ready to answer any questions."

"Of course he isn't," Westcott agreed. "Now, Mr Marston, how are you, sir?"

"Who are you?" Marston asked, in a slow, lifeless voice. "Are you another physician come to torment me?"

"Dear me, no, sir. I claim to know nothing about diseases, but I know about men and I know when I see one cowed and degraded."

For a moment, the words did not appear to have sunk into Marston's mind, but, suddenly, he gave the weakest of weak smiles. Becoming solemn again, he whispered, "I live in fear. If, as they put it, I do not behave myself, I am shut away on my own. No one answers my cries. For every time I call, they say that they will add an hour to my imprisonment in the tiny cell. Sometimes I scream. I cannot help it," he added, turning to his sister for her to forgive such a weakness. "Then it is an ice-cold bath. They take my clothes away and leave me naked." This last sentence was said in a low voice for Westcott's ears only.

"Do you talk to no one, James?" Maria asked in disbelief. "Is there no one you can appeal to for a little kindness and care?"

"To my fellow sufferers who utter a stream of words with no meaning but to themselves? To those who sit curled up like animals with never a sound? To those as cowed and desperate as I? Or the attendants, less wise and less educated than our own servants at home?"

Gazing straight at Westcott, whom he sensed to be in charge, Marston pleaded, "Take me back to my home, sir. Take me back to my wife and children." Aware of the expression which crossed Westcott's face, he added in haste, "They are dead, I know. I have been told so a hundred times in harsh, plain words by my attendant, who treats me as though I were as ignorant as he. But they lie buried in the churchyard and...." A look of fear crossed the vicar's face. "The churchyard," he muttered several times and was silent.

"One thing at a time, sir," the detective said quietly, realising there was something the man could tell him about the churchyard, even if he were reluctant to recall it now. "If we take you home, will you promise to rest, to eat good food and regain your health?"

"Will you promise?" Marston repeated in a dull voice, seeming to shrink back into himself. "If I break my promise, what will my punishment be? They punish me here when I displease them. If I displease you, will you return me to this dreadful place?"

"There can be no worse punishment," Westcott claimed, "than the one you impose upon yourself. This melancholia. It comes from within you. You must fight it with the help of those who love and care for you."

"It is my punishment for sin," Marston answered. "The dreadful penalty for my sins. Just as God has taken away my wife and children for my sins, He has settled this empty blackness upon my soul."

"What shall we do, Mr Westcott?" Maria asked, her hand upon his arm.

"Let us take your brother home. This is no place for a healthy man with strong mind and spirit, let alone a man sick in his soul."

Maria walked over to her brother and leant over him. "James," she said quietly, "we are going to take you home. You must rest and recover your spirits. Do you hear me?"

As she had spoken, Marston had seemed to retreat into himself once more. He beckoned to Westcott to come closer. Maria walked to the window.

"I cannot trust myself," Marston whispered to the detective, "not to cut my throat. I must stay here, after all, for the sake of my child and my sister." Trying to smile, he added formally, "Thank you, sir, for your concern."

To his surprise, Westcott heard himself saying, "We'll have to put our trust in God's mercy, Mr Marston."

To his greater surprise, he heard Maria say, "I cannot manage alone.

I trust you will move into the vicarage to help us, Mr Westcott."

Again he surprised himself. "Of course, Miss Marston. I cannot be a worse attendant than the ones your brother has endured."

Immediately, Westcott began to question in his own mind what he was doing, but he managed to face up to Dr Chilvers with confidence. "Miss Marston wishes to take her brother home."

"That is impossible. I advise most strongly against it. You cannot have discussed this with his friends, who will be most annoyed at what you plan to do."

"It is most certainly possible and we reject your advice."

"But my fee," the doctor whined, not sure whether he would do better to agree with them or to resist. "It may be weeks before I fi..."

Maria finished the sentence for him, "find a suitable patient. I shall pay for an extra week."

"It may well take two or three," the doctor ventured to mention.

"One week," Westcott said firmly. "Now please fetch everything belonging to Mr Marston. We, the three of us, shall walk in the garden."

James Marston stayed close to his rescuers. Seeing his fear now that he was about to re-enter the world, Maria took his arm. "Alice will be so happy to see you."

"Alice," the clergyman repeated, smiling slowly. "I have missed my little Alice. She has suffered too, has she not?"

"You must comfort each other," Maria urged. "Sit in the garden with Alice and the dogs. Teach her her lessons. Then, when you are stronger, you may walk in the fields and the woods and feel God's presence once again."

Her brother stood still. "He has deserted me, Maria. God has turned his face from me."

"God never deserts those who trust in His grace. You will come to know his presence again amidst the beauty of the fields."

"But not in church," Marston whispered. "The Devil rules in the churchyard."

"What have I done?" the detective asked himself. "I know nothing of how to help this man. Should we let him stay?" Aloud, he said, "The Devil is not there, sir. Evil is the work of man."

For a second, the clergyman appeared about to speak, then, his face pale and his eyes dull, he muttered, "I am so weary." All animation left his

146

expression and he stared ahead, waiting to be led wherever they wished to take him.

"Here comes a servant with your belongings, James," Maria said. She, too, looked tired enough to drop.

"Let me help you both to the carriage," Westcott said encouragingly. "Half an hour and you will both be safe in the vicarage."

CHAPTER 28

Though not given to questioning his own decisions, Westcott did, on the return journey, begin to doubt the wisdom of his decision to bring James Marston home. At first, the clergyman seemed to have returned to a world of his own, but, the nearer they came to Upton Market, the more restless and agitated he became. On dismounting, he stared towards the graveyard and mumbled, "God forgive me."

"What a situation this is," Westcott mumbled to himself. "I'm more certain than you that you are not the killer, but you should know better than I do." Then his attention was drawn to the sounds of galloping hoofs and a horseman swung in through the gates.

Captain Skinner Montague yelled at a servant to take his horse and walked straight into the house behind them. Immediately, James Marston turned and attempted to climb the wide staircase. "Please take me to my room, Mr Westcott. I do not wish for company."

"But I have come to see you, James." It took little effort for the Captain to jump the stairs two at a time and turn to face Marston. "I cannot believe that, against all the advice of your friends and of Dr Chilvers, you allowed yourself to be led away from a refuge where you were comfortable and safe." Tactlessly and angrily, he demanded, "Who put this mad idea into your head?"

Instantly, the vicar appeared to crumple into a heap on the lower steps. The Captain's tone changed to that of a man speaking to a young and misguided child.

"Let me take you back, James. No harm has been done. The local police are not aware of your escape and we can have you back before anyone learns of this unfortunate occurrence. Your friends, James, amongst whom I place myself first and foremost, have only your good at heart."

Westcott stepped forward. "Come, sir. At least have a night in your own bed."

"Who are you, Westcott, to give orders in this house?" Skinner Montague demanded.

"Who are you?" the detective was about to say, but, at that moment, Maria Marston, who had run upstairs to prepare Alice for her father's unexpected return, appeared with the child. Alice ran to her father and, as they embraced, Maria urged her to take her father upstairs to his room.

Angrily, Skinner Montague repeated his question. "I asked who this man was to be given charge of James?"

"My brother has placed himself in Mr Westcott's care and I have agreed." In making it her brother's decision rather than her own, Maria was beginning to waver. Here, once again, was someone to whom she looked for love and support, unpredictably turning against her, just as Mrs Jakes had in her childhood. She had few defences against domineering bullies.

"Mr Westcott's care! Is Mr Westcott," the Captain demanded, spitting out the name with contempt, "a physician? To my knowledge, he is a man given to plodding through the vilest and meanest streets of London, no doubt taking bribes from those who can pay and hauling before the courts those who cannot. What knowledge has he of the sensibilities and intelligence of a gentleman such as your brother? He has mixed only with those members of society as coarse and hardened as himself."

"Please, Ernest, Mr Westcott is a guest in this house. I will not have him spoken to in such a way."

Weary as he was, James Marston made a decision and, taking his daughter's hand and gaining strength from her, climbed the stairs and disappeared into his room.

Not wishing to leave Maria alone, Westcott remained downstairs, observing the young man intently. The charm had vanished to be replaced by a distasteful mixture of arrogance and petulance, both expressing his belief that nothing and no one must thwart his wishes.

At last noticing that he was being watched, the Captain adopted a more tolerant, teasing attitude to Maria. Approaching her and smiling, he placed a hand on her arm and said in a soft voice, "You are a woman, just a girl, and do not understand these matters." Gently lifting her chin to look straight into her eyes, he added, "I know that you have not, as you will at our wedding, promised to obey me, but humour me and give way to my greater experience and to my manly right in these matters."

"Oh, my," Westcott thought cheerfully and without regret, "You, sir, have just said the wrong thing." Maria, he was sure, had been trained by Kersey not only in the rights of man, but of women, too.

Even Westcott was surprised by the intensity of scorn in the young woman's tone and expression. "You are an expert in both the minds of women and in my brother's illness, are you Ernest? How did you acquire such extensive learning? Merely by being born male?"

The detective, whom both had forgotten, had never seen anyone's lip really curl, but, watching now, he could have sworn that Ernest Skinner Montague looked, for a second, like an angry cur about to attack. Then the man's charm returned, like a mask falling over his face.

"I have angered you, my dear Maria. Please forgive me. It is only my love and concern for you which led me to risk your disapproval. I apologise, my dear, without reserve." Then another mask came across his face, – that of a naughty, spoiled boy who has seen the error of his ways and, having apologised, is sure his wheedling ways will ensure his forgiveness. "You do forgive me, don't you Maria?"

To Westcott's surprise, Maria seemed to forgive him everything. What it must be like to be a charming, handsome young man, he thought. He had never had that experience. Was it jealousy which made him not only dislike the fellow, but suspect him of disposing of his rival, Peter Kersey?

"Come, Maria," Ernest coaxed, smiling even more beguilingly, "let me take this burden from your shoulders. My only wish in life is to cherish and serve you, my dearest. Let us take care of James together."

Looking from one man to the other, Maria hesitated, until, glancing around, she caught sight of Constance at the door, nodding her disapproval.

"It is most kind of you," Maria decided, "but my brother has placed himself in Mr Westcott's care."

Turning to see where Maria was looking, the Captain threw a look of contempt at the housekeeper, who, by now, was standing meekly waiting for orders.

"Miss Marston," she asked innocently, "is Captain Skinner Montague to dine with us?"

They watched the Captain sweep from the room, striding out, chin raised and eyes straight ahead.

"It would appear not," the detective said with satisfaction, but he was aware that such a man was not to be underestimated. If the Devil were in Upton Market, it was in the form of Ernest Skinner Montague.

CHAPTER 29

While James Marston was settling back into his former life, Westcott took the opportunity of arranging matters with Constance and the curate. He and the curate were to be constantly with the vicar, or, while he was with his daughter or sister, somewhere close by. Tom was to move into the vicarage, too, and sleep outside Mr Marston's room. All razors and sharp instruments were to be kept under lock and key, except when in use, and checked every hour along with anything which might be used in a hanging. Vigilance was to be constant, but, as far as possible, not oppressive.

Matters were made easier by Marston's attitude to Westcott. Either because the detective had released him from confinement or because he had immediately transferred to him the dependence he had felt upon his doctor and attendants, he liked Westcott to be close at hand. Sensing that the vicar would feel betrayed if it were kept from him, Westcott insisted on the vicar's being told his true identity and purpose in being in the village.

James Marston's first response to this news was not encouraging. "So I did not kill the man. I did not think that I had, but even old certainties of God and His Word have turned to doubts."

The detective, although longing to hear whether the vicar knew anything of the murder, did not press him on the matter. Against all the evidence, he had convinced himself that Marston was not the murderer. In one of the spells when he joined Constance for a few minutes away from his new duties, the detective told her this.

"Ernest Skinner Montague is rapidly moving to the top of my list, Constance, and I think Miss Marston should not be left alone with him."

"I have already presumed to suggest this to her, Charles, but that young lady has a will of her own."

"You noticed, then, how thin is his veneer of charm?"

"He displayed that for all to see," Constance remarked, with a shiver of distaste. "Do you think he killed Kersey to rid himself of a rival?"

"I am coming to that conclusion. I knew that he was intent on marrying Miss Marston, but I had no idea until very recently how much of a rival Kersey had become."

Nodding in agreement, the housekeeper replied, "Miss Marston would, I am sure, never have married Skinner Montague while Peter Kersey was alive, even if Peter were a hundred miles away." She went on to raise a thought, which had occurred to her earlier. "It was Skinner, remember, who seems to have planned this marriage. Do you think that he had any part in the murder?"

"How can you measure guilt in these matters? Even if Skinner gave no direct encouragement to murder, he brought up the boy to see such an alliance as his right and as necessary to fulfil his uncle's ambitions." Then Westcott admitted, "An active part in the murder? I have my doubts. The killing has the stamp of recklessness in its execution as well as deviousness in covering it up. I think Skinner Montague acted impulsively and alone."

"And poor John Howard, is he free from suspicion?"

"It would seem so."

A little voice in the detective's head did say that, had he been able to talk with and observe Howard as closely as he had watched Skinner Montague, he might have discovered equally strong cause for murder and equal recklessness and deviousness in his character, but he ignored it.

"My money's on the Captain.....or," he added hastily, "it would be, were I a betting man."

"I am sure you are right, Charles," Constance agreed, offering the new resident more cake. "But we must not forget Kersey's interest in Mrs Jakes."

"I have not forgotten," the detective replied, taking the largest piece. "Skinner Montague may well have had more than one reason for killing Kersey."

Refreshments over, Westcott stood up and brushed the crumbs from his trousers. "Back to duty," he announced. "I must keep Mr Marston company in the library."

Constance wondered whether, in summing up a man's character and worth, a strong sense of duty, which Westcott possessed, out-weighed a marked tendency to shower carpets with crumbs.

Long before the housekeeper had made up her mind on that point, Westcott had returned to the library and was thinking of his reply to the clergyman's question, put the second he entered the room, on whether he was a well read man.

"Dickens, Trollope, Marryat, that's about my line," he answered, without great thought. He had examined the titles on Marston's shelves before and realised that, where literature was concerned, they lived in different worlds.

"I must read those authors at some time. They are, after all, what my parishioners read. They may need my guidance." The vicar considered this before he continued. "Dickens I always thought, from the little I read and from what I heard, guided people through the meanest parts of London and exposed his readers to evils they need never have known. Oliver Twist, with that villain Sykes, and the Jew and his gang of young thieves. They do not lift the mind and spirit, but drag them down and corrupt."

"They provide a little entertainment for dull lives," Westcott explained.

"But literature should be uplifting," Marston began, as though about to start a lecture. Then he stopped. "Does it matter, Westcott? Does anything really matter? I know it does, but, sometimes, to me, it does not."

"Your spirits are low, sir," the detective commented, realising how weak that sounded and that it did nothing to raise the man's spirits. Trying to think of something cheerful, he added, "Little Alice is so much happier, now."

"Young Alice. My little daughter has become very spoiled, I fear. But Maria tells me that I must not scold her, but treat her with gentleness and understanding. Does gentleness drive away sin, Westcott?"

"Hangings don't seem to work, sir. What are we left with?"

"Spare the rod and spoil the child. My father said that on many occasions." Marston recalled. "Does it not hold good anymore? Sin was to be beaten out."

"A happy medium, in all things, is my motto," the detective said, wondering if that was in fact true. He was longing to be off or to have the clergyman tell what had really taken place in the graveyard. "We'll let the women spoil you while we men point out the error of your ways." It was an empty remark, but Marston took it, as everything else, on face value.

"Please do, Westcott. I have many faults. Spoiling, as you call it, I see as spoiling the character. I must know my faults to correct them. Maria says that I must be forgiving of the sins of others. Perhaps that is true, but one's own sins, of those we must be unforgiving."

With scarcely a pause Marston continued, "You will forgive me, Westcott, if I talk too much. I think that I talk to turn my thoughts outward – to keep my mind busy. Melancholia will not leave me. It sits there, on my shoulder, ready to fill my whole body, mind and soul the minute I look in its direction. I dread its return. Death would be preferable, Westcott, but I must not take that road, for Alice's sake."

There was the sound of knocking at the front door and fear returned to

153

Marston's eyes. "Do not let anyone near me, Westcott. I cannot face people yet. Their eyes bore through me and I have no defences."

Westcott walked to the door and turned the key. "There, you are quite safe. You are in control, sir. You need not be afraid."

"I am not in control, but I trust you," Marston said, earnestly, "I see you as my other, stronger self. You must stay with me and be my strength until I am myself again."

Looking at the empty wreck of the man, words of a poem came into Westcott's mind. The words of another man who had known madness. He spoke them over to himself.

"'I feel I am, I only know I am
And plod upon the Earth as dull and void...' then," Westcott thought there was a line 'my soaring thoughts destroyed.' Something, something ...
'I was a being created in the race
Of men disdaining bounds of place and time –
A spirit that could travel o'er the space
Of earth and heaven – like a thought sublime,
Tracing creation like my maker, free –
A soul unshackled like eternity,
Spurning earth's vain and soul-debasing thrall
But now I only know I am – that's all.'"

CHAPTER 30

Lost in his own thoughts, Westcott almost missed Marston's next remark. "You are a detective. Yes, they told me that. What evil you must have seen, but you have not been dragged down. Now, I suppose, you would like me to tell you what happened that day."

"We can leave it until you are well, sir." Westcott, totally alert again, was forcing himself to be patient.

"I am well enough. It might help you in your investigation. The guilty must be punished."

Without reply, Westcott waited to hear whether the clergyman was ready to tell his story. For a while, it seemed that he had forgotten what he was about to do, but then he explained.

"My memory Westcott. It comes and goes. Just as I am about to grasp a fact, it fades back out of reach. Please be patient with me."

"Our time is our own," the detective reassured him. "Take your time."

"I think that I have always been in a hurry. A hurry to preach, a hurry to condemn, a hurry to censure — myself, as well as others." Marston's tone became confiding. "I was too strict with my boys, Westcott, with those sweet boys I shall never see again."

Deciding there was no answer he could make to that, the detective was silent. After a moment, Marston's attention came back to his companion. "What were we saying, Westcott? I can see that I have wandered from the subject."

Before Westcott could answer, Marston continued, "Oh, yes. I found poor Kersey's body." Again, he took time to gather his thoughts. "I often went to the grave of my wife and young boys. Being there gave me some contact with them — even if it were only the thinnest thread. In my condition, Westcott, the imagination plays tricks, and, as I sat in my chair that afternoon, my thoughts were full of pity for my family alone in the damp, chilly weather. I had to be with them. I left the house and took the path to the church. I paused by the wicket, struck by the silence, a deep silence made all the deeper by the tiny sounds to be heard all around — droplets of moisture falling from the trees, the chirruping of a sparrow in the hedgerow."

"I had pulled the gate to behind me. It squeaked noisily on its hinges. I still had my hand upon it. Something was keeping me back. Have you noticed, Westcott, that when there is silence, the imagination fills it with sounds, sounds so quiet that you do not know whether you have heard them, or not?"

Part of the detective wanted to urge the man on, to propel him forward to the point of the story, but he knew that he must let the clergyman relate it in his own way, or risk losing small details, which might prove of the greatest significance. And he must remember, he told himself, to return to the subject of these imagined sounds later.

"The next sound I heard was not unusual. It was the huffing of a horse, as it shook the moisture from its nostrils. Still, I felt a presence and waited, straining every sinew of my body to see and hear." A wild look came into the clergyman's eyes, as he continued, "Through the mist and the eerie stillness, a small voice called, 'Papa! Papa!' No more. No other words. Even in my melancholic, deluded state, my reason told me that it could not be my boys. But in my heart and soul I so longed for them to step out of the mist and run into my arms.

"It is hard to recall exactly what I did. I hurried forward, stumbling over hummocks and kerb stones, half running to my children who had come back to me. I called their names. I thanked God for answering my prayers."

"I came, at last, to the grave." Marston shook from head to toe. He shut his eyes, but whether he was seeking to blot out the scene or recreate it, the detective could not tell. "Mr Kersey's body," the vicar said, courteously giving the man, in death, a title he would never have bestowed on him in life, "lay back over my family's grave. His eyes, staring at the sky, showed horror and amazement. A knife stuck from his chest. Blood had soaked his clothes and run onto the grave. I tried desperately, with my bare hand, to rub it away. My wife and children must not be touched by such evil."

From staring ahead, Marston turned to Westcott. "You must remember that I was not acting as a rational man or, as I realise now, as a Christian. I did not take his pulse. After a while, I did close his eyes. To be quite honest with you, Westcott, I must admit that I did not do that as a mark of respect for the dead. In even the most educated of us, I realise, pagan fears are not far below the surface. I was foolish enough to recall the belief, held by most of my parishioners, that a likeness of the murderer is etched into a murdered man's eyes. I looked there, and my punishment was to see that deep emptiness, which I had seen in my wife's eyes when she had taken her last breath. I see it in my own, now, when I gaze into the mirror."

James Marston looked down at his hands, was quiet for a moment and then admitted, "I envied that man, Westcott. I thought, 'This man might be in Heaven with my family. Why, God, have You chosen to take him and to leave me?'"

There was now a longer silence, in which the clergyman seemed to sink into himself. He was, once again, the pale, haunted figure Westcott had seen in the asylum. His instinct, which he followed, was to try and drag the man back. Perhaps, if Marston shared this terrible story, it would not weigh so heavily on his mind.

"And the knife, Mr Marston. What of the knife?"

"The knife?" the man echoed. He seemed to be collecting his thoughts once more. "The knife? At last I began to act more rationally. I thought that I would drag Kersey to the house and see if there was anything we could do for him. As I reached for him, to lift him to my shoulder, I pulled out the knife and tossed it aside. Yes, I am sure that I threw it aside. It was in my way, you see, Westcott."

The detective made no comment. He knew only too well when a witness was playing for time or hoped that he would turn to another subject. To his surprise, the clergyman looked at him sheepishly, half smiling at himself and what he was about to say.

"It was thrown back." He braced himself for the detective's laughter.

"So there was someone there, in the mist," Westcott commented simply.

Relieved and encouraged by the detective's acceptance of his story, Marston went on. "I have had the time and the solitude to think of the happenings of that day over and over again. Now you can tell me, Westcott, did the murderer, if it was he, want me to have the knife? Did he want the blame to fall at my door?"

"Most certainly."

Marston waited again. He was clearly reluctant to name the man he suspected of the murder and the detective did not want to put ideas into his mind. The clergyman was not yet ready to name the suspect, but, to waste time, he added, "He threw the knife too hard. It flew past Kersey's face and snicked his cheek."

There had been, in the coroner's report, mention of a gash on the cheek. This seemed to confirm the truth of Marston's account.

"It was my duty," the clergyman was saying, "to apprehend the murderer.

157

Yet again, I failed in my duty. My thoughts burst into a thousand pieces, leaving just confusion and panic. I grabbed the knife and ran back towards the house. At the wicket I paused. I began to shout wildly that this was the Devil's work. I threw the knife down. Next day I returned to the spot as dawn broke. The knife had gone. As so often, Westcott, the Devil's work is done by the hand of man."

"Which man, in this case, sir?"

Marston looked up at him. It was some seconds before he answered. "How do you know, Westcott?"

"I sense," the detective replied, "that there is something you have not told me. Something which happened when you first approached the churchyard from the vicarage,"

"To name someone, Westcott, I must know for absolute certainty that I am right in what I think I heard. Remember, my senses were dulled by my sorrow, yet my imagination raced, spurred on by the strange light and chill of the fog. I cannot be certain. Even as I heard it, I was not sure. How can I be sure after all this time? It may have been…"

"Tell me, Mr Marston, to the best of your knowledge, what did you hear?"

"As I approached the churchyard, I paused and felt in front of me for the latch to the wicket half hidden in the fog. In that second, I thought that I heard a word uttered in surprise and then a terrible shriek."

"The name, sir."

"It would not be true to say that it was a name. The word was 'Captain'," the clergyman admitted, speaking slowly. Then regrets came in a rush. "I should not have told you. He may be an innocent man. They say that he is a hero. The shriek may have come twice, without a name. We try, do we not, to make sense of any sounds. Think how we imagine a bird saying 'bread and cheese' or …"

"No Marston," Westcott said, addressing him as a social equal. "Think of what must have happened there in the churchyard. Kersey felt someone behind him, turned his head, saw a man holding a knife raised, uttered the man's name and was then stabbed in the back. He gave his last shriek of pain. His assailant withdrew the knife, threw Kersey back on the tomb and plunged it into his chest. Then, almost immediately, he heard the sound of the gate opening. He must have tampered with it before hand to ensure it gave him warning. He hid nearby and softly called, 'Papa' to bring you to the grave."

"What wickedness! So you think that Ernest Skinner Montague is the murderer?" The clergyman shook his head in sorrow. "I have never liked the young man. I did not encourage him to seek Maria's hand and would have been most reluctant to give my consent."

"That is a good enough reason for his wanting to get rid of you, while courting your sister. And shutting you away had the extra benefit of allowing everyone to think they knew who was the murderer, without looking further." Thinking of how the deed was done, Westcott continued. "The Captain must have left a note for Kersey in a place where he looked for messages from your sister. You knew, of course, that they were friends."

"I knew that no good could come of it."

"And Skinner Montague is an excellent horseman and a daring one. He would risk riding in the fog and jumping a hedge here and there in country he knew well from hunting. I am sure that he is a man ready to act on impulse and think on his feet. He is impatient and arrogant with no regard for others. Who else would have tossed back the knife?"

"He must have known that would be the final act to make me lose my senses. I must make up for my past failures. I must go to him, make him repent and accept the Earthly punishment for his crime."

"No!" Westcott pronounced firmly. "At the best he would flee the country. At the worst he would continue to put the blame on you and it would be you who hanged instead of him. You have shared your burden of knowledge with me. Now let me bear its whole weight on my shoulders. You rest. I shall need your advice soon enough."

"Advice!" Marston said regretfully. "If only I had helped poor Kersey. Have you discovered what troubled him?"

"No, but that, too, falls on my shoulders, not yours. Go and rest, sir."

Having called Tom to help the vicar to his room, Westcott remained in the study, thinking over all he had been told. It had convinced him that Skinner Montague had killed Kersey, but it had provided no solid proof. Who would believe Marston, against the Captain? He sat there, lost in thought, until the sky outside grew dark and a servant came to light the candles. They shed no light on the question of what, as Marston had put it, troubled Kersey.

159

CHAPTER 31

Leaving the questioning of James Marston to her new cousin, Constance Brown had given her thoughts over the last few days to a line Westcott had attempted to follow. He had asked Tom whether Peter Kersey had left a note book or piece of paper on which he might have jotted the nature of his business in the Uptons and the results of his inquiries. When Tom had shaken his head and mumbled that he knew 'nothing about any bit of paper,' the detective had asked permission to search the cottage, but had found nothing.

Constance, who had been present when Tom had been asked about a note, thought she knew when a servant was lying and Tom had been concealing something. She could not let the matter rest, certain that the reason for Kersey's coming to the Uptons lay in a connection between his brother's death in the Crimea and the men who had gone from these villages to fight in the war. Having now been taken into Maria's confidence and been told much of her conversations with Peter, Constance was certain that he had been on a mission to right a wrong and that he had felt his life to be in danger. The first she had deduced from what she had learned of his character and the second from the care with which he avoided telling Maria anything which might put her in danger.

If she had been in Kersey's place, amongst strangers and unable to confide in friends for fear of endangering their safety, Constance knew that she would have written something down. She would have wanted someone to carry on her mission and she would have wanted to point the finger at those responsible should any harm come to her.

The housekeeper's determination to get to the bottom of this matter had been rekindled in the class she ran for servants to teach them to read. Carrie brought a scrap of paper to the class with a word scrawled on it by her brother, saying they had come across it in something they were reading and could not spell it out. Constance knew the time to act had come. The word was 'Crimea'.

There had been doubts about going behind Charles' back and Constance knew that she would be in trouble if things went wrong, but she was sure that she could do better than he had. Not only was persuading servants to tell the truth one of the skills she had learned over the years, but she had the advantage of not being a policeman. Practically the whole village had heard rumours about West's real identity. Those, like Tom, given to a little poaching had instantly become suspicious of him as part of the new police force intent on their destruction. The boy might have taken to Westcott as a good employer, but he would not have forgotten that you thought twice before talking to policemen of any sort.

Choosing a time when Tom was taking a rest from his duties with James Marston, Constance came straight to the point.

"Tom. Please show me the letters or book which Peter either left with you for safe keeping or which you found amongst his possessions."

At once, the young man was on the defensive. "What letter? 'Oo said nothing about a letter?"

Constance had not missed the accusing glare he had aimed at Carrie. "Look at me, Tom. Peter knew that you could not read. He expected you to ask for help."

"Ain't got no letter."

"Now I am going to confide in you, Tom, and you must confide in me. Mr West is really Mr Westcott, a police detective from London...."

"Knew that. Everyone knows that."

"But they do not know that he came here at Miss Marston's request to find out who murdered your friend."

"Guessed that." Then he blurted out, "The police ain't no friend to the common man."

"Did Peter teach you that?"

"Didn't 'ave to, Miss. I worked that one out for meself."

Constance tried again. "Mr Westcott needs your help to find Peter's killer. Don't you want him to be found?"

"'E ain't found 'im so far. I reckon it's Mr 'Oward."

"Perhaps," Constance admitted, "but we don't want to accuse the wrong man and let the murderer go free. Please, please, Tom, give whatever you have to me or to Mr Westcott."

"I can take me own revenge," Tom claimed. "I knew 'im and you didn't, nor this Mr West or whatever 'is name is."

Against her better judgement, but desperate to persuade Tom to tell the truth, Constance said quietly, "You know that Miss Marston was Peter's friend, too."

"Yes," Tom admitted, grudgingly. "We talked about it, once. I told 'im as

161

'ow it wouldn't lead nowhere. She were leading 'im up the garden path. 'E said 'e knew it couldn't lead nowhere, with 'er so rich and 'im so poor. 'E couldn't change the life 'e'd chosen and live 'ere and she wouldn't be 'appy cleaning and cooking in one little room in London."

"Doomed from the start," Constance muttered to herself and found herself asking, "Did he love her?"

"Ain't 'ad much to do with love, meself, yet," Tom replied with honesty, "but I think so. 'E were always spotting things to tell 'er and picking up little presents for 'er."

"Like what?" Carrie demanded, joining in the conversation at last. "'E couldn't afford nothing a lady would like."

"I know 'e couldn't," Tom agreed. With obvious embarrassment at speaking of such matters, he mumbled, "Little things don't cost nothing. Little things like a lad gives to a lass as 'e's courting."

As Carrie mocked, "You're blushing, Tom Osborne. You've got a lass of your own," Tom struggled on, "A flower from the 'edgerow, a bright woodpecker's feather, a little doll 'e whittled out of wood. You know, don't you, Mrs Brown?"

Carrie looked very doubtful that anyone of Mrs Brown's age would know any such thing. Constance passed over the question rapidly.

"So you see, Tom, Miss Marston wants Peter's killer to be found and Mr Westcott is the man to find him, with your help. It's what Peter would have wanted. He wouldn't have wanted you to get into trouble seeking out the murderer on your own."

"I want to read it meself," Tom said doggedly. "Peter left it with me for safe keeping, not with Miss Marston."

Realising that the lad was still young enough not to understand that Peter put Maria's safety before his, Constance was loathe to point out that he had not wanted to put Maria in danger by leaving it with her. Instead, she made the boy a promise.

"I promise you, on Mr Westcott's behalf, that he will read the document, whatever it is, to you out loud. You shall hear it at the same time as the rest of us learn its contents."

"Go and get it, Tom Osborne," Carrie ordered. "Do what your betters tell you." The girl, Constance knew, was no revolutionary. Praised and appreciated, she was now content with her lot in life.

"Can I go and fetch it, then, Miss?" Now he had decided to give the note-book up, Tom was eager to know its contents.

"Yes, but take Joseph, the groom, with you. We don't want anyone to steal it from you or harm you."

"Someone tried to find it," Tom laughed, "but when you're brought up in the workhouse there's a few useful things you learns, like where to 'ide all your worldly goods."

The moment Tom left, the housekeeper sent Carrie to ask Miss Marston and Mr Westcott to come to the library. With all that Marston had told him still fresh in his mind, Westcott came along only to please Constance, expecting to hear her latest theory on this or that. When he knew the real reason for the summons, he was surprised that Constance had acted without him, but, on reflection, accepted that the ends justified the means.

As Tom re-entered the room, he hesitated, not knowing to whom he should give the book, Miss Marston, who was his employer, the housekeeper, who had asked for it, or Westcott, who was a policeman. Then Westcott held out his hand and the two women indicated that he should give it to the detective.

"You'll read it out loud to me, won't you, Mr Westcott? Mrs Brown promised."

"Oh, did she indeed!" Westcott commented. "Only if you give me your solemn promise that you will not act upon anything you hear. You must leave that to me. If you go off at half cock, you may allow the culprit to go free and escape justice. Have I your word?"

A grudging, "Yes, sir," just escaped Tom's lips.

"It could be something or nothing," the detective said, trying to quell his excitement as he opened the book. Carefully folded within the front cover was a sheet of paper. The detective unfolded it and, after a brief glance at it, began to read to his three eager listeners.

"Notes made on my conversation with Corporal Jonathon Smith, formerly in the Crimea and now of Mile End, concerning matters related to him by my brother, Mark Kersey, in the field hospital."

"Corporal Smith told me that he had met Mark in the hospital after the battle of Balaclava. Mark, not far from death, had asked the corporal to bring this report to me. While on the battlefield, tending those who had been wounded, he found Major Frederick Storr, who had suffered heavy loss of blood from a wound to his leg. Mark applied a tourniquet and, having called over stretcher bearers, turned to help others. A little later, Mark was surprised to find the major still on the battle field. The tourniquet had been removed and the major was dying. Mark asked what had happened, and attempted to replace the bandage. The major reached out his hand, as though to attract Mark's attention to something he wanted to say. He struggled, with his dying breath, to pronounce a name, which Mark, with some difficulty, made out to be Jack Sanders."

"Mark looked round for the two bearers he was certain had gone to the major when he called them. He saw two figures watching him, but they did not answer his calls or respond to his waving."

"No more than an hour later, Mark was hit by a sniper's bullet when he thought that he was within the safety of the camp. The surgeon who removed it said that it came from a captured Enfield. Mark was sure that the gun had not been captured by the enemy, but that he had been shot by one of the men he had seen near the major and that it had been their intention to make sure that the major died."

"Mark died two days later. He passed to me, his brother, the duty of seeing that justice was done for himself and for the major. And he told the corporal to pass on the message to me that I was right about the pointlessness and cruelty of war.

"Corporal Smith had inquired within the regiment and found that the major who had died, the Honorable Frederick Storr, was the son of Lord Storr of Upton St John. His younger brother, Henry, had also ridden with the Light Brigade. Unfortunately, the corporal could find nothing of a Jack Sanders."

Making no comment, Westcott looked through the pocket book itself. It contained notes on Peter Kersey's doings in the Uptons. It recorded his attempt to seek the advice of James Marston on what to do and of his conversations with some servants of the Storrs. It was noted that, hearing of the death of her husband, Frederick Storr's widow had been distraught. Her brother-in-law, Henry, had advised her to return for a while to her parents, leaving their baby son in the care of Mrs Jakes. Another note was added that, on his advice, Maria Marston had persuaded her friend to take the baby with her and not leave it with Mrs Jakes or anyone else. All the servants, it seemed, had told Kersey that it was a pity it was Frederick who died and not Henry.

Having had a few moments to absorb what had been read to her,

Constance burst out, "Frederick and Henry would have gone to war not knowing that an heir was to be born to Frederick." She stopped speaking as suddenly as she had begun, recalling that Tom was listening.

Maria finished the conclusion for her. "Then Henry would have expected to inherit the title and the estate, had Frederick died in battle. When he returned and found an heir had been born, he..." At last noticing Westcott's warning frown, Maria, too, kept her thoughts to herself, simply adding, "It is true. I did advise her not to give the baby to Mrs Jakes' care."

"Well, well!" Westcott said, adding, "Now don't let's go rushing to conclusions. This may have led eventually to Kersey's death and it may not. It may be connected and it may not." Slowly and carefully, the detective turned the pages of the little note book. On one was written, "What shall I do if I find Mark's killer? I do not agree with hanging, but he was my brother and I wish to see justice done." Within the back cover was a letter, folded into a small square. Westcott glanced through it and promptly handed it to Maria. She read it silently to herself.

"My Dear Miss Marston," it had begun, but this had been crossed out and replaced by, "My dearest Maria." It continued, "Now that I am dead and all Earthly conventions are removed, I can say how deeply I have loved you. How stupid that I, who put no store by birth or riches, should have let them stand in the way of our happiness. Think kindly of me now and again, my dearest one, but, above all, live a happy and full life for us both. Your Peter, eternally."

Maria, clutching the letter, turned and ran from the room.

"Hell and damnation," Westcott swore, rubbing his eyes. "If I can prove it, the murderer will hang and I shall lose no sleep over it."

CHAPTER 32

After a while, Constance went to Maria's room to comfort her, but the young woman had all the comfort she needed in the note she held close to her and read over and over again. Spoken words and phrases fade with time. The words themselves are hard enough to recall, but the tone and emphasis with which they are spoken are even more elusive. In moments of cheerfulness, one can imagine the words said with warmth and affection, while, in moments of despair, they are recalled as insincere or as a jest. Now Maria had words before her eyes in Peter's own handwriting. There was no doubt as to their meaning and they would never fade.

When Constance returned, Westcott was giving Tom detailed instructions on how to travel to London by train and how to reach Philip Robertson at St George in the East. He gave him a note, with instructions to keep it in an inner pocket, asking Robertson to find Corporal Smith and question him closely. The note also, although Tom did not know it, asked for the lad to be provided with an escort of two burly men. Finally, the detective gave Tom a lecture on the dangers of the streets of London, both from anyone who might follow him from the Uptons and from undesirable inhabitants of the Great Wen itself.

"Are we putting the young man in too great a danger?" Constance wondered, when Tom had set out for the station.

"No," the detective replied. "If anyone is watching him, they must know that we have the notebook. They might want to get him drunk to find out what he knows and," he admitted, "certainly a stranger alone and drunk on the streets of London is always in danger. I have told him to drink nothing intoxicating unless he is with Robertson, or someone that young man has recommended to him. He is to speak with no one from the Uptons and, if at a loss, to approach a policeman and mention my name."

"Would ...?" Constance began.

"Yes. The lad will even talk to a Peeler if it means finding his friend's killer."

The detective pulled up a chair for his 'cousin' before settling back into his own. He waved aside her objection that housekeepers do not make themselves comfortable in their masters' libraries.

"Will the corporal have anything else to tell you, Charles? He was only

166

a messenger and may have told all he knows."

"There is some truth in that," Westcott agreed, "but we must extract every scrap of information from him. And a trip to London will do Tom no harm. It will widen his horizons and help him to imagine the life his hero, Kersey, lived."

"Carrie will not sleep until he has returned safe and sound, of that I am certain."

"There is always a chance that he may give us a lead on Jack Sanders, or Sanderson, or, even, Anderson."

"Perhaps that is not what the officer said. He was in the throes of dying and must have been suffering greatly."

"It is all we have to go on," the detective pointed out. "I have tried to pronounce the name while pretending I am breathing my last, to hear what else it might sound like. I have written down anything which sounds remotely similar."

"Will you follow up Mrs Jakes, as Peter Kersey was doing, to see whether you come across anything?"

"Jakes," Westcott muttered, as though his mind was on something else. Then he suddenly jumped up. "Jakes!"

"What is it, Charles?" Constance asked, anxious to know what had occurred to him.

"Send for one of the servants to rush to the station and catch Tom. I'll scribble another question for him to ask."

Obediently, but dying to know what the question was, Constance did as she was told. When the servant had gone, she could contain her curiosity no longer.

"What was it that struck you when you spoke the name Jakes?"

Pleased with himself and with the fact that he had been quicker than Constance, he took his time telling her.

"As I said the name – Jakes, that is – it...."

"Tell me this second," the housekeeper burst out.

"As you wish. What if the name was not Jack, but Jakes? What if this was not followed by a surname, but by 'and'?"

"Jakes and Erson?" Constance pronounced, not greatly impressed with the theory.

"No, my good woman," the detective argued, "Jakes and Ernest. He would have called the servant by his surname and his friend, or the man he had been used to calling a friend, by his Christian name."

"Or," Constance commented, warming to the idea, "his life slipped away before he had finished the name. "'Jakes and Ernest Skinner Montague' is a long speech for a man who is dying."

"Exactly. My conclusion, exactly." He looked at Constance and became very serious. "Now keep this to yourself. And do not go out alone."

Not even, in his wildest dreams, considering that Constance could produce a nervous laugh, he was amazed when she did. She apologised at once.

"Whatever came over me! It's all this talk of breathing one's last and suspecting people I have known for some years. It is all so melodramatic. I am quite in control of myself again, believe me, Charles." Then, as a thought occurred to her, she said, "Oh, dear!"

The detective was following his own line of thought. "Tell me, Constance, is Skinner Montague, by any chance, in line of succession for the Storr title and estate?"

Raising her hands to waist level, the housekeeper counted off names, saying finally, "I know the first six in line, but Skinner Montague is not amongst them. I am sure that Skinner would have boasted about it, had his nephew been. The Marstons would probably have a claim, which, should he marry Maria, his children would receive. You are wondering why the Captain would wish to kill Frederick Storr and his baby son?"

"Then if not for his own benefit, for whose? And why do their dirty work?"

"It must have been as a favour to Henry Storr. As to why…"

"Perhaps Henry Storr fired the shot which wounded his brother and was then unwilling to wait for dirt and disease and the butchery of army surgeons to finish him off. I know old scores are often settled on the battlefield. Whoever first wounded Frederick Storr – his brother Henry, the Captain or the Russians – it was Captain Skinner Montague who tried to complete the task. Henry Storr must have had some hold over him and I can guess what it was." Recalling Constance's exclamation a few minutes before, Westcott inquired, "Were you going to say something about my Jakes and Ernest theory?"

"Unfortunately, yes," Constance admitted reluctantly, not wanting to burst the bubble. "Mark saw these two men after the Charge. I am afraid that it was the talk of the servants' quarters at the time that Jakes died a

168

hero's death charging the Russian guns."

"Damnation," Westcott swore and Constance found herself pleased that he felt so at home with her that he did not immediately apologise. "Are you certain?"

For an answer, Constance gave a tug on the bell-pull and, when a servant promptly arrived, sent for Carrie.

As Carrie arrived outside the door, they heard her say, "Ain't to be no dinner today if I can't get on with the vegetables." A pause suggested that she was smoothing down her apron and making herself presentable. It lasted so long that Constance remarked that she felt like a constable ushering in a witness.

"You're too polite for a constable," Westcott remarked.

Finally in the room, Carrie flopped into a chair, mumbling with some satisfaction, "That Sally'll 'ave to do the taters today." Then she reminded herself to sit up straight and perched herself on the chair's edge. Her eyes darted here, there and everywhere.

"Now pay attention, Carrie," the detective urged.

"I am, sir. I'm looking around with me eyes, but that don't stop me listening to you with me ears. I ain't listening to nothing else."

Deciding that would have to do, Westcott began, "When you visited your brother, Carrie, and Peter was alive, did he ever ask you about Mrs Jakes?"

"Yes, sir. I wanted to forget 'er in the odd hour 'ere and there what was all I got of me liberty, but 'e kept asking about 'er."

"What were the questions, Carrie?"

At last Carrie paused in her detailed inspection of the room. "Let's think. What were she like? That were one. 'Orrible, truly 'orrible, I told 'im. What were 'e like, the son? The same, I told 'im, 'cept being a man 'e were always trying to get 'is way with any girl what come in sight." Before the detective could ask another question, the servant went on, "And 'e asked me what the old crow said about the way 'er son died."

An expression of deep satisfaction crossed Westcott's face. Kersey had questioned whether the son died in the Charge. "And what did the old crow say?"

Normally, the housekeeper would have remarked that the servants should not be encouraged in the use of such language, but she, too, wished to know the answer.

"She were very proud, weren't she, of 'er Frederick? 'Oo wouldn't be, 'im dying in the charge into the Valley of Death against the Ruskies. It were the only good thing what 'e ever done. Surprised me 'e never jumped off 'is 'orse and 'id till they passed 'im on their way back."

"'Out of the mouths of babes!'" Constance remarked.

"Who," the detective asked, "did this Frederick Jakes work for?"

"Sometimes 'Enry Storr and sometimes the Captain. Like you borrowed me from 'ere and Tom works for you and for Mr Marston. Ain't it true that 'e died in the Charge?" Carrie asked, having worked out where the conversation was leading.

Ignoring the question, Westcott continued, "What other questions did Peter ask you?"

"Now," Carrie said, having let her attention wander to the large globe standing near the desk, "let me rack me brains 'ere a minute. Oh, yes, 'e wanted to know where she got 'er money. Lots of people ask that one. She's always got plenty these days, I can tell you."

"Where does she get it, Carrie?"

"Ain't sure," the girl answered, considering the question. "Now, I mustn't pass on rumours, must I Mrs Brown? Like you said, we mustn't pass on lies we ain't sure about. I ain't sure about this one."

"I'll decide whether it's true, or not," the detective said impatiently. "Just tell me." Then, seeing the servant's hurt expression he apologised. "Sorry child, but rumours are all we have to go on. They might lead us to the truth in the end."

"Well," Carrie said, sensing her importance and giving up her inspection of the room, "I once see John Blackburn...."

"That's Henry Storr's man," Constance exclaimed.

"The quiet one," Westcott thought, recalling Mansfield's description of the man.

"I once see 'im giving 'er money. 'Ow I know what it was," Carrie explained sheepishly, "was I see 'er put what 'e give 'er in a drawer and I peeped in. I ain't never seen a sovereign before, let alone five of 'em all at once."

"So," Westcott concluded, when Carrie had gone. "Henry Storr was behind the killing of his brother. It had to be, after all. He would have inherited the title and the estate had he managed to get rid of the brother and his baby son. Now there are two questions to answer. Was Jakes killed

170

on the battlefield? Leave that one to me. What hold did Storr have on Skinner Montague to persuade him to help? May I leave that one to you, Constance?"

CHAPTER 33

When Westcott suggested Constance should pay visits to her friends among other housekeepers, she agreed readily. But she expressed the reservation that, if she did visit the housekeepers to the Storr and to the Skinner households, they would be surprised if she wished to engage in gossip.

"Come, come," the detective laughed, we all like a little gossip now and again. Even men indulge in it from time to time."

"A little gossip! Even men!" Constance echoed. "Have you ever watched two men at work within earshot of each other, chattering away like sparrows? And when they finish work, leaning over the garden gate or drinking in the public house?"

"Peace! Peace! I apologise, but please Constance, engage in gossip just this once. See if you can find out what hold Storr may have had on Skinner Montague. But do not make it obvious. This is a dangerous business. Above all, Constance, take care."

Moved by his concern, Constance reassured him, "It happens that Mrs Maxwell, the housekeeper you met at the Skinners, is my cousin and my cousin german at that. No one will think it strange if I am seen visiting her. But you realise that she is very discrete. After all, she did not remark on the fact that you suddenly appeared as another cousin of whom she had never heard."

"And the housekeeper at the Storr's. Is she related to you by any happy chance?"

"My sister's daughter's second cousin thrice removed," Constance answered solemnly, but, seeing Westcott looking awkward, not sure whether or not he was being teased, she added, "Too grand to be related to my family, I fear. My mother claimed some link, but I have forgotten the details and it was a very tenuous one, to say the least."

"Then you will be safer if you try to obtain the information from Mrs Maxwell. If she knows anything, you need not go to Storr Hall. Do take care. We must consider that Skinner Montague did not kill Kersey simply to remove a rival. It is far more likely that his reason was the knowledge that Kersey was close to finding out the truth about Frederick Storr's death."

The housekeeper shook her head in sorrow. "Kersey must have known that he was putting his life in danger asking the questions he did. He was a brave young man."

With that thought in her mind and determined to see justice done, Constance lost no time in arranging to visit her cousin, Mr Skinner's housekeeper.

"How lovely of you to call," Mrs Maxwell greeted her, when the day arrived at last. "It's so long since you've been here, but, then, we housekeepers never have a moment to call our own."

She looked long and hard at Constance. "I have the feeling you have some special reason for coming."

"To tell you the truth, there is," Constance began, having carefully thought out her story on the way. "I have developed a great regard for Maria Marston. The poor child has not had an easy life. She has never known a mother's loving care and I worry so for her future now that she is an heiress."

Having put on an act of reluctance to go further, Constance burst out, "I must ask you, Emily, is Captain Skinner Montague a suitable husband for such a trusting young woman? If he is not, then I could drop a gentle hint to her."

"Hint of what?" Emily asked cautiously.

This was what Constance, knowing her cousin, had expected. She would confirm something Constance already knew, but would not start gossip.

Stabbing in the dark, Constance replied, with more certainty than she felt, "Women. I have heard he is a ladies' man."

"What young man," Emily wished to know, "does not pursue women and often, I might add, catch them with their full co-operation? Times have changed, Constance, even though we do not wish to change with them. He is no worse than many and better than some."

Thinking her inquisition over, Emily showed her cousin her new brooch, and as Constance admired it, told her, "I am well paid for my services, Constance. Though I should, perhaps, not say it, Mr Skinner lacks some of the social graces and looks to me to set him on the right road. He says that servants are in a good position to watch and see how people behave. He has asked me frankly to point out any little errors or deficiencies I notice, so that he does not repeat them. I would never say a word against Mr Skinner."

Taking it as a good sign that her cousin had not included Skinner

Montague in this speech, Constance, recalling what she had heard of Ernest's father, made another stab in the dark. "But the Captain, Emily, there is the gambling, is there not?"

"How has that reached your ears?" Mrs Maxwell demanded, but, at the same time, she seemed relieved that she could now talk about it with her cousin.

"How yours?" Constance parried, avoiding having to invent an answer.

"The usual route," Emily admitted. "Young men keep their masters' secrets until they wish to impress a young girl. We have an exceptionally pretty maid, who is courted by a young groom at Storr Hall. He told her how Skinner Montague regularly loses large sums to Henry Storr and his crowd. I am afraid you are right. He can only pay his debts by marrying Maria Marston."

"How long has this state of affairs existed?" Constance inquired, anxious to establish that the Captain was in debt when he left for the war.

"If the truth is to be believed, his uncle, that is Mr Edward Skinner, forbad him to gamble on pain of losing his inheritance. He never bet one farthing, it is said, until he went away to the war. On the journey to the Crimea he fell in with Henry Storr, who enticed him into betting beyond his means. It was the same old story, each time he sat down at the gaming table he was convinced his luck had changed. The men say," she added, "that it would have been better for the Captain had he been brought up to gamble. He was a lamb to the slaughter, it seems."

"A lamb well-fleeced, you might say," Constance commented.

"But now he has grown into a black sheep, ready to recoup his losses from Miss Marston's fortune. I fear, too, that having spent her fortune he will neglect her. I am told that Miss Marston, quiet and thoughtful as she is, is not the type of woman his fancy usually lights upon."

"So my fears were well-founded. Is there no hope of his uncle paying his debts?"

For a moment, it seemed as though Emily was going to confide a secret to her cousin, but she changed her mind. "No hope at all," she said bluntly. After a pause, she added, "Mr Skinner has always said that his money was hard won and he would not have it squandered on gambling."

"So Mr Skinner would disown his nephew if he knew of his debts?"

Emily muttered something, which sounded vaguely like agreement and then changed the subject. "Have I told you, Constance, that I have been offered an excellent post quite close to our cousin Mary in Essex?"

While inquiring about her cousin Mary's health, Constance made a note that Emily's reluctance to continue that conversation, her uncertainty that Mr Skinner would, after all, disown his nephew and her leaving Mr Skinner's employment, suggested that Mr Skinner had invested all his wealth to bring about such a marriage and needed it as much as his nephew did. She had always been able to read Emily's real thoughts. Patiently, she talked of family matters, but longed to return to the vicarage and tell Westcott of her discoveries.

By the time she eventually arrived back, the detective had discoveries of his own to relate. He read her a letter from Philip Robertson containing answers to the questions sent with Tom Osborne. On the question of Jakes' character, it seemed, he knew little except that Jakes had a reputation for stealing from the dead, and not from the enemy alone. As to Jakes' death, Corporal Smith had reported that he was shot within seconds of Mark Kersey. The two had, in fact, been seen having something of an argument at that moment. Jakes died on the spot and Kersey a few days later."

Having listened, in turn, to Constance's news, the detective asked, "Now how do we prove these things?" The housekeeper, not knowing that he often asked much the same of Tom Cat, was pleased that he had said, "we".

"What have we so far? We have a report conveyed all the way from Russia by a man, Corporal Smith, from a dying man, Mark Kersey, who alleged that another dying man, Frederick Storr, had claimed that a Jack Sanders had been eager to help him die. No, we do not even have that much. Frederick Storr simply uttered that, or a similar, name, without saying why. Had he lived a little longer, he might have been going to recommend the man, or two men, for their courage in the battle."

"But Mark Kersey was shot because he knew too much," Constance protested.

"The surgeon who extracted the rifle ball was quite willing to accept that it came from an Enfield captured from us by the Russians."

"But Peter Kersey's death...," Constance began.

"Again, the only evidence we have that it was Ernest Skinner Montague is a name supposedly uttered by another dying man, Peter Kersey, and overheard by, with all respect to Mr Marston, a man losing his mind. No, it was not even a name he heard. It was just a rank – 'Captain.'

"I am convinced," Constance asserted stubbornly, that Skinner Montague, aided by Jakes, killed Frederick Storr to please Henry Storr and that Skinner Montague then killed Mark Kersey and Frederick Jakes to protect himself. On his return to England, he killed Peter Kersey for the same reason and, of course, to rid himself of a rival."

"You are probably right, Constance, but we cannot be certain that Henry Storr asked the Captain to kill his brother or even implied that he wanted him dead."

"Does it mean nothing that Henry Storr enticed Ernest to gamble and to fall into debt.?"

"It might have been Ernest's own idea in order to mix with the nobility."

"And who was the sniper in the Crimea? John Blackburn, they say, is the best shot for miles around and acted as a sniper on our side in the war."

"The Captain might have called on his services," Westcott suggested, "or Storr, but Blackburn will never admit it. In short we have no proof of anything."

"Surely," Constance asserted in disbelief, "it is not beyond the police to make the man admit his guilt."

"The rack and thumb screw are no longer used, Constance. Remember, too, that we are dealing with heroes of the war. The police are already unpopular. If they accused such men without firm proof, there could be a riot fermented by those who still wish to do away with the very idea of a police force."

"What more can you do?"

"I can find out why Frederick Storr is paying money to Mrs Jakes and I can delay telling my employers, the Marstons, what I have learned to avoid their rushing to the police and putting the men, whom we suspect of the crimes, on their guard."

"For mercy's sake do," Constance pleaded. "Mr Marston will face them and ask them to confess their sins and Maria will not let them go free for the murder of Peter Kersey."

CHAPTER 34

As he knocked on the brand-new brass knocker on the Jakes' cottage door, Westcott noticed that the door itself was roughly made of old planks, cracked and split and scarcely water tight. Feeling disgruntled, he paid it little attention. By now certain that he had identified the guilty men, he wished he could have been arresting Captain Skinner Montague and the Honourable Henry Storr, not coming to see an unpleasant and avaricious woman, who would not take kindly to being questioned by him.

By way of answer to his knock, a large, ugly mastiff galloped around the side of the house, came to a stop a yard away and dared him to move.

"Good boy," Westcott said weakly, to the delight of a group of grubby children who had appeared from nowhere. As he slowly lifted his hand, keeping it close to him out of sight of the dog, the detective felt the last vestiges of his authority slipping away. He knocked again at the door, feeling foolish to realise that he was smiling at the dog to win its favour.

At last, when the family had wrung the last drop of hilarity from the detective's plight, the door was opened by a child. This one looked surprisingly clean in a new apron with shoes on her feet.

"'What d'yer want?' Ma sez," she demanded in a voice which probably echoed the tone in which her mother had asked the question.

"Don't yer like dogs, mister?" a young lad asked, unwilling to give up his sport of detective baiting until, receiving no reply, he led the animal away with one small hand on its collar.

"I've come to see Mrs Jakes, my dear," Westcott answered, trying out his smile on the child. It had no more effect than it had had on the dog.

"Ask 'im what 'e wants," came the order from the dark depths of the cottage.

"I done that," the girl replied with an exaggerated sigh. At around thirteen years of age, she was beginning to use to her mother the tone her mother had always used to her.

"Me Ma says, 'What d'yer want, mister?' and I ain't standing 'ere all day with this door open."

Determined to retain some control, however weak, over the situation, the detective raised his voice and answered, "If Mrs Jakes will kindly come to the door, I shall tell her my business personally."

177

The children, all four of them by now, were pushed aside like skittles and Westcott found that the stare of the dog had been replaced by the cold stare of Mrs Jakes. Her eyes were smaller and meaner, but every bit as threatening. Westcott had seen her about the village, a large, flabby woman who waddled rather than walked. If there had been times, as with all poor people, when she had known hunger, those days were past.

"Well?" Before Westcott could attempt any reply, she went on, "If it's about the murder of that young feller in the churchyard, 'is killer's in the vicarage, ain't 'e? The Reverend done it and that's that. No one wants some stuck-up peeler from London coming and pointing the finger at innocent people as never done nothing wrong in their lives."

Such people did not live in this cottage, the detective was sure. Stung by her stare and her protestation of innocence, when he was sure she knew something of the crimes, he went straight to the point.

"I am not seeking information on the unfortunate death of Peter Kersey, but I have some information on the equally unfortunate death of your son, Frederick Jakes."

Mrs Jakes' expression was at once guarded and suspicious, but she tried to bluff it out. "E died an 'ero's death beside 'is master."

"That is not my information, Mrs Jakes," Westcott said, gaining confidence. "If you will let me step inside for a moment and send the children to play, we can talk quietly together."

A clip on the ear of the nearest child sent all the children at the front door tumbling past Westcott onto the common opposite the house.

"Play until I tells you to come in," was the instruction they were given and each knew the penalty for disobedience. "Come in then," Mrs Jakes went on and, to Westcott's amazement, seeing the earth floor, she ordered, "Wipe your feet."

Like most cottages in the village, the one the detective entered was low and dark, the only light coming from small windows designed rather to cut the cost of glass and to exclude the cold than to illuminate the interior. In most such cottages, however, the scarcity of furniture gave the tiny rooms a spaciousness their dimensions did not deserve. Here, odd pieces of cheaply and shoddily made furniture crowded in on each other.

Aiming for a chair large enough to support him, Westcott swore under his breath as he knocked into item after item, only to be told, "Don't sit in there. That's me 'ubby's and 'e don't like no one sitting in it but 'im."

As he dropped lower and lower into the low chair he was directed to, Westcott wondered if his hostess had deliberately chosen this one to make him appear small and put him at a disadvantage. Though thoroughly uncomfortable and apprehensive about picking up a flea or two, he tried to look relaxed.

"So," Mrs Jakes sneered, "You're the great detective from London, paid by them Marstons to 'ave the Reverend escape the 'angman!" Before the detective had thought of a crushing reply, the woman continued, "That Maria, same bad blood as 'er brother. I see signs of it from 'er first few days. Tried to do what I could "

"With punishments, I understand."

"Is that what she's saying? Well," she added, with a smug smile, "she didn't get that Peter Kersey did she, throw 'erself at 'im as she did?"

"About your son, Mrs Jakes…"

"You want to besmirch 'is name, do you, Mr Detective? 'E died a 'ero, killed by the enemy in the glorious charge of the Light Brigade. They should all 'ave 'ad Victoria Crosses, if you ask me."

"I think you know perfectly well how your son died, Mrs Jakes. He survived the charge and was shot a day or two later."

For a while, Mrs Jakes stared at him, at a loss what to say. Westcott realised that she did not know the truth. She was clinging to the version that he was a hero.

"A real Mr Knowall, ain't yer? What if 'e did come through the Valley of Death? Some of them as died only 'ad to charge 'alfway. If you're telling the truth, our Fred went all the way there and all the way back. And 'e were still shot by them Russians, weren't 'e?"

"I agree with you all the way, Mrs Jakes, except for the last little bit. He was a hero. All those who rode into the Mouth of Hell on that day were heroes. That is why he did not deserve to die as he did, killed by friend, not foe."

Mrs Jakes was no longer staring at Westcott. Behind the tears, there was a pleading look in her eyes, begging him to tell her this was not the truth.

"They sent John Blackburn to tell me 'ow 'e died. 'E were Fred's best friend."

"The evidence I have, Mrs Jakes," Westcott told her, "and I am sorry to bring you this news, suggests your son died alongside Peter Kersey's brother, shot by the same man. By an Englishman. By someone from the Uptons."

Again there was silence while Mrs Jakes compared this information with what she already knew. Something she knew already, the detective suspected, stopped her rejecting his news outright.

"'Oo done it?"

"You probably know that as well as I do," the detective said, not wanting to admit that he was unsure who pulled the trigger.

Mrs Jakes turned away from him and stood gazing at the sky, her hands pressed against her lips. She was grieving for her son all over again with a dignity which made Westcott admit to himself that he had tried to score over her and was ashamed of it.

"Please go, now, sir. Let me think about me son in peace. 'E were no less a 'ero for being shot by a coward."

"I am truly sorry, ma'am," Westcott said quietly. He had hoped for some revelation, some small piece of information from her which would prove Skinner Montague's guilt. While her behaviour had confirmed his suspicion that she knew something, Mrs Jakes was giving nothing away,

For two days, Westcott played for time. Finally, he told the Marstons that he would take his report to the police. They knew all he did about Peter Kersey's death, but not all the details of the murders in the Crimea. To delay telling them everything, he said that the police would want matters kept secret until they were ready to make an arrest. He wished that James Marston had been stronger and could give him advice, but, if too much were asked of him, the man was still liable to fall into an agitated and low mood.

About to climb into the carriage for a meeting with the Head Constable, Westcott heard a footfall on the drive. He turned to see Mrs Jakes. She was no longer crying, but the redness of her eyes betrayed hours of weeping. At once the detective, his heart racing, took her aside and prayed that she had irrefutable proof of Storr's and Skinner Montague's guilt.

Without a word and still making clear her disdain for the police, Mrs Jakes handed the detective a letter. As he opened it, he could see that it had once been carefully bound in oiled cloth and tied with string, which had been sealed with wax on every knot. It was written in a neat hand difficult to associate with the Jakes family.

"Another voice from the grave, courtesy of state aid to elementary education," he thought.

"Ma," it said, "I know Betty will be reading this to you and I send her my love and tell her to keep her mouth tight shut about what is in this letter. In case I do not return, I want you to know that I have been trying to earn all the money I can anyway I can to enjoy life in comfort. If I cannot collect the wages of sin, I want you to collect them for me and buy yourself all the little things I have always wanted for you.

In short, the Hon. Henry Storr has asked Skinner Montague to get rid of his brother in some way as won't call attention to the crime. The Captain asked me to help and I agreed, at a price. We done the deed in the battle at Balaclava. I have been promised £100. If I die, see you get that and the extra money I would have asked for now and again to keep my mouth shut. Your ever loving son Frederick Jakes."

So Fred had been too greedy!

Mrs Jakes waited for him to finish reading and then remarked with pride, "'E were a real scholar, my Fred. 'E'd 'ave made something of 'iself, 'e would, if they'd give 'im the chance." Her thirst for vengeance taking over again, she asked, "'Ow did you say 'e died?"

"As I've said," Westcott replied, "I can prove nothing, but it seems that Mark Kersey, Peter's brother, saw the Captain and your son making sure that Frederick Storr was dead. The Captain or Storr, or both together, decided to kill him. They sent your son to talk to Kersey, no doubt to lead him into a position for the sniper to do his work. Perhaps it was planned, or perhaps not, but then they saw the chance of killing two birds with one stone. They shot Kersey and your son, leaving no witnesses. My guess is that two people were involved at this stage, one to aim at each man. It was risky enough to kill within the camp, without having to take aim twice and give one a chance to hide. And they fell together, it would seem. Your boy died at once and Mark died later."

"That'd be John Blackburn. 'E never misses and kills clean as a whistle." She took a deep breath. "Leave 'im to us. 'Ave you got enough proof against the other two, now?"

"Not water-tight proof. The Captain killed Peter Kersey, too."

"We all guessed that, but we thought it was cos 'e blocked the way to Maria Marston's fortune." That seemed a good enough reason to her.

After a little thought, Mrs Jakes seemed to decide she was in for a penny and might as well be in for a pound. "I were doing as me son asked me, getting money from Storr. They knew I must 'ave a letter, but they didn't never find it. The soldier as brought it couldn't keep 'is mouth shut about bringing it, but 'e didn't know what was in it. My boy knew I wouldn't never pay the man a penny, if the seals was broke. 'E 'ad writ on it the amount I were to pay."

"My old man says I'm as mad as the reverent, but you can 'ave the letter to use in evidence. I couldn't take no more money from 'im, it would be blood money for me boy." Her old character broke through, "I'll be out of pocket, you know."

Westcott rose to the bait. "We can't pay for your evidence, but I am sure that Miss Marston will reimburse you if you are out of pocket."

"See she do," Mrs Jakes ordered. "If justice don't pay more than crime, you bobbies'll never get rid of criminals."

"You know," the detective pointed out, "that the lawyers will say that your son made this up to extort money."

"Then why did 'e pay?"

"He'll say that he didn't."

"Then where did I get me money?"

"They will learn of a dozen ways you have used in the past. They will discredit you as a witness. They can even say that the letter was not written by your son and that you had someone write it when you knew that Frederick Storr and your son had both died in the Crimea. Storr, if cornered, will certainly deny that he asked the Captain to dispose of his older brother."

"Then," Mrs Jakes said, in a cold, detached voice, "you can tell 'em 'ow Storr sent John Blackburn to tell me that there'd be something in it for me if I took the baby who's heir to the estate and 'e 'appened to die?"

"Did he ask you to kill it in so many words?"

"I can say 'e did if you want me to."

"But you didn't have charge of the child?"

"It were all arranged when that Maria Marston butted in. Did she think I'd 'ave 'armed a baby? 'E'd 'ave been safe with me. I've nursed many a baby."

"And how many have died?" Westcott asked, knowing the high death rate amongst babies put out for wet nursing.

"Babies is weak little creatures and God often calls them to be with 'Im in 'Eaven." Her work done, as she saw it, Mrs Jakes waddled off down the drive.

The detective's heart sank. This woman was the worst witness he had ever seen. Her appearance, her past history and the words from her own mouth would condemn her as a cruel, dishonest and grasping woman. To raise his spirits, he told himself that, at least, they now knew that Henry Storr was involved in the murder of his brother, that Jack Anderson had been Jakes and Ernest Skinner Montague and that the other murders followed from Frederick Storr's death.

Climbing into the carriage, he sat down and placed Fred Jakes' letter on the report he had written of all his findings since his arrival in the Uptons. It was out of his hands, now.

CHAPTER 36

The Head Constable, John Croft, did not take long to make up his mind. The very next day, Westcott was standing before him again, having received a command to present himself at the police station at 3.00pm, sharp. Immediately on entering the room, Westcott realised that he would receive no thanks for his work from this quarter.

Irritably turning the pages of the report, first this one and then that to suggest that none was worth focusing his attention upon, the Head Constable pronounced, "There is a great deal to be said, Westcott, for letting sleeping dogs lie. You have stirred up a hornets' nest here."

"I have found a trail of murder from the Crimea to ..."

"Where is your proof, Westcott?" Croft asked in a tone of despair which suggested he was convinced none existed. "Let's consider your evidence, if you can give it that name. At the bottom of this plot, you have Jakes, a self-confessed crook who is now dead, appearing to claim in a letter that a member of an ancient and honourable family asked Skinner Montague to kill his brother. Jakes does not even claim to have heard the making of this request. The Head Constable's irritation giving way to firmness, he stated, placing the matter beyond discussion, "No. You have no evidence against Henry Storr."

"Perhaps," the detective persisted, "you will find some when you question Skinner Montague."

"Question a hero of the Charge on such flimsy evidence! The mob would riot. Do you realise the effort I have made to have this police force accepted against opposition from rich and poor, saints and sinners?" Patting his chest, he claimed, "I deserve a medal for all I have done and I am not throwing it away."

In a voice of sweet reasonableness, he appealed to Westcott. "Come, my man, you have had some experience of battle." Stress on the word 'some' showed that Croft did not consider Westcott's experience as great as his own. "There was a battle raging. Have you a shred of evidence that Frederick Storr was killed by anyone other than a Russian?" He paused barely a second. "No? I thought not."

"There is the evidence of Mark Kersey."

"Evidence! He, too, is dead and cannot be questioned. He knew neither

184

Jakes nor Captain Skinner Montague. If he did see two men, he could not identify them. In any case, if a crime had been committed, he identified the culprit, from the supposed dying words of Frederick Storr, as this Jack Anderson."

"But the tourniquet?"

"There is Storr, lying dying in agony. Do you not think," he questioned, grabbing at his own leg," that the officer might have pulled it off in his pain and suffering, convinced he was dying and wishing to end his agony?"

Westcott made no reply.

"There," Croft pronounced with satisfaction, "I see that you had not thought of that." He pushed the report in the detective's direction. "I shall take no action against Henry Storr . As you are not working for the police, I wish you to take these papers away. If you take my advice, you will destroy them before the gentlemen you accuse bring down the full force of the law upon you."

"There is still Skinner Montague," Westcott began, when he had recovered his power of speech.

"I'll hear nothing of attacks you make upon a brave officer while he was serving Queen and country. What if he were on the field after the battle? Coup de grace, Westcott. It is the unfortunate duty of an officer and a gentleman not to allow his men or his fellow officers to suffer unnecessarily. That is, of course," he added smugly," if he were the man your so-called witness saw."

Looking at the man and trying to compose his thoughts, Westcott found himself thinking that the only things this man had achieved in his life were to grow a fine set of whiskers and to carry out the orders of officers of higher rank than himself, one of whom had no doubt obtained this post for him.

"There is still the question of Peter Kersey's murder. Some saw him as an angel, some as a devil, but murder is murder just the same."

"Ah!" Croft smiled condescendingly, "I wondered if you would ever get round to that subject. It is, after all, the crime you were invited here to investigate."

Still trying to take a firm stand, Westcott asserted, "I am satisfied that Skinner Montague killed Kersey."

"Are you? Well, I am not. I see no evidence against Captain Skinner Montague, to be courteous and give him his correct title. If you force me to say it, you are going against your own evidence. I say this in the strictest confidence, but you have convinced me, though not entirely, of course," he added hastily, to explain his lack of action against the man, "that the killer may have been James Marston. He saw Kersey as the Devil and I must say that, as a sane man, I can see other reasons beside his red hair to see him as an evil spirit tempting simple men from their work and their duty by promises of an easy and idle life if only they would rise up against their masters."

"If we forget the Crimea, sir, the Captain still had cause to kill Kersey because he stood between him and a fortune."

"Nonsense," the Head Constable laughed, "You have no children, Westcott, have you? Girls are, by nature, given to silly fancies. Their minds and affections flit like butterflies from one man to another. This Kersey fellow would have been forgotten all too soon. I can see Miss Marston safely married to Captain Skinner Montague in six months from now."

"Hardly safely," the detective ventured.

He received Croft's harsh gaze. "As I was saying, a few babies and Miss Marston will be laughing at her childish fancy for Kersey."

As Westcott felt that he had been knocking his head against a brick wall, the Head Constable roughly gathered up the papers and handed them to the detective.

"Leave these matters with me," he said, in a firm voice to convey the impression that this was equivalent to taking decisive action. "A job well done," he stated, without conviction. "You will be returning to London today, I expect. You will be pleased to leave the sleepy Uptons and return to the pulsating metropolis."

At the door, Westcott stood his ground, "You forget, sir, that not only the Storr family are involved in this matter. There is Frederick Storr's widow. From an excellent family, I hear, outranking the Storr's."

"You may no longer be a policeman, Westcott, but I will not accept this insolent tone from you. You are not familiar with the ways of the country. You are certainly not familiar with the ways of the aristocracy." In his annoyance, Croft forgot himself and added, "Neither Lord Storr nor his relations want these matter aired. They settle them within the family. Many an errant younger son has been sent to the colonies and redeemed himself."

186

CHAPTER 37

Why Maria Marston, having just learned of all Skinner Montague's crimes and received the news that the police intended to take no action, sent a note asking him to meet her in the very place where she had so often met with Kersey and been spied on by the Captain, Westcott was never sure.

Deciding later that day that this had been an action understandable only to a woman, Westcott had asked Constance, "Why, oh why, did the foolish young woman go alone and without telling anyone?"

"I don't think," Constance had replied, having already asked herself the very same question, "that she can have known herself why she went. Perhaps she thought that the murder of the person she held most dear to her in the whole world touched her as it touched no one else."

"So why didn't Maria stay in her room crying and mourning her loss and thinking of the times they had together?"

"Hers was the greatest loss. Perhaps she thought only she could make the Captain repent and confess his crimes. Perhaps she believed his protestations of affection for her and thought, as many women do, that she could influence him to do the right thing. Perhaps she wanted to believe that it was Storr alone who was to blame."

"It makes no sense to me," the detective asserted, making it clear that it could make no sense to anyone.

"It may be," Constance suggested, after further thought, "that she did not wish to lose a moment of Peter's life, even the moments in which he died. Only Skinner Montague shared those moments and knew the truth of them."

"I shall never understand," Westcott said. "Never."

Whether anyone would ever understand, Maria made her way to the wood. When she arrived there, the Captain stood waiting for her. He had been warned by Henry Storr that all was suspected, but nothing proved. Being the man he was, he had decided to bluff it out. Being a conceited man, he believed his crimes had been the perfect murders. Who, he asked himself, would take the word of a madman and an aging detective from London over his word as an officer and a gentleman? He came, not as a truly penitent man to confess murder – his conscience was untroubled – but in mock penitence for having been, as he put it after greeting Maria and apologising, 'so disagreeable' about James' return.

"I can only say in my defence, Maria," the Captain began, "that the news of James' return came as a complete surprise to me." Quickly edging the blame for their quarrel onto her, he chastised her, "Why, my dear, did you not tell me of your plan? Why did you not consult me? I am always at your service, Maria."

"It was on Mr Westcott's advice. That was a dreadful place, Ernest. How could you leave my brother there? He was so unhappy."

This was not the deferential or teasing reply Skinner Montague usually received from women and he had only two possible responses to such a situation. He could lose his temper or increase his charm.

Taking Maria's hand, Skinner Montague urged, "Come, Maria, let us return to our happy, former relationship before I was foolish enough to offend you. Believe me, I spoke and acted only out of my concern for you and James."

Maria seemed particularly interested in his hand. She turned it over and gazed at it intently. The strangeness of this behaviour impressed itself on Skinner Montague, usually concerned only with the impression he was making on others. For a second he felt, unusually for him, that he was not in charge of the situation. He hesitated, the first small doubt questioning his belief that he could win her round.

Within seconds, the Captain's confidence returned. Instead of drawing his hand away, he stretched out both and, taking both of Maria's hands in his, attempted to draw her to him.

"When we are married ....," he began, but stopped as she shuddered and pulled away. For a second, his smile faded, then, "My dear," he asked, his face and voice, as well as his words, expressing affectionate concern, "are you cold? Come, take my jacket."

Removing his coat, he lifted it to Maria's shoulders. She stepped back.

"What is it, dearest Maria? If I have offended you in some small way, please tell me. I would not hurt you for the world." When Maria did not answer, he pleaded, "Speak to me, Maria. I am the man you plan to marry."

"Are you?" Maria asked in a quiet, calm voice. She seemed to expect an answer, but whether it was to come from him or from herself was not clear.

"Of course," he laughed. "All this trouble over James' return has upset you." Again having little doubt that he could win back her affection and still determined to win her fortune, he urged her, "Let us sit down and rest for a while."

The Captain spread out his jacket on a fallen tree trunk, beneath overhanging branches and beckoned Maria to join him. Without protest, she walked over and sat down. He sat beside her, confident she was coming under his spell once more.

"Ernest," Maria began, her voice steady and her manner calm.

"Yes, my dearest," Ernest smiled, taking her hand again and pressing it to her lips. Again she shivered, but did not withdraw her hand.

"Ernest," she began again, and even Skinner Montague could not ignore the unnatural quality of her calmness. "I know that you murdered Peter Kersey."

Outrage, the captain guessed, would be the emotion an innocent man would show and he showed it. He stared at Maria in horror and disbelief. Then his natural instinct for acting the part of a devoted, open and honest gentleman took over and his expression turned from outrage to deep hurt.

"This is not your doing," he claimed, "Westcott feels he must earn his fee and keep his reputation and has corrupted your mind against me. And your brother, has he been talking some mad nonsense?" Unable to suppress all resentment from his reply, he added, "I am sorry, my dear, but the fact of his madness must be faced. I know that this is not your doing. I shall not be angry with you, but your words cut to the quick."

Still following his instinct for drama, Skinner Montague, as though to compose himself in the light of her unfounded and dreadful accusation and to hide his distress, stood up and turned away. Then he leaned gently over Maria. "You are ill, my child, otherwise you would not have said these things. When we are married, I shall protect you from all matters which might upset your feelings and cause you distress."

Greatly sensitive, as she was, to hints of over-excitability or even madness, Maria showed her real anger for the first time. "Marry you, Ernest! I said that I would consider a proposal of marriage from you, in time, to try to live a normal life. I said that I could never love you. Now I say that I would only marry you to make your life a misery, to taunt, to mock and to belittle you every minute of the day. Our lives would be Hell on Earth, but I would gladly suffer to make you pay for taking Peter's life."

Disgust overcame all of Skinner Montague's other emotions. How could this slip of a girl belittle and refuse him! But for her fortune, he would have run a thousand miles from her. All the hours he had humiliated himself speaking sweetly to her little dogs, instead of kicking the useless things aside! All the miles he had walked with her, communing with nature! All the views he had admired in the most poetic language he could compose or recall! There were a hundred livelier, jollier, more beautiful women ready to fall about his neck and to join him in hunting, riding recklessly over the countryside and in making love without protests about their virtue. There were many longing to bask in the reflected glory of his fame and his military career. Some would even have admired his daring and coolness in murder, had they known.

Standing up, Skinner Montague grabbed Maria's wrists and tugged her roughly to her feet. "Look at me, Miss Marston, look at me, I say. How could you prefer that red-headed apology for a man, a man who would not fight to defend himself? How could you prefer an uneducated dolt with wild ideas, a man from the gutter to a gentleman of education and taste, welcome in the homes of some of the greatest in the land?"

Although she struggled to free herself, Maria was barely aware of the pain from the grip on her arms. She was aware only of his expression of contempt and hate. This was the face Peter had seen in the last seconds of his life. She was looking in the face of death. And in her expression, Skinner Montague read what Maria would not admit to herself, that part of her would welcome death to be with his rival.

The Captain did not kill from kindness, but he had killed for some real or fancied slights. He looked from the scarf draped around Maria's neck to the branch above the log. He could strangle her with that and make it appear that she had stood on the tree trunk, reached up to the branch, tied the scarf around it, made a noose for her neck and then jumped from the log. Her feet would be only inches from the ground, but that was enough. He could claim that he had arrived and found her already dead.

The Captain felt the exultation of danger and revelled in it. He could think on his feet like no other men he knew. There were men like Storr, who needed others to do their dirty work. There were men like Jakes, who had to be told what to do. No one touched him in the planning and execution of murder. Then, as a cold voice within him told him that Maria was no use to him dead and that he had invested too much time and trouble in pursuing her to give up now, the moment for murder passed.

"Maria, let me take you home. We are both upset. It is not, after all," he laughed, "every day that I am falsely accused of murder."

190

Maria had seen the wild exultation in his manner, the glance from scarf to branch and back to the fallen tree trunk. The instinct to live broke through her despair and she was overcome by the folly of her action in coming here alone with this murderer. She let Skinner Montague place his jacket around her shoulders and meekly let herself be led from the wood. She and her friends must think of a more sensible way of proving Ernest Skinner Montague's guilt.

CHAPTER 38

As they walked, Skinner Montague's jacket around Maria's shoulders, he, as though to read her real thoughts, walked a few inches ahead, staring down at her. She, to keep her real intentions from him, fixed her eyes on the ground.

Until he spoke and they looked up, neither was aware of Tom Osborne standing in their path. "So you've forgiven Peter's murderer, 'ave you, Miss? That's 'ow deep your affection went, is it? All forgive and forget, is it, Miss? Peter thought as 'ow you wanted to marry 'im and you was just leading 'im on."

"Oh, no! No!" Maria wanted to cry, but she dare not. Tom's presence had not eased her fear, but made it even more intense. If he said the wrong thing and provoked Skinner Montague, she might read the evil in the Captain's face again. "I feel ill and confused, Tom. I am going home."

Tom had his own demons driving him on. This was the woman who had taken so much of his hero's time, the time he could have spent telling Tom of the world outside the Uptons, stretching his mind and his hopes far beyond the 'God put you on this Earth to toil and obey your betters' philosophy he had been taught in the workhouse.

"I tried to tell Peter you was no friend of 'is, but 'e were besotted with you. Can't see why. You've forgot 'im as soon as 'e's been put in the ground."

Without ceremony, Skinner Montague stretched out his hand, planted it squarely on Tom's chest and pushed him aside. The action unleashed the fury built up in the young man by society's neglect and by his frustration at not having been there to defend his friend from his murderer. He pushed aside Skinner Montague's hand, leapt on him and wrestled him to the ground. Tom knew all the tricks of workhouse brawls and the pain of his attack stung Skinner Montague into an immediate reply. He, in turn, knew all the tricks, fair and unfair, of public school brawling and he replied to Tom in kind.

To Maria, it seemed only seconds before blood ran freely from both men, soaking their clothes and mingling with the dust on the ground. Cries of pain and anger punctuated the stream of abuse from both.

Equal in anger and hate, in recklessness and in contempt for each other, they yet proved far from well-matched opponents. Tom had the wiry build of a young man who had been too insufficiently fed and too overworked to achieve his full height and weight, while Skinner Montague, some eight or nine years older, was well built with ample stamina to outlast his challenger.

Maria's pleadings for them to stop and her screams had fallen on deaf ears, but now that the Captain stood over his defeated opponent, she ran forward and attempted to pull him away. Holding her off with one hand, Skinner Montague kicked viciously at Tom's body and was positioning himself to kick at his head.

"Enough's enough," an authoritative voice called, and John Howard emerged from a copse at the side of the path. As Skinner Montague brought back his foot to aim a blow at Tom's head, which would have killed him or turned him into the village idiot, John Howards' mastiff sprang at the Captain and held his ankle between strong, white, slobbering teeth until told to let go.

"Get up, whatever your name is," Howard ordered Tom. "Go home and keep out of trouble."

Painfully, Tom pulled himself up, spat blood and a tooth or two and stared at Skinner Montague with unabated hatred. He had not finished yet. "'E killed Peter Kersey and 'e killed Frederick Storr on the battlefield and anyone else 'oo got in 'is way."

It would have been difficult for the Captain, trying to stem the blood from his ankle and cursing the dog, to think of a reply. He kept silent, planning his next move. Maria, seeing a chance to appeal to a gentleman of influence, outlined Skinner Montague's crimes.

"More Skinner than Montague in him, I always said," Howard remarked, looking at the Captain with obvious contempt. "There may well be self made men, but there is no such thing as a self made gentleman. Gentlemen are born and bred, not moulded out of grime in the gutter. Bad blood will out."

Skinner Montague had sat down to tie a handkerchief around his ankle. He said nothing.

"Don't know what you're plotting, Skinner," Howard said, "but make one move to run away and I shall let you have both barrels."

The Captain looked up and checked. It was double barrelled. If he pushed Tom into the gun, could he avoid both shots? He stood up.

Howard was firmly in charge. "You run ahead, Miss Marston. My house is closer than yours. Get a half dozen servants down here, without delay.

Ask for a couple of good shots amongst them." Seeing Maria trembling with emotion after watching the brutal fight, he added, in a voice reserved for women and children, "Come, Miss Marston, there's a good girl. I'm depending on you."

To Howard's surprise, the young woman laughed. Seemingly shocked out of her trance by his words, she turned and hurried off muttering, "Good girl. Good girl," and laughing as she went. His surprise abated when he recalled that she was, after all, a Marston.

Howard, who had taken his eyes off Skinner Montague for a few seconds, turned to face him. "The catch is off, Skinner. I'd shoot you as readily as I'd pick off those pigeons. It's all one to me."

"My name is Skinner Montague. Have the grace to use it, Howard."

"'E means you're a bastard," Tom laughed, causing more blood to trickle from his mouth. He glanced at Howard to see if he appreciated the joke. Skinner Montague took his chance, grabbed Tom's arm and threw him onto the barrel of Howard's gun.

The idea had been to let Tom take the blast of both shots while Skinner Montague ran for his life before Howard could reload. It is doubtful whether he would have got far with the mastiff at his heels, and he had not reckoned with Tom's being too exhausted and beaten to try to regain his balance by staggering in the direction of the gun. As it was, Tom crumpled to the ground. The first shot passed both Tom and Skinner Montague. The second missed Tom and hit the Captain in the eye, shattering his brain. He was dead before he hit the ground. There were no last words. The luck of the Devil had deserted him.

The dog, which had moved to seize the ankle again, released it in great haste. As it sat back on its haunches, it fixed Howard with large brown eyes, anxiously telling him that it was not the cause of this death. Howard came forward and patted its head.

"Self-defence," he said, not bothering to look at Tom.

"Yes, sir," Tom agreed. "I'm your witness, sir. 'E went for your gun."

"No," Howard corrected, "a simple shooting accident. Let us not sully the name of the courageous Light Brigade by revealing all this man did."

CHAPTER 39

On the journey to London, Maria was glad that they were travelling by railroad. The excitement had left this form of travel, as it had left everything in her life. She had to admit that the noise and grime were far from pleasant, but she could no longer bear to travel by coach, imagining each figure they passed on the road was Peter, alive and well, strolling on to meet her at her destination.

The young woman was glad, too, that she was making this journey with people she had come to love and trust. Beside her was her brother, James, who needed her so much and young Alice leaning on his shoulder. And there was Constance, whom she had come to depend on as an older sister, or even, a mother. Following Peter's principles, she was trying to let rank no longer come between them, any more, that was, than the smooth running and discipline of the household required.

As for Augustus Westcott, Maria smiled to see him feeling and examining the comfort of the first class carriage and murmuring to Constance, "I could become used to this." They all knew him well enough to be sure that he could not. Left to himself, he would have been travelling in the second class with Carrie and Tom Osborne. Maria had wanted them all to travel together in the third class or the first, but Westcott had counselled against it. "Take things gradually, one at a time," he had said. "You cannot throw everyone into a mixing pot without unsettling them. It would be like the child's game of twisting someone round and round until they became giddy and did not know whether they were on their head or their heels."

When they had learned the truth that Lord Storr had sent his son Henry to Australia, together with the servant, John Blackburn, James Marston had, at first been greatly upset, by the news. "The guilty must be punished," he had said. "An eye for an eye." Then, after much soul-searching, he had decided, that vengeance could be left to God, who alone knew what was in men's hearts.

The news had left Maria quite calm. "Peter and I talked of many things. His ideas seemed so strange to me, even though, in essence, they are there in the Bible for all to read. He always said that no man should take another man's life, even in the name of the law."

"That's all very well," Constance had answered, using her new found freedom to state her opinions on this, that and the other, "but a murderer should not be free to make a new life in the colonies, as though nothing had happened. They say that he showed no remorse. What do you think, Charles?" she appealed to Westcott.

The detective, who preferred to answer to the name of Charles than that of Augustus, replied, "I have always found that the old saying, 'Give a man enough rope and he will hang himself,' often works out in the end."

The housekeeper was not impressed and gave Westcott a dismissive glance to which he replied with a smile. The detective would always keep to himself the knowledge that, Lord Storr, not wishing to besmirch the family name and admit that his elder son had been murdered instead of dying a hero's death and that his younger son was behind the murder, had paid Mrs Jakes to keep quiet. She had used some of the money to pay the passage of a cousin, sailing on the same ship as Henry Storr to Australia. If he obeyed her instructions, Henry Storr should be overboard before they reached Cape Town.

Rocked by the rough rhythm of the train, Maria thought of her life ahead. How different it was from the one she had envisaged travelling less than a year earlier from London to Upton Market. Now she was returning to the capital to join Philip Robertson in his work for the poor in the East End, the work from which Peter had been so cruelly taken. She, along with James, would give their time and wealth to the work, so sorely needed. It would pass the time for them both, Maria thought, until they died and were reunited with Frances and the boys and her dearest Peter.

Westcott, looking round the carriage, was glad that he had been able to help the Marstons. Those who had known James Marston before had found him a stern, unforgiving man, but Westcott saw him now as courageous, travelling alone through a life which had seen more than its share of pain and suffering. Maria, he hoped, would find the happiness and peace Kersey had wished for her. As to Constance, she would make a reliable friend. For the rest, he could not decide whether she had set her cap at him and whether he would regret most that she had or had not. Time alone would tell. Until then, he would jog along with Tom Cat.